Skinny Dipping in Cane River

Skinny Dipping in Cane River

Phylis Caskey

This is a work of fiction. All of the characters, organizations, and events portrayed in this novel are either products of the author's imagination or are used fictitiously.

Petite P Imprint

Cover Art by Melissa Ringuette
www.Melissasgraphicdesigns.Com
Visit Phylis at her site:
www.Phyliscaskey.Com

ISBN: 0692362711
ISBN 13: 9780692362716

*This book is dedicated to the one person
who has always believed in me. To the love of
my life: David Caskey.*

Table of Contents

Hyperkinetic Memory Syndrome is defined as a neuropsychological disorder. Characteristics include random and/or frequent memories involving all five senses. Negative symptoms include, but are not limited to, flat affect, confusion, and disorientation. The most essential clinical manifestation is the sensation of reliving the remembered episode in real time.

Prologue

Night wind strums the few gray hairs left on my head, and I glance over at my brother huddled in the passenger's seat, snoring louder than a congested pug dog. Neglected, sputtering neon signs coax me to a blinking yellow light, and I flinch looking both ways for oncoming traffic. Nothing. My hands itch, and I twist the steering wheel, but it doesn't help. It's too late to turn around. I'm back in the slowest town south of the Mason-Dixon Line.

My headlights reveal whitewashed cypress columns of a French Creole townhouse masquerading as a bed and breakfast, and a petite woman wearing running shorts over spider-thin legs opens the front door. Her puppet-show shadow interrupts the soft yellow light glazing the wide planked porch.

"Dr. James!" She prances toward the car and extends one hand while twirling her sun-bleached ponytail into a tight coil. "Welcome to Cane River B & B. What brings you to Natchitoches?"

I start to groan, but my brother nudges me, cutting me a look. He thrusts out his hand and gives her a smile reserved for strangers and small children, one that engenders automatic trust. "I'm Brett James. Please, don't pay to any attention my brother. It's been a long day."

Exactly, don't pay me any mind. If I'm acting like a curmudgeon, who cares? Just find me somewhere to sleep. I grab our carry-ons from the back seat, cradling my bag under my arm. Tension builds in the back of my neck.

"To answer your question, we lived in Natchitoches as kids… haven't been here in fifty years." Brett thumbs the luggage strap onto his shoulder.

"I'm Patty, by the way." She clasps her hands together, clearly delighted. "So you lived here a while ago. What brings you back?"

Brett squeezes my upper arm. "We're pretty tired. Rough drive."

Oblivious to our fatigue, Patty leaps onto an ornate rug, and for a minute, I worry she's going to grab pom-poms and break out into a spirited dance. However, she clears her throat with a small cough, then extends her hand in a sweeping gesture around the room. "We're standing in the entry of what was originally known as the Davion House. Built in 1848…"

Her perkiness annoys me. All I want to do is crawl into bed and get tomorrow behind me. I've dreaded coming here for weeks. Patty twirls around and directs us deeper into the house. Once we've completed the two-dollar tour, she unlocks our rooms.

"The St. Denis Room. Named after the city's founder. This is the oldest town in Louisiana." She hands me a skeleton key. "Pleasant dreams."

"A dreamless night is more what I have in mind." I push past the door. Patty and Brett stop at the next room. I imagine him giving her another smile.

The room smells like crushed gardenias. Sad memories crowd into my head, and for a moment, I can't move. I struggle to drive the shifty impressions back into my mind. Can't let a single remembrance through, no matter how precious.

Hyperkinetic Memory Syndrome—a one-line diagnosis defines me. I have a gift wrapped in a curse; detailed memories so life-like, I mistake them for reality. Biting the inside of my lip, I quickly search the room for a distraction, grounding me in the moment. When my fingers dust the duffle bag I remember where I am and why I'm here.

The lock snags, but after two frustrating attempts, I unzip my bag and gingerly extract a cream-colored ceramic urn swaddled in bubble wrap. It's so unexpectedly light. My throat catches like I swallowed a fish bone; I try unsuccessfully to clear it.

The crinkly wrap clings to the urn when I pry it away. Each ridiculous tug creates a pop, and I clench my teeth. My exhausted brain is as fragile as the tiny pockets of air lining the stupid wrapping, but I have to find the perfect place to leave the urn. I spy an oval table near the window. It'll have to do. The room is filled with antiques only a Victorian woman would appreciate, but the bed is firm and inviting.

I cross back to the bed where the bag gapes open. Inside, a small bone-white envelope lies on a folded blue oxford shirt. I pull a satiny card from the envelope before angling it toward the light. Black calligraphy flows across the page. I can almost hear my wife whisper in my ear: *Written Instructions.* When I run my index finger over the two short sentences written in mirror image, a sigh catches at the back of my throat and a weary, hollow longing fills my chest. Regardless how complicated the backwards writing looks, I know the words by heart. I lean the envelope against the ceramic urn.

Someone knocks. I trudge to the door and Brett steps inside. "Wanted to check on you one last time before bed. You sure you're all right? No memories triggered?"

"No. Don't worry. I haven't had one break through in a long time."

"Well, you've been under tremendous strain these last few months. I'd hate to find you face down, unconscious, frozen in some memory."

"I can control it." My words are sluggish, and I wave Brett away. "Let's talk about this in the morning. I promise. I'm fine."

Brett almost touches my shoulder, but drops his hand and leaves the room. I stumble to the bed and flop on the bedspread, hungry for sleep. A yawn escapes and hangs above me. I close my eyelids. If only I can shut out the world for just a few minutes.

Light pours through slatted plantation shutters. I scrunch open an eye. Good God, I'm still in my clothes, shoes and all. I haven't slept through the night for two weeks.

A return to my morning routine is what I need—a scalding shower and coffee with two sugars. I pull on a starched oxford shirt with soft khaki pants, then with my eyes closed, slide on soft well-worn topsiders, jamming my toes into the knotted seam. Pain shoots through my foot, but is a welcome distraction. I glance at the ceramic urn and wince.

Just about to leave the room, I hear a conversation and press my ear to the wooden door.

"And, what about the old dude with the bag? What do you think he has inside? The way he carried it you'd think it was the Crown Jewels." Patty's words are fast, her tongue on speed dial.

"Shh. Keep your voice down. I'm sure they're still sleeping," An older woman answers with a pleasant southern drawl. Their chitchat tapers off and disappears.

Nice to know Patty has more on her mind than what color shorts to wear. Clearly, she's the local form of social networking. I listen and wait a few minutes, then slip from my room and head to the main dining room. A silver coffee server sits between delicate cups in razor-thin saucers and basic brown Styrofoam to-go cups. If I'm quick, maybe I can sneak away before anyone spots me.

Tipping the server, I slide a to-go cup underneath. Thick, chicory-flavored coffee curls into the cup. The moist scent fills my nose. A memory pushes the cusp of my consciousness. A trill runs through my diaphragm and my breathing hitches. No, I won't let even the smallest thought slip through. With great effort, I change my focus. I plop two sugar cubes into the cup, and stir until every speck of sugar dissolves. My mind relaxes.

I dip into the hall, opening the back door before anyone sees me. This morning, of all mornings, I must be alone. A magnificent Magnolia tree choked with ivy shades the entire yard, its umbrella unfolding over a narrow back alley. I hurry under the tree and speed-walk onto the cracked asphalt. After a block or two, I slow to check my pulse. Can't afford to have a heart attack right here on the sidewalk.

The neighborhood I stroll through is filled with remodeled antebellum homes, but I'm careful not to dwell on any one thing too long. Unwanted memories are sometimes triggered by familiar scents, Charleston-green doors surrounded by spikey pink mimosa blossoms, tiny white honeysuckle strung like Christmas lights across iron balcony railings, uneven red brick streets glued together with creeping moss, or even cypress trees whispering in the wind.

I glare into my coffee cup and concentrate so hard I can actually see wax specks. When I glance back up, I spot Patty jogging one block over. Shit!

She spies me and waves. "Hey! Dr. James, wait up!"

I ignore her and increase my speed. Another alley appears on my right so I veer down the winding blacktop, half running, half walking. The alley splits only a few feet away. I take the right path and check over my shoulder once more. Thank God, she didn't follow me.

Why can't she leave me alone? I suck in a deep breath and clip on to the alley's end. Suddenly, I stop. Across the street a yellow stucco building, stained with graffiti, spans the entire block. There's no sign, but I immediately recognize the abandoned railroad station. My body floods with electricity, zipping up my spine, shooting through my arms and legs– filling my rubbery guts.

Had I headed in this direction all along? Above the station's entrance, an arched stained-glass window stippled with Venetian greens and blues shimmers in the sun. Oh God, no. A trigger. I want to run. My legs shake, refusing to move. The station's double doors creak open. Dull, cracked tiles undulate like thick dark oil in the entrance. Please, not today.

I dread the confusion more than the claustrophobia associated with tunneling into the past. I strain hard, fighting the memories, but they won't have it. The last few weeks have exhausted me. My head pounds. Then, a freezing cold sensation clamps around my brain like icy fingers–a sensory aura. Shadowed faces, coded words, and tiny brass keys shove each other, trying to be first. Their cool images rush through me, replacing the searing electric heat, and I can't resist anymore.

No one was there to meet me. I rubbed the pitted glass window, smearing grime in cloudy circles. I squinted to see through the dirt, scanning the platform once more, searching...

I

1962

"Hey, Julian. Where's your dad?" A pimple-faced teen sitting next to me looked through the dirty window. His rank butterscotch breath hits the back of my neck like sticky sweat.

"He'll be here. He's just late." But my dad was never late, never. I looked past the clustered parents and hoped I'd glimpse Dad's brown fedora, but I didn't see it. Woody, his wood-paneled station wagon, wasn't in the parking lot, either. My stomach shifted into a tight fist.

The kid pointed through the window. "Look, that's my dad. Why's he here with Mom? He hates train stations. Says hellos and goodbyes are for sissies."

He elbowed me, shoving past two other kids in the aisle, causing me to drop *Of Mice and Men,* my eleventh-grade English teacher's idea of class punishment. The kid nearly tripped on the last step, but he managed to be first off the train.

His dad, a muscular baldheaded man, squeezed his son as if he were a spy just returned from some dangerous mission behind the Iron Curtain. His mother wrapped her arms around them both.

Snap! Brilliant light flashed through my brain. I tucked away the image. Whether the man's shiny head or the family hug triggered the picture is anybody's guess. But one thing's for certain, when I least expected it, I would later relive this exact moment with each cough, whisper, and sniff, not to mention the greasy train smell. I constantly struggled to suppress my memories, but sometimes it was impossible, especially when all five senses kicked in.

No one moved or said a word when I stepped onto the platform and inched forward, yet everyone stared at me. Why? I wished my dad were here. Surely, he had a simple explanation. Maybe his car didn't start, or he had a flat tire.

Whispers and shushes hurried through the solemn adults. The bald man dabbed his sweaty forehead with a wrinkled handkerchief. "Poor kid. Tough break."

Was he talking about me? A sliver of fear zipped up my spine. Every head swiveled toward the train station's entrance. A slender woman paced along the brick walkway, a white gloved hand to her throat. Lila Dupree was my mother's best friend, a lifelong Louisiana debutante, and a tried and true member of the Natchitoches Ladies Historical Society. Her platinum blonde hair was wound into a French twist so tight blue veins pulsed under her pale skin. She stopped. Her eyes locked with mine.

I lurched into the crowd, weaving through the silent onlookers. A man gripped my shoulder, slowing me for only a second. A woman whispered, "He doesn't know."

I didn't turn. I didn't want to see who said it.

Mrs. Dupree swished over. Her cool cotton sundress fluttered around her calves. If I needed verification something was wrong, her presence was enough, and my stomach twisted the last bit of burning acid up my throat. I wanted to gag.

"Hello, Julian." She plucked at her dress, the motion uncharacteristic for a smooth southern belle.

I nodded. "Where's Dad? Is Mom alright?"

She tried to smile, but her mouth collapsed. She pinned her red-stained lips between her teeth and spun on her heel as if I disgusted her. Her attitude stung, especially when she assumed I would follow her like some well-trained dog. I ran to catch-up with her.

She didn't slow down for a second, just sashayed to her car, answering over her shoulder. "Let's get your suitcase in the trunk. We'll discuss your mom and dad on the way home."

Mrs. Dupree owned a white Oldsmobile with a shiny metal grill that grinned from headlight to headlight. The car was showroom new in 1956, but now, six years later, the paint looked more like day-old cream curdled under a thick coat of yellowed wax.

Broken plastic stitching snagged my pants as I slid into the passenger's seat. The car smoldered with southern heat, and the smell of dried gardenias rose from the floorboard. Mrs. Dupree tied a flimsy scarf under her chin and turned the key. The engine rumbled to life. Fanning the air, she pressed a chrome button, and the windows whirled down.

She cleared her throat. "Your mother wanted to meet you, but she just couldn't." She clutched the turquoise steering wheel. "Now Julian, you must be brave."

I hated that particular southern euphemism. It meant one thing: Mrs. Dupree was about to tell me something so terrible I needed to brace myself. I prepared the best I knew how. I held *Of Mice and Men* to my chest, not quite a shield but close.

The car jolted over a pothole. A steady roar whooshed past my ears. I couldn't hear her. What did she say? I didn't want to hear her voice, but no matter how much I tried to ignore it, her nasal singsong voice kept rising and falling, filling the entire car with garbled words.

"I didn't hear what you said." My hands trembled around the book.

Mrs. Dupree eased off the gas. Her expression changed, softened. "Your father walked to the college like he's done for a thousand mornings. Oh Lord, help me. But today he had an accident…"

She slowed for a caution light. My heart hammered so hard against my chest I just knew it would bust out and fly across the car any minute. What? What happened to him? Why didn't she just spit it out?

"I know this is hard to believe, but your father fell from his office window. A student found him on the ground near Russell Hall. Honey, he wasn't breathing when they found him. I'm so sorry...so terribly sorry. I wish I had better news, but... well... he didn't make it."

"Huh? Didn't make it?" I repeated the phrase, letting the words sink into my muddled brain. "He didn't make it?"

"This is a terrible shock, I know, but he's gone, Julian. Nothing could be done. This can't be easy. But at least he's with the Lord now." She eased her grip on the steering wheel as if the worst was over. But wasn't the worst just beginning?

"I don't believe you. I talked to Dad last night. He sounded fine." My throat ached. I couldn't pull up enough spit to swallow. I croaked. "How could he fall from a window?"

"No one knows why these things happen. But God called him home and there's nothing else to say." Silence sat hard between us, but not for long.

I dropped my face into my hands so she couldn't see me. She droned on, a run away engine I couldn't shut off. I stopped listening. I didn't have anything else to say, not to her anyway.

Dad wasn't sick or old. And he would never fall from a window. He hated heights. He dreaded climbing a ladder even to change a light bulb. He took the stairs before he ever rode in an elevator with glass doors. And he *never* looked out the window of a plane. The very idea made him dizzy.

I didn't want to be stuck in this car with Mrs. Dupree. I wanted to go home. She yammered on and on, and I couldn't think. My dad was the heart of everything, how could my life go on without him? This wasn't happening. I wanted to rewind the clock. Go back to this morning.

A hot breeze rushed into the car window, carrying the sickening smell of summer roses. I wanted to stick my head out the window and yell at the top of my lungs.

When I lifted my head and looked out, houses blurred together, white-washed buildings in one long strip. A crushing image of Dad spread-eagle on the ground came from nowhere. I couldn't stand it. I didn't care what Mrs. Dupree said. She was wrong. What did she know anyway? My dad didn't fall from his office window. I didn't buy it.

I I

The Duprees' car lumbered into the drive and everything looked perfectly normal until I spotted Police Chief Hendricks standing on the front porch. He tipped his felt cowboy hat as we drove past the house and parked beside my Dad's old Ford station wagon. The waning afternoon sun played through the branches of a sagging oak tree, casting short summer shadows across Woody's gray-green hood.

I pulled my suitcase from the dusty trunk and trudged up the gravel walk with Mrs. Dupree trailing behind me. I stood on the top step, unable to accept my father's death, trying to reconcile other homecomings to my new reality, but it was too fresh. In the mudroom, wet clothes hung above the washing machine, and tennis shoes with crimped heels were abandoned beneath a thin-legged cast iron sink. The wooden floor was freshly waxed, and my reflection eased with me to the kitchen.

Tudy stood at the sink, washing dishes. She shook her sudsy hands, then wiped them on her crisp apron. *Snap!* Blue light zipped through my brain followed by a click like the clatter of an old movie. Every moment would be recorded, no matter how excruciating.

I blinked and gazed down for several seconds, focusing on Tudy's legs. Strange things hitch in your head when bad things happen, and her loose hose wrinkled around her ankles were more interesting than her face. The truth is I didn't want to look at her. If I did, everything Mrs. Dupree told me would be true.

Tudy sidled over to me, and I struggled with my composure, pulling in a ragged breath. I mustered all my courage and looked into her face. Tear tracks stained her coffee-colored cheeks, her dark eyes so sad I couldn't stand it. She didn't say a word; instead, she clutched me to her bony body. Familiar scents–coffee and Ivory soap–permeated her neck and dress. Her hands were still damp, and warm moisture seeped through my dress shirt. I wanted the warmth to seep through my muscles and wrap around my heart. When she backed away, shiny tears clung to her lashes, and the enormity of my father's death crashed around me.

"What we gonna do, Julian? How we gonna manage without him? Ain't nothin' worse 'n this." Tudy reached down, tugged at the corner of her stiff white apron, and scrubbed her face. "I made breakfast same as usual. He ain't never left this house without a good breakfast. This morning he didn't touch a thing. He was low, didn't ask me how's my day. Didn't say a blessed thing."

I let this new information roll around in my head as if it were a new word rolling over my tongue. He never left without eating. He said breakfast was like gas in the car; you had to begin each morning with a full tank. It didn't surprise me he left without saying goodbye. Sometimes he went into himself, especially if a new archeological theory was spinning in his brain, or if he was leading a new excavation. He was often in deep thought and didn't join in conversations. Mom always said he lived in his own world. I squeezed my eyes closed, but I couldn't shut out the nightmare.

"Where's Mom?" I asked.

Tudy glanced over at Mrs. Dupree, then blotted her face once more. "She's upstairs. People been dropping by all afternoon, paying their respects and leaving food. I don't know what we gonna do if one more chicken leg walks through that door."

Mrs. Dupree floated past us and headed to the dining room. She casually dipped a finger into the mile-high meringue of a banana pudding crowded between two other lavish desserts. I inwardly groaned.

"Your mama's upstairs." Tudy grimaced at Mrs. Dupree. "She says no more visitors today. She can't take another soul crying on her shoulder.

Probably laying down trying to soothe her nerves. Go on up now. She's been waiting for you. Can't believe he's gone."

"Where's Brett?" There was an edge to my voice. I loved Tudy, but it irritated me when she referred to Dad in the past tense.

"He's real upset. Left as soon as Chief Hendricks done drove you mama to the funeral home. And he ain't been back since."

Tudy trudged back to the kitchen. She'd lived with us as long as I can remember. Most days she sang family hymns about heaven and the glory.

I made my way into the foyer. Mrs. Dupree spoke to Chief Hendricks in hushed tones. A toothpick wiggled in the corner of his mouth, and he flicked it occasionally with his tongue.

I wanted to shoot upstairs to my mom, but something bigger bothered me, and I asked. "Chief, what happened? How exactly did Dad die?"

His gaze swiveled toward Lila Dupree. She looked at the floor. His glanced back to me. "Well son, we're not rightly sure, but it appears he fell from the top floor of Russell Hall. No one saw him this morning, so it's kinda like putting a jigsaw puzzle together."

"Sure. I understand." I thrust my hands into my pockets to stop them from shaking. But in truth, I didn't understand.

"I gotta go. Thanks." My voice sounded husky. I needed to go upstairs and find Mom before I lost control. Chief patted my head when I walked past, only making matters worse.

Mrs. Dupree stepped to my side just as I grasped the handrail. She didn't try to take my hand or touch me in any way. "Your mother is in a bad state. Be careful what you say to her."

Even though she was solicitous, it struck me wrong. "She's my mother. I won't say anything to upset her."

"I know this is difficult. But that's no reason to be rude." Mrs. Dupree smoothed her hair. No more fidgeting, she was back in her element. "Be mindful of your elders."

Her little statement was typical of what I'd endure over the next few days, and I dreaded it. Anyone who ever shook hands with Dad would show up with a platter of food. Then his body would be displayed for all the world to see at Buckner's funeral home, more visitation, more food, and then the high point a day or two later: the actual funeral. Afterwards, our living room would be crowded with people, and everything would be smothered in enough chicken fried gravy to comfort even the most miserable soul.

I plodded up the stairs to my mother's bedroom. The shutters were closed, making the furniture look lumpy and gray. A smoky haze hung over the room, and the bitter tang of cigarettes stung my nose. Mom only smoked when distressed. I guess *now* fell into that category. The smoke trail led to the summer sleeping porch where Mom sat in a cedar rocker, creaking back and forth.

Before I went to the porch, I checked Dad's side of the room. It was neat, nothing out of place, as if he'd return any moment. The bed was made, and his khaki pants were folded in a chair. I still couldn't grasp he wasn't coming back. I missed him, his absence more evident here than anywhere else. Another thing struck me hard: nothing he left behind, not one single possession, could replace him. How did this happen? Why did this happen?

Golden light outlined two Egyptian perfume bottles on my mother's dressing table, gifts from my father. I shuffled to the sleeping porch. Mom brought a cigarette to her lips, and the rocking stopped. She knew I was there.

My shadow fell over her, and she looked up. Her blue eyes were ringed with red. I couldn't bear any more pain. All the energy left my body, and I dropped to my knees. Mom grabbed me, hugging me with brittle desperation. A noise escaped from me, a low choking wail. I couldn't help it. I hated seeing Mom miserable and broken.

After a while, I let her go. She tilted her head, easing it into her palm like a fragile, thin-shelled egg. We didn't speak for a while, consoling each other the best we could. She started rocking again, and we watched the day slip into night.

"I wish I had something comforting to say, but all I can think about is how much I already miss him," she said.

"I don't understand how this happened. Chief Hendricks said he fell from a fourth floor window." I bristled, suspecting he hadn't told me the truth.

She didn't say anything for what seemed like an eternity. "I guess you know Brett found him." She gazed into the back yard. "He left a homework assignment at home and cut through the campus at lunch. Since finals are over, the campus is all but deserted."

"God. No. He did?" A ridiculous sense of relief washed over me; I was glad it wasn't me. I felt sorry for my brother. Finding Dad was bad enough, and lately they'd argued over the dumbest stuff, like Brett watching too much television or coming in after curfew. Some days their arguments were so hot the house expanded with tension; the walls stretched so thin I heard every angry word.

Mom rubbed her hands over her pants before she picked up a tiny bell-shaped glass filled with clear liquid. I smelled alcohol. My guess was gin. Her face looked wan. She'd never be the same. She'd followed Dad all over the world on his excavations, letting him make all the decisions. Mom wasn't weak or anything, but she was an artist, a dreamer, and glad to leave the decisions to him.

She brought the glass to her lips and paused. "He acted funny from the moment he discovered the open window with the screen off in his study last night. I wanted to call the Chief, but your dad said it was probably the wind."

I wanted to ask her what she meant by funny, but I heard singing coming from beneath us. A deep masculine voice, slightly off key, lamented *Five Hundred Miles*. It was Brett. I held my breath, listening to his slow, distinct clomp up the stairs. When he reached the porch, he slapped the door facing with his hand.

"Well, I'm back. See ya made it home safe and sound, J. J." Brett had called me J. J. from the get go. Mom said Julian James was more than a mouthful for a little kid.

"Honey, where have you been?" Mom's speech slurred, more from exhaustion than alcohol. Her eyelids were so puffy from crying she could barely open and close them.

"I couldn't stay home one minute longer. I was about to explode. All the people, all the questions, all the shit. I dunno. Somehow, I ended up at the river. No one bothered me there. So I stayed," said Brett.

I touched his shoulder. His shirt was wet with sweat. He shrugged my hand away, a small movement, but effective. My emotions, once raw, were now dull, and I was unfazed by the gesture.

"Some homecoming, huh J. J.?"

"Yeah. I keep expecting Dad to come walking in and whistle up the stairs." I wanted it to be the truth. "I still can't believe it."

"Oh… you can believe it. He was crumpled on the ground when I found him. So still with his legs all twisted underneath him. He couldn't have gotten up if he wanted to. No damn way he could have walked." Brett's voice broke. He slumped against the doorframe, turning his face toward the wall, then unexpectedly he pummeled the door so hard with his fist, the door splintered under his knuckles.

If I was expecting solace from my brother, I realized in this moment, he was incapable of giving it to me. It was asking too much. He was going to handle Dad's death differently than me. He was going to distance himself as quickly as he possibly could. I felt as if I was swinging in the wind with nothing to anchor me.

Mom rose. Her legs buckled, and she held onto the rocker for support. "I need to see Lila out and help Tudy close the house. We have a long day tomorrow. You boys need your sleep." Mom kissed us on the cheeks, her fingers lingering on the side of our faces. She sighed as she stepped into her bedroom.

I was right behind her and made one more sweep of the room. A polished barrister's bookcase stood next to Dad's chair. I ran my hand over the cool, clear glass and peered inside. The top shelves held his favorite authors: Michener, Camus, Wells, and Hemingway. Crowded on the bottom shelves were his diaries, all thirty-one, all the same size, in black leather with red stitched seams. He'd written his thoughts every day since he turned thirteen.

The only diary outside the case was this year's diary, usually on his bedside table. *Click!* My brain added the tabletop image to a string of images from today. His diary wasn't there. Instead, *The American Revolutionary War* lay on the bedside table. His black-framed glasses were folded cleanly on top. I picked them up, and looked through the smooth glass. No finger smudges, nothing. A cold sensation like eating ice cream too fast spread through my chest and head. A memory bloomed in my mind.

The room changed to bright daylight, and Dad sat on his bed, writing in his diary. His fountain pen scratched across the page. He stopped writing and nodded at me, then smiled. The room flashed dead black, like the night sky after a fireworks display. My heart actually hurt with each thud. Was he really so careless? Was his death really an accident?

III

The phone downstairs clanged so loudly I was sure the firehouse was on alert. *Good grief. What time was it?* I glanced at my Big Ben alarm clock. Midnight. I jumped out of bed and raced down the stairs to head off Widow Laborde. We shared a party line with her, and she shared our business with all the old ladies in her bridge club. If the phone rang more than six times, she answered and stiffly announced into the receiver that we weren't home. With any luck, she'd sleep through it tonight. Somehow, I wasn't feeling very lucky.

Fully awake, I jerked the receiver out of its cradle before the sixth ring. "Hello?"

"Julian. Oh, I'm so glad it's you." Priss. Her voice was thin, as if she'd held it so long she barely had enough breath to finish the sentence.

I was more than a little grateful to hear her voice, and for a moment everything was okay. Priss was Lila Dupree's daughter. We'd been friends forever despite her mother's insistence she attend a private boarding school instead of Natchitoches High School, where, I might add, I received a perfectly fine education. Her mom had forced her to travel on the school's end-of-the-year mission trip and according to the newsletters sent home, they were building a cinder block church for the desert heathens. Apparently, you couldn't truly understand self-sacrifice or get final grades unless you participated.

Mrs. Dupree practiced Old South traditions, and to her, appearances were everything. Priss sipped tea and ate cucumber sandwiches like a perfect lady, especially when the Demoiselle Club met each month. But when her mom wasn't around... well let's just say, Priss liked to throw a good party, and she knew more about sex than just how to spell it. She had plenty of secrets, and that's why I liked her.

"Glad you called. It's been hell around here." I didn't mince words.

"I'm so sorry I can't be there. We're in the middle of nowhere. Some tiny town called Tuba City. Sister Alberta let us call our parents, though. Five minutes apiece. Mom told me about your dad. I wanted to call you right away, but I only have enough money for a few minutes. Sister gave me special permission to call after midnight."

"Thanks. It means a lot." I shifted the phone over to my shoulder. Mom appeared at the top of the stairs. I pointed to the phone and mouthed Priss's name. She went back to her room. I plopped down in the cushioned chair beside the phone table carved from a single block of Lake Cypress.

"Did you hear a click?" Priss stopped talking. A slight wheeze passed through the receiver. Uh-oh. I could feel Priss's back straighten over the phone. "I think someone's listening on your party line.... Is that you, Mrs. Laborde? This is a private conversation if you don't mind. You can hang up now, you old Bitty."

It was all I could do to suppress a laugh. A soft click traveled the line. "I don't think she's listening anymore."

"Nosy ole crone." Priss's voice changed. It became soft and sad. "I can't believe it. How can your dad be gone? When Mom told me, I cried right in front of Sister Alberta and the other nuns. I can't imagine what you've been through. How is everyone? Are you okay?"

This is the Priss few people knew: a kind, tender person. I had no idea why she liked me. We weren't similar in any way, especially when it came to risks. She took on more dares than my brother and his super cool friends. But, her recklessness was a sticking point in our friendship.

"I'm all right. It's crummy though. Sort of like when he goes on excavation, but this time I know he won't be coming back."

"This is awful." Priss swallowed, making a wet clicking noise. "Mom said he didn't suffer. We have to be thankful for that."

Why did people say such ridiculous things? How much worse could it be? He was dead. I didn't say anything, and a vacant hum traveled the phone line for a full five seconds.

"How's Brett? Poor thing, he must be taking this hard. Several girls want to know how he's holding up." A little sing-song tone slipped into her voice, the kind of sound she used when she wanted something.

It was inevitable. Somehow, our conversations eventually wandered to Brett. I'm sure her friends *were dying* to know if he needed consoling. They probably had every intention of *caring* for him as soon as they hit town.

"He's handling it." I tried not to let any bitterness creep into my voice. It wasn't as if Dad's death had brought Brett and me any closer.

"One good thing. They won't make you and Brett take finals. Hello, senior year. Look, I'll be home in a few days" Priss drew in a breath. "I'm bringing a friend to Natchitoches for the summer, and I want you to meet her. In fact, I'm throwing her a party as soon as we get home. She goes to the Academy with me, but she's from New Orleans. She's the smartest girl in our class. She's so nice. You have to meet her. You'll really like her."

"Nice? Come on Priss." I couldn't believe she'd just used girl lingo for ugly.

"She's so sweet, and she could use another friend."

This just kept getting better—sweet, nice, needs a friend. What next? "I don't know."

"No really. Her name is Sara Glorioso. You'll see. She's kinda shy. You'll like her. I promise."

"If you say so."

Some girls had their sidekicks: the girl they could talk into anything, and the guy-friend she wouldn't dream of dating. That's what I was to Priss, her good ole sidekick.

An operator came on the line and in a nasal tone said, "You have one minute remaining."

"Hold on a sec." Priss's receiver made a rustling noise, and I heard coins clink into the pay phone. "My last two quarters. Where were we? Oh, yeah. When I come home."

When the operator hung up, the connection sounded as if I held a sea-shell to my ear, and Priss was deep inside.

"Tomorrow will be so hard for you. But, pretend I'm right next to you." She paused. "Oh no, I just thought of something. Is your dad's funeral open casket? Will you have to actually look at his body?"

Sometimes a stop sign was needed between Priss's brain and her mouth. My father lying lifeless in satin-lined box depressed the hell out of me. "I guess so."

"Oh my gosh. If it were me, you'd have to zip me into a straitjacket to get through it. I wouldn't trade places with you right now for a queen's crown."

"Priss, are you supposed to be comforting me? Cause you're not doing a very good job."

"Yeah. I guess I am, but I know you. You'll get through this." The phone clicked a warning. Time was up. "Listen, I have to hang up. I'll call you as soon as I'm home. Okay?"

"Okay. Oh, Priss... Thanks."

Silence.

I'm not sure if she heard the last part or not. The phone probably cut me off in midsentence, but her voice was gone, and the house became exceptionally empty. I missed Priscilla Dupree. Her intentions were good, even a bit self-centered. No doubt, when she returned home, her number one priority would be to cheer me up. God, I didn't know which I dreaded most: Dad's funeral or Priss's good intentions.

I returned to my room and sat on my bed, unable to sleep. Thoughts jumbled together, and images clacked around in my brain as if they'd spun off a film spool. I stared out my window not really looking at anything, but something moved near the driveway between two pine trees. Rising, I focused on the shadows and spotted a dark figure carrying a backpack, partially hidden by a thick pine. It was difficult to see his size other than a lean form, but he was there, wavering behind the tree for a second, then he split across the lawn, blurred in the darkness. I raced to Brett's room.

He was harder to wake up than a redneck boozed up on bargain beer, but I shook him until his head bounced around on his pillow.

"What?" He cocked open one eye and swiped my shoulder. "Get off."

"There's someone outside."

"So."

"Get up." I kicked his leg. "Someone's outside the house. Looks like a burglar."

"Awww, Jeez." Brett followed me. "This better be good."

We slipped to the window, and using my finger, I tracked an imaginary line on the mesh screen. The yard was quiet except for a summer breeze rustling through the white oleander under my window.

"He came around the driveway between those trees and ran across the yard."

Brett yawned and pressed his head into the screen. "Are you sure it's not a memory?"

"It wasn't a memory."

"Yeah, but a burglar? Come on."

"Mom said Dad felt a draft and was checking the downstairs windows when he found one opened with the screen off last night. She wanted to call the Chief, but Dad convinced her it was the wind. Then tonight I saw someone dressed in black running across *our* yard."

"J. J., there's nothing out there. Mom probably planted the idea in your head, and you just pulled up a memory. Besides, we don't have anything to steal, except ancient clay pots, and who'd want those? You know what happens when you're tired."

I didn't need to be reminded that I was most vulnerable to false memories when I was tired or stressed, but this was different. "Brett, I saw something. I'm telling you someone was out there."

"Look. It was probably the neighbor's black Lab. He's always crossing our yard. You're just tired and confused. We've got the stupid funeral tomorrow. Let's get back to bed." Brett moved away from the window and yawned, scratching the back of his head. "Just so you know, Mom's upset they won't bury Dad in the Catholic Cemetery."

"Huh? What do you mean?"

"Father John said Dad couldn't be buried in the Catholic Cemetery because Chief Hendricks thinks maybe his death wasn't an accident."

"What?"

"Chief thinks it was a possible suicide."

"Dad... committed suicide? Why would they think that? The Chief told me Dad had an accident. He told Mom the same thing. She's never said anything about suicide." My dad would never harm himself. It didn't make sense.

"Time to grow up, J. J. Of course, Mom didn't say anything. She isn't going to either. Don't forget, I'm the one who found him. All bloody on the ground. When the Chief got there, he said Dad must have fallen. He said he'd ask around, see if anyone saw something." Brett pushed back his hair, his light brows furrowed. "Later, he changed his mind. Said he thought Dad may have jumped."

"He wouldn't commit suicide. He wouldn't do that. Dad loved us. He'd never leave us." My voice shook and my hands clenched into fists. I wanted to hit Brett. Why was he saying these things?

"You're such a know-it-all. Maybe this once you didn't get it right. Dad was a man like anyone else. He wasn't perfect," said Brett.

"I don't believe you."

"The only reason I'm telling you is so tomorrow you don't cause a scene at the cemetery. Don't ask Mom any questions. And don't say anything about a burglar. I'm warning you."

Brett left the room, and I just stood there, too stunned to move. This was our Dad he was talking about. Surely Brett didn't believe it. I considered the concept even though I hated to even speculate that it was possible. Did my father kill himself?

The prowler's image running across the yard came back. I definitely didn't imagine him, and he wasn't a memory. I shivered and crept to the bed.

IV

Dad's funeral was the worst day of my life. An entire day dedicated to his memory.

I was depressed, uneasy from the night before, and searched the faces of everyone who walked through our door. No one resembled the lean shadow traipsing in our yard. Falling to sleep last night was almost impossible. There were too many unanswered questions, and no one to ask.

The next morning, Dr. Pasquier called. He asked me to work for him. He was the only general practitioner in our town who still delivered babies at home and sewed head wounds right in his office. He knew I wanted to be a doctor so last summer he showed me how to take vital signs and let me do little things around the office. This summer, he said he'd teach me to stitch, listen for heart murmurs, and set broken bones. Needless to say, I didn't turn him down.

As soon as I hung up the phone, I started for the clinic. Like everything else in Natchitoches, it was within easy walking distance. I couldn't wait to leave the house. Staying at home only made me think about Dad.

Tudy stood in the hall with the phone pressed to her ear when I came home late in the afternoon. She batted her eyelids together like some silent film star and held out the phone.

"The little princess done made it back..." she muttered as I grasped the phone.

"Hello."

"Julian... how are you?" Priss never identified herself. She assumed everyone knew her voice. "The bus driver pulled an all-nighter so we could get here by morning. I called earlier, but Tudy said you were at work."

"Yeah. Dr. Pasquier is teaching me this summer."

"Wow! That's great. Are you really okay?" Her voice sounded gentle, concerned. "I can't wait to see you. Listen, I'm throwing a party tonight for Sara."

"Tonight? You just got home."

"I know, but you have to meet her." She paused to take a breath before rattling on. "Look, I have a ton of things to do. So I'll see you tonight?"

"I don't know, Priss. I'm pretty tired." I kneaded my neck. Truthfully, a party was the last thing I wanted to do.

"Come on. I've told Sara all about you. She's dying to meet you. Besides, you need something to get your mind off things. Say you'll come. Oh... and you'll bring Brett?"

Foolish to argue, Priss would pester me forever or swing by and pick me up if I didn't go to her party. Once she made up her mind, changing it was a like taking a bone from a Doberman. I just had to buck up and go.

"Sure, I'll bring Brett."

Priss giggled. "Great! See ya later alligator."

The phone clicked. Great. A party.

The Duprees' pre-civil-war plantation, Sweet Magnolia, rested in the crook of Cane River. The main house was an enormous, dove-gray rectangle with column-lined galleries wrapping around the broad front and narrow sides. Magnolias twice as tall as the house occupied either side of the front walk, sentinels for generations. Everyone in Natchitoches Parish knew about Sweet Magnolia. It faced the river like the main diamond in a tiara.

Brett parked Woody, the old station wagon, next to a rust-colored El Camino. We stepped onto a circular drive made of crushed seashells. Dusk settled in, and fireflies flitted along the main house's steps. Mrs. Dupree,

Priss's mom, sat on the front gallery sipping a Pink Lady from a martini glass. I hadn't talked to her since she told me about Dad. She held up her glass as a greeting.

"Good evening, boys. If you're looking for Priss, she's in the back. Follow the lights."

We waved to her like polite southern boys. "Yes ma'am."

Once we were past the house, Brett tossed me the keys. "You drive Woody home. I'll ride with some of the guys."

This didn't surprise me. He never stayed for an entire party because he and his friends liked to cruise Main Street on the weekends.

A mosquito landed on my neck, and I slapped it off. I walked under Christmas lights strung all the way from the main house to the old mule barn. Dry splinters, easily mistaken for miniature wooden stakes, studded the barn walls.

Inside, hay bales were piled in each corner just in case some lucky guy ran into a good-looking girl willing to make out. Bare light bulbs formed an X across the barn ceiling and hung in huge arcs. My eyes darted around the outside of the barn. For some reason I couldn't shake the image of a prowler running across our yard, and every dark, shadowy corner gave me the creeps. I needed to get a grip.

Priss stood near the entrance under the garish light. Her hair was cropped so short she looked like a platinum Audrey Hepburn, her idol. Her denim shorts were cuffed just below her butt, emphasizing her lean tanned legs. She'd tied a matching plaid shirt at the waist. She spotted us and grinned from ear to ear. Opening her arms, she waited for us to step within hugging range. She smelled flowery sweet, probably some expensive perfume her mother gave her.

"Gosh, I've missed y'all. I can't tell you how much." She leaned into Brett. "I'm sorry I wasn't here when your father died."

Brett raised his brows. "What could you do anyway? Why fret about it?"

He pushed past her and tramped over to a few guys standing near an aluminum tub filled with brown beer bottles coated with chipped ice. It wasn't long before bees came flitting around the honey. Two girls kissed him before he even opened his beer. It came so easy for him.

"Did I say something wrong?" asked Priss.

"He's been mad since Dad died. He's angry at the whole world right now. And we're both tired of people asking, 'How're y'all doing?'"

Priss gave me a peck on my cheek. "I won't say another word."

Someone else walked up, and Priss blossomed into full-blown hostess mode, tapping the aluminum tub filled with ice and bottled drinks, then pointing toward other people in the room.

Brett caught my eye. He leaned into a girl I didn't recognize. He cradled her hand and squiggled something on the inside of her wrist. She giggled.

She wasn't from Natchitoches, that was for sure. She wore a thin white cotton shirt tucked into beige shorts, like clothes worn on safari. I half expected her to pull a pith helmet from behind her back. She laughed at something Brett said, and her dark hair shimmered blue-black in the light, dropping in thick layers to her waist. All the girls in Natchitoches teased their hair until it screamed, but not this girl. She was a knock out. Priss tapped my shoulder.

"So what do you think? I told you. Gorgeous. Right? Just like I said. Do you want to meet her?" She grabbed my arm, and before I knew it, she'd dragged me over to Sara and Brett.

My brother snickered at something he'd said. Sara brought a paper Dixie cup to her lips, nibbling at the rim. She hadn't noticed me. Her eyes were immense and an odd dark amber. The angles in her face were soft. She casually moved the cup away to answer Brett, but I didn't hear what she said. I stepped a little closer. She smelled like summer, like honeysuckle. Her fragrance went straight to my head.

"So you've met one James brother. The dangerous one." Priss draped her hand over Brett's shoulder.

"This is the other James brother, the safe one, Julian…" Priss gestured to me.

Safe? Me… safe? Nobody wanted somebody safe. Priss should have just punched me in the gut. Here was my lifelong friend insulting me in the worst way. If she said I was Jack the Ripper, I'd have more appeal.

Sara angled toward me and smiled. I swear my heart quit beating right there in my chest. I wanted to touch her, just run my finger down her back, all the way… I lifted my hand. It hovered at her waist. *What was I thinking?* I stopped.

"Hello." The little paper cup still rested on her bottom lip above a glistening drop of moisture. Man, I wished more than anything I could suck that drop off her lip.

"So how did you end up in Natchitoches?" A nerdy question, I know, but it was all I could come up with since my body was revving up like a Formula One Racer.

Brett grunted. "She goes to Sacred Heart with Priss. You know that."

A guy clicked a button on the portable record player, and music exploded through the barn. A brunette with a lacquered beehive hairdo jostled into me and yanked Brett to the room's pulsating core. Within seconds, a group of mostly girls were twisting the night away. Priss, of course, leaped in the middle, pointing her toe into the loose hay and twisting it back and forth, pretending to grind out a cigarette. But I wasn't interested in them.

Sara removed the cup. I moved closer ostensibly so she could hear me, but really so I could casually bump into her. She was driving me crazy. "Why would you come to a small town for the summer?"

"Priss made it sound quaint and unique. She said it was full of ghosts and farmers. She swore I'd love it." I strained to hear her. Sara ended the word Priss with a whispered *th* instead of a *s*, a barely-there lisp. She angled toward me and studied my eyes as she spoke. I knew why she was looking. Brett had blue eyes like Mom, but mine were pale green like Dad… pale green circled with gold rims. She shifted closer, and honeysuckle clouded my brain. Mother Mary, this girl was killing me.

I glanced at the makeshift dance floor, trying to get it together. I'd never been this jump-started before. I stepped back before I did something absurd. Priss backed into Brett, her ample butt mashed against him, twisting furiously to the music's beat. She turned around when the music stopped and pecked him with a kiss. Her actions didn't help. Made me think about Sara.

"Sorry. Gotta steal her for a bit." She clasped Sara's hand and led her over to a clutch of girls. The honeysuckle smell dissipated, and the fizz bubbling through my body with it.

Brett stood near the beer tub, and when I walked over, he tossed me a bottle. "Think fast."

He was always trying to catch me off guard. I almost missed the bottle and juggled it from one hand to the other, nearly dropping it. Luckily, I knew the opener would follow.

"Heads up," Brett yelled.

I looked up just in time. A metal opener almost hit me in the head, but I caught it and popped the top. Beer spewed all over the ground, and I jumped back. I looked around—thank God no one saw.

Brett elbowed me and gestured to the barn door. The air felt only slightly cooler outside. For a few minutes, we stood near the entrance, watching several couples slow dance.

"That girl, Sara. She's pretty neat, don't you think?" Brett tapped his beer in her direction, and I nodded.

"Yeah. She's cute."

"I wasn't talking about her looks. She's definitely not a brown bagger, though. I'm talking about how good she is at lip reading. You'd never know she's deaf."

"She's deaf?" My mouth dropped open like the hinge popped.

"Yeah. Watch her. See how she studies people. See." Brett aimed his bottle at Sara again. She scrutinized Priss and another girl. "Look how she leans in when people talk to her. She's reading their lips. Man, she's so cool. I mean she's stone deaf."

I noticed it earlier, when she was studying my eyes. She did the same thing now. She stepped in front of the girl with the beehive hairdo, crowding her when she talked. The girl craned back as if Sara made her uncomfortable.

"Don't tell me you didn't notice how strange she talked. Kinda quiet, with a slight lisp. She learned to speak without ever hearing a sound. I wouldn't have figured it out, but Priss told me."

Brett gulped down his beer, and brushed off a frothy trail above his lip. He moved back to the aluminum tub, but before he made it there, a buddy of his pulled him away. I nursed my drink and watched Sara. She chewed on her lower lip, concentrating on what the girl next to her said.

"Hey, J. J., I'm gonna head out. I'll meet you at home." Brett chuckled and clapped my shoulder. "Don't have a wreck."

After he left, I went back into the barn, past a couple so into making out they flipped backwards on a hay bale. Everyone laughed, and I chugged on toward Sara. Chuck, a guy from my high school, had planted himself next to her. His legs bowed in the middle, giving him a lost cowboy look. He must have raided his dad's cologne because he smelled like he'd been dipped into a vat of Old Spice.

"Yeah, my dad's determined to have our fallout shelter finished by August. He's not taking any chances. All the rumors about the Russians and their nuclear missiles." Chuck shook his head, his tone deadly serious. "My mom's collected every kind of canned food you can imagine and stored water in empty milk bottles. My dad bought special cots and a chemical toilet. If you want, I can come pick you up sometime and show you."

Sara's face tipped up, and she studied Chuck. She didn't reply, then a beat later she said, "I don't think I heard you correctly. You want to take me where?"

"To my fallout shelter."

Her forehead creased, and I jumped in. Speaking slowly, distinctly, and loudly, I drew a square in the air with my finger. "His... family... has... a... fall... out... shelter...."

Sara stepped back. Her voice sounded small and thin. "I understood that part."

I nodded. "Gooooood."

"Hey man, why are you talking that way?" asked Chuck.

I didn't want to embarrass Sara, so I said, "You were babbling, and I don't think she understood a word you said."

"You have shit for brains, Julian. Did anyone ever tell you *that* before?"

"Was… he… speaking… too… fast…?" What did he know? My mouth formed each word to perfection.

"No. I don't think so." Sara stepped back and brought a hand to her cheek.

"Go away, Julian. We were fine until you came along." Chuck glanced back to Sara.

"I need to help Priss with something." With a puzzled expression, she hurried away.

"Jeez, what's with you? You acted like she was a retard." Chuck stomped off, and dipped his head to avoid a string of lights.

I stood there by myself for a while. Did I do something wrong? I only wanted Sara to be comfortable. Oh no, she thought I was helping Chuck. He was a nut. She must have thought I was nuts too.

"What did you say to Sara?" Priss snuck up on me.

"I was just interpreting. You know, slowed down the conversation for her. Chuck talks way too fast."

"Why? He's such a spaz, no one listens to him anyway."

"Brett told me. You know, about her being deaf." I faced Priss. "Why did you tell Brett–"

Priss exploded with laughter, clutching her sides like she might split in two. Between cackles, she said, "You fell for it?"

My entire head was on fire. At least, Sara wasn't in the barn. Priss and a little entourage drawn to her cackling left me standing in the middle of the barn like a fool.

I was going to kill Brett.

Priss circled back, her shoulders shuddering. "Oh God. Let me catch my breath. You goober. He set you up. You should've seen it coming. You of all people know how Brett is."

"Yeah." So much for making an impression on the new girl. "Sara probably thinks I'm the weirdest person she's ever met."

"She does kinda think you're an idiot." Priss rocked back on her heels. She was enjoying this a little too much.

"Great."

"Wait here. She went to the house for a sec. When I tell her what happened, she'll think it's funny. You'll see." Priss half turned, and I swear she muttered under her breath, "She needs a good laugh."

"Uh?"

"Nothing. Just talking to myself. I'll find her."

"I don't know. I think I've done enough damage for one night. Maybe I'll just go home." Did Priss honestly think I would wait around for more humiliation?

"Stay here. Don't move. I'll be right back."

If the ground quaked and opened into a gigantic crevasse, I would gladly fall in. But I grabbed another beer instead. Brett was so sullen lately; it never occurred to me he might pull a fast one. This signaled a return to the old Brett.

Someone tapped the overhead lights and sent them swaying. When Priss and Sara returned to the barn, dancing shadows bounced across the splintered walls. The light played tricks with the girls' expressions, and I couldn't determine what they thought as they ambled across the floor.

Sara walked right up to me, but Priss hovered near the entrance, spinning beers in the icy tub. She looked our way, and I swear, her lips twitched to keep from laughing.

"Great trick. Kinda mean, but funny." Sara glanced at the swaying lights, then back to me. "I wish you'd seen your face. You were so earnest forming those long E's. I have to admit, though, it was kinda weird."

A smile kicked up at the corner of my lip. "Can't believe I fell for it."

"Me either. Maybe you aren't as smart as Priss says." Sara didn't blink.

What? My smile vanished. She was serious. I was beginning to think she wasn't shy like Priss said, just a mean snob.

Priss walked up. "So how does it feel to be in the middle of a little family rivalry?"

I shot her a look. "Wouldn't go so far as to say a rivalry."

"What would you say? A harmless prank meant to make you look like an idiot-stick?"

"I'd better go."

"Wait. Let's go to Shell Beach. It'll be midnight soon." Priss's words slid together.

"I'm not interested." I'd had enough fun for one evening. "I'm going home."

"Why?" Priss wrapped her arm around Sara, and I knew from the way she melded into Sara, she'd drunk her quota of beers for the night. "We can swim later…. Without our clothes."

Sara glanced into the dark sky like this was the most boring evening she'd ever experienced. I expected her to stifle a yawn next. No, I didn't want to stay.

"Not tonight." I stuffed my hands in my pockets and walked toward the front drive. Why didn't I leave before Priss came back? I'll never understand her. And Priss's so-called friend was too stuck up to even think about a small town guy like me, anyway.

"Tomorrow then." Priss yelled after me. "After lunch. Come on, don't be mad. It'll be fun."

I didn't turn around. The night was over for me. Priss had succeeded at one thing though. I hadn't thought about Dad or shadow figures for the last two hours. Right now all I wanted to do was kick the shit out of Brett.

V

The next morning, I went to the kitchen, poured a glass of cold milk, and grabbed some leftover biscuits from the refrigerator. Mom sat at the kitchen table, completely absorbed in Saturday's Natchitoches Daily. She never looked up.

I slathered two biscuits with grape jelly and shoved them on a plate. I split two more biscuits, stuffing each one with a glob of grape jelly mixed with enough hot pepper sauce to launch a bottle rocket, then plopped them on a plate and scooted them to the center of the counter. I had serious plans for them.

Mom turned the page and read the top line. She slurped her coffee, combining air with the hot liquid. It smelled so strongly of bitter chicory, I don't know how she drank it without cream and sugar.

"How's Priss?" Her eyes moved along the page.

"Fine." I swigged my milk and wiped my upper lip with the back of my hand.

"I hear Priss brought home a friend. Sara's her name, right?"

"How did you know?"

"Priss called this morning. She gave her condolences." Mom's face crinkled into a strained smile. "She mentioned Sara. And said you were meeting them at Cane River this afternoon."

"I'm not going to Cane River." I blew my hair off my forehead. "Don't really wanna be around Priss."

"You've said that before. I think it's a good idea. I told her you'd meet her."

"You didn't really tell her I'd go to Shell Beach, did you?"

"Yes, I did. It'll be good for you." Mom blew across her coffee cup, then sipped the dark liquid. Her nose was back in the paper.

I couldn't believe it. Why would she say yes to Priss without asking me?

She stopped reading, then folded the paper back into a neat rectangle. "Julian, something's come up, and I'm traveling to Shreveport today. I'd planned to clean your father's office, but since I can't, I need you and Brett to bring his things home. I hate to ask you to do this, but it can't be helped."

The entry stairs creaked, and Brett scuffed sleepily into the kitchen. He wore gray sweat shorts and a t-shirt with Natchitoches Track and Field across the front. He yawned his good morning.

"Have any plans for the day?" I asked.

"Yeah. I'm meeting Jack and Austin. We're gonna drive their boat down the river." Brett loped across the green linoleum tiles and poured a whopping glass of milk. Just like I'd hoped, he spied the biscuits left on the counter and brought them to the table. When he dropped into his seat, he beat a drum roll with his index fingers.

Mom lowered the newspaper. "Can you go to the Crawfords' this afternoon? You need to help Julian clean your dad's office."

"Aw Mom. We're gonna ski before the river turns choppy."

Mom gave Brett a look, one that said she wasn't asking.

"Okay. I'll meet up with them later." He was miffed until he rediscovered me. "So, little brother, how did it go last night? Did you talk to *Sara* any more?" He snickered, his nose scrunching like a comic book villain.

"Not really. She was busy meeting everyone else at the party. You know, reading lips and all. It's a slow process."

Mom's interest piqued. "Sara reads lips?"

Before I could answer, Brett popped an entire biscuit into his mouth. He made a loud smack with his lips just before his eyes bugged out of his head. He jerked up. His chair screeched across the floor. He streaked for the kitchen sink, spitting and gagging. Mom flitted behind him, patting his back. He shoved the water faucet on and gurgled water between breaths. I laughed so hard I nearly fell off my chair.

He spun around, inadvertently shoving Mom into the cabinet. Water spurted everywhere as he stomped over to me. "What the hell? You're dead, you little shit."

"Revenge is a dish best served cold." I grinned. I knew better than to swat at a mad hornet.

Brett punched me, full force, in the middle of the chest. I fell backward on the table. Plates crashed to the floor, and food splattered all over the cabinets. Coffee and milk zipped over the table's Formica top, pooling at the back of my shirt. Mom's hands whirled around her head, as if flapping the air would actually stop the fight. Brett punched me again in the chest.

I bounced up before he jabbed me again. He hadn't expected it and was rattled for a split second. But it was more than enough time. I used my chest like a battering ram and shoved him clear across the kitchen. At the same time I brought my fists up, protecting my face. Brett, however, didn't go for my face. He doubled over and shot forward with a head butt, bashing me hard in the stomach. My breath whooshed out. *Oh God*. I was dying. I couldn't suck in a breath. My lungs burned, and I swear, my heart slowed to a single thud. Brett yanked the front of my shirt, and my feet scuttled over the floor.

"Stop!" Mom shouted. Brett dropped my shirt so fast I tumbled into him. I struggled to breathe, but my lungs were completely paralyzed.

All noise left the room, and for a few seconds, Brett's hoarse breathing was the only sound. My diaphragm unhitched, and I sucked a lungful of cool air.

"What in heaven's name?" Mom's voice quaked.

"He spiked my biscuits with hot sauce," said Brett.

"He told me Sara was deaf. Like an idiot, I fell for it. Thought I'd get him back." I leaned toward Brett. "You're such a jerk!"

Brett snorted with laughter. "You're such a smartass know-it-all. What did you do? Try to speak to her in sign language? You did, didn't you? Oh man, I wish I'd been there."

I glared at my brother. Mom touched my arm. It held me in place.

"I have enough to worry about without you two fighting. You've got to stop this. I can't tolerate much more."

"But Mom, Brett embarrassed me in front of everyone..."

Mom's head drooped. I didn't need to see her face. She was tearing up. Anger seeped out of me, and my hand relaxed. I wanted to take it back, the fighting and the name calling, but it was too late. She bit her lower lip until it lost all color, and she wouldn't make eye contact with Brett or me.

"Mom. What's wrong?" I asked.

"I didn't want to worry you, but I've never been very good at hiding anything from y'all." She dropped into a kitchen chair. "A suicide clause is written into your father's insurance policy. He probably never thought a thing about it. But the life insurance money is frozen until the sheriff makes a firm decision concerning his death. We may never see a penny."

Good God, first Dad's death. Now this. He always told Mom not to worry. If anything happened to him, everything would be taken care of. Without the insurance money, what would happen to us? Where would we live?

Dad's death was an accident. Had to be. Things just didn't add up. He would never leave us in such straits. There must be clues, something.... The shadowy figure came to mind, but Brett didn't even believe me. All I really had was a hunch.

"What if we could prove Dad's death was an accident?" I asked.

"Then the insurance company would surrender the entire cash benefit to his beneficiaries, us." Mom rose from her chair and wearily collected the broken dishes off the table. "I don't know how we'd prove it, though. It rests with Chief Hendricks. We can only pray he finds something. There's nothing we can do."

She made it sound so hopeless, but I wasn't ready to give up. I knew my father. I knew he wouldn't commit suicide. And Mom hadn't mentioned

Dad's missing diary. I'd wondered if she'd even noticed. She hadn't noticed a lot of things lately.

She cradled the dishes to the sink. Brett pressed his back against the kitchen door, sulking. I stood by the table and traced spilled milk with my finger. I hadn't meant to hurt Mom. If only I could redo the last few minutes.

"I have to leave, or I'll be late. Y'all clean up your mess." Mom carefully positioned each dish in the sink. "Rebecca Sharp is taking me to Shreveport to meet with a lawyer."

Weird. What was she talking about? She worked with Dad. She wasn't one of Mom's usual friends. "Why are you going with Miss Sharp?"

"She's been very kind. She even talked the lawyer into coming in on his day off." Mom's tone turned defensive. "You know, she admired your father a great deal. Oh, she did ask if we'd seen his research folder. It seems to be missing. Have either of you seen it?"

Brett and I shook our heads. The only thing we agreed on.

"Ah well, I'm sure it'll show up."

Once she left the room, Brett stomped toward the table, and I grabbed a mop off the back porch. The only sounds in the room were dishes clattering, and the mop swooshing across the floor.

"Maybe we should cool it around Mom for a while. She has enough on her mind without you losing your temper every ten minutes. You could take some responsibility every once in a while." I swiped the floor under the table, leaving a thin trail of milk.

"Who do you think you are... God?" Brett tossed Mom's coffee cup in the sink.

"I was thinking of Mom." I took another swipe.

"You're wrapped so tight I don't see how you walk down the street." Brett slammed his hand on the table. "As far as Mom goes, I do think about her, but you don't always know what goes on around here. You've always got your nose stuck in some book."

"I just said—"

Brett tossed the remaining dishes in the sink. "Don't say another word. And don't ever lecture me again. Leave it alone."

He made for the back door. It fanned open and slammed shut behind him.

Dad's office occupied a space on the top floor of Russell Hall. I looked up at the framed glass windows facing the campus and wondered what really happened to my father. I traipsed over a worn path, around drooping aza-lea bushes and a row of fuzzy purple iris, to the side door.

When I entered Dad's office, Brett stood akimbo, looking down through the very window where Dad fell.

He didn't say anything when I walked in, and I couldn't tell whether he was still mad or not. He nudged a box with his foot. "Let's get this over with. I'll start with the desk, and you empty the book shelves."

"All right."

He didn't budge and ran his foot along the windowsill. I moved in closer and squatted near the window. I ran my finger over a snaking, deep gouge disfiguring the entire lower panel. Something scraped the window-sill, something sharp. It wasn't there before.

"Dad was always so careful. He didn't open this window and fall out." I rose and pressed my forehead against the glass. "He was petrified of heights. Remember when he cleaned the gutters? He always tied a safety rope around his waist."

"Yeah, kinda weird."

"I know. There's no way he jumped." I bit my thumbnail while mulling over it. "Brett, did Dad seem melancholy to you? Everyone keeps talking about his depression."

"Mom said he was down, but he wasn't that way around me." Brett stepped back from the window.

"Me either." I turned back to the room. It just didn't make sense. Dad wasn't sad. In fact he was happy, especially about the recent discoveries at the archeology site. When did that change? Why didn't I notice?

A sliver of iridescent blue caught my eye. Five large shadow boxes filled with rare, richly colored butterflies stretched across the wall. Some specimens were from remote parts of the world, captured while Dad was on excavation. A cold aura started. Frost formed like a crust around my brain, and thin cool images thawed into bright, intense colors.

A striking yellow and blue butterfly flew through the glass and darted around the room. Dad waved a net past several intense green plants, the leaves bent into the wet path. Light filtered past loopy vines studded with giant trumpet-shaped flowers. The butterfly flitted just past my eye.

I bit the inside of my lip. Could have pinched the webs between my fingers or jabbed my nails into my skin, but biting my lip was always the quickest way to come back. I knew the memory wasn't real, but it made me sad to come back to the real world, a world without Dad. I closed my eyes and regained my bearings. When I opened them again I checked out the shadow boxes. Odd, the box closest to the window was knocked askew.

To collect butterfly specimens, he had to catch them and preserve them. He kept all the necessary items in a white stand-alone medicine cabinet behind his office door. I opened the glass door to the cabinet. A crimson tin of ether, label turned to the back, rested on the top shelf, and below it on the next shelf were two navy blue cardboard boxes containing raw cotton. Next to the tin sat a jar filled with powdered alum and some watercolor brushes. Specimen jars lined the bottom shelf; four were empty and pushed to the back. And icy finger jabbed my brain. *Snap! Dad held up the jar with the powdered alum and nodded.* I somehow had backed all the way across the room and into Brett. My eyelids flew open.

"Hey. Watch it." He smoothed his hand over Dad's worn leather writing pad. Several photos surrounded the pad on Dad's desk. A picture of Mom and Dad waving from the Eiffel Tower rested next to the phone, apart from the other photos. My chest ached. They looked so happy. Another picture, a family portrait snapped at the British Museum two years ago, was surrounded by vacation snapshots and school pictures. I could hardly look at them.

An unremarkable black telephone took up the right corner. An alabaster fountain pen in a wooden cradle lay next to it. *Snap!* Lightning flashed across my brain, again. An image saved and added to others. I couldn't put my finger on it, but something about his desk looked wrong.

I swallowed and concentrated on Dad, letting a few memories in. It hadn't been that long that I'd learned to control some recollections. They hovered at the door of my consciousness, waiting to take over. I'd been able to open the door and let a few in, but I had to be careful an aura didn't start, signaling a full-blown hyperkinetic memory.

Old images of Dad's office played like a slide show inside my head, only faster, blurred at a thousand images per second. One picture halted and enlarged. I mentally scanned it. In the image an over-sized coffee mug on a wooden coaster sat next to the phone. It had a blue and white Scottish flag on it to remind him of the year he spent studying the mounds in Scotland. I ran my hand over the worn coaster next to the phone. The mug was missing. Odd. He drank coffee from that mug every day. Why wasn't it there?

Brett was right. This wasn't easy. I grabbed a box and scooted it over to the built-in file cabinet. I tugged on the drawer, and it easily opened. It was unlocked. Each week, Dad paid me a dollar to file his papers. The last time I came to his office, several folders hung in color-coded slips inside the file cabinet, one for each excavation. He always filed them by date, and I'd memorized their positions. Right away, I noticed all the folders were there except the one for the current excavation.

"Not all of Dad's folders are here." I pointed to a vacant slot in the file drawer. "His diary wasn't on his bedside table, and his favorite mug isn't on his desk."

"They're probably at home. Why are you so wound up?" Brett removed the writing pad, a stack of site maps, and several framed pictures. He dropped them into a box and opened the top drawer.

"Because he stored all his research notes and new theories in his file cabinet. He kept the cabinet locked." Maybe Dad gave Dr. McKnight the missing file? He had become department head now Dad was gone.

Come to think of it, I hadn't seen him. He didn't attend the funeral, either. "Rebecca Sharp asked Mom about Dad's folder. She knew already it wasn't here. And where's Dr. McKnight?"

"Dr. McKnight left at the end of term like he always does. Dad said the man would have lived on an island if he could get away with it. You'll never make any sense outta this. Give it a rest."

If the file wasn't in the cabinet, where was it? Maybe he did take it home. I'd look later. I closed the file cabinet and turned to the bookshelves. Dad was a true bibliophile and always said, "A man is made better by the books he reads."

He kept every book he'd ever read. There were bulging boxes at home along with overflowing shelves in his study and bedroom. His philosophy was the main reason I always had a book in my hand. He allowed me to read any novel as long as I replaced it on the shelf where I found it. Not too difficult with my so-called photographic memory.

He was astonished at my ability to memorize an entire book. When the teachers complained about my daydreaming at school, Dad defended me. He knew I'd fallen into in a memory, but he always came up with some convincing excuse. He protected me. It was his idea to tell everyone I had a photographic memory. He said most people had heard of that, making it easier to explain than a hyperkinetic memory. Who would defend me now?

I opened a small ladder and climbed up until I reached the top shelf. My hand skated over the top row of books. I touched something about the size of a deck of cards. It fell through my fingers and bounced onto the desk before landing in the same drawer that Brett had rummaged through. It collided with a heap of paper clips, scattering them across the floor and under the desk.

Brett picked up the book and thumbed through it. "*Mastering Simple Codes*. I'd almost forgotten about this book."

When we were younger, Dad taught us simple codes. Later, he introduced us to book ciphers and more difficult types of decoding. It became a game for a while.

"I wonder why he kept this?" Brett showed it to me before tossing it in a box with photos.

"Wow. He kept our first codebook. No telling what else we'll find." I removed more books from the upper shelf. But the codebook had triggered a memory, and the aura began. Icy cold surrounded my brain, and images expanded, warming in my mind.

I smelled birthday cake and burned wax. Five candles smoldered on the cake decorated with iced cowboys, and a string of smoke led to a birthday card. A coded message was written inside. Dad stood beside me, sucking on a candy cane while I decoded four numbers. Peppermint stung my nose. I scribbled with a pencil converting the numbers into letters. A simple code...

"You can do it, son." He stroked my hair. "Just one more letter."

I bit my tongue and concentrated, converting the last letter: BIKE.

I knew it. I jumped up and yelled. "A bike. A bike."

I raced for the back door. My first bike leaned against the bottom steps, a red Schwinn Hornet. I turned. Dad stood right behind me. He grinned with the candy cane stuck in the corner of his mouth.

"Hey." Brett thumped my leg. I shook my head and opened my eyes. I hated reentry. My head and body ached like I'd squeezed back through a tunnel. My nose still tingled with the smell of peppermint.

"Are you listening?" He fanned Dad's daily planner at me.

He plopped it on the desk and opened it. Monday, May 20, 1962, was circled in red and marked with a big X. The day I came home, the day Dad died.

"Why would Dad mark the day he died? Maybe he did plan it," said Brett.

"That's nuts, Brett." Why was it so easy for him to believe Dad committed suicide? I stepped off the ladder. "Think about it. It's too weird."

"Everything's weird," said Brett. "I can't go anywhere without someone coming up and saying it must have been awful to find Dad. The old ladies are the worst, slobbering me with kisses or giving me a pity pat."

I felt like I'd stepped in dog shit, and no one wanted to tell me, so I kept walking around with the damn putrid stuff stuck to my shoe. But every time I brought up a reason Dad wouldn't have jumped or fell, Brett shot it down. Was I the only one who thought this was strange?

I threw some books in a box. Dad was careful, meticulous, and dependable. If he'd planned his own death, he would have left things much more organized. He would have arranged everything for Mom, like his life insurance. His research would have been easy to find. This whole thing stunk.

Brett finished the desk and helped me with the books. We heard a cough. Miss Rebecca Sharp was standing at the door. Her long blond hair flipped at the shoulder, and she patted a shiny black headband into place. She flicked a pair of white gloves over her wrist as she walked in. Professor Noble stood behind her in the doorway, wearing a threadbare tweed suit. Even in this heat, he wore a vest underneath. A gold chain, draped from one pocket to another, stretched tightly over his rounded belly. His thin hair, coated with smelly pomade, shone as if he'd polished it into a fine slick mat. He held a handkerchief to his face.

"I stopped by to pick up a site map before taking your mother to Shreveport." A northern accent chopped into Miss Sharp's words. "This is such a delicate time. I truly want to help."

Brett and I just stared. I hadn't expected anyone to be here on the weekend. Before we could respond, she turned to leave and spoke to Professor Noble, placing a hand on his arm. "Good luck. I'll be back later today. Bye, boys."

"I hope all turns out well." Professor Noble lowered his handkerchief. A puckered expression on his face, as if he'd eaten something sour, had been hidden behind the pale cotton cloth. He stuffed his handkerchief in his breast pocket, leaving his wrinkled initials hanging over the edge, and fiddled with his watch chain.

"This has been such a tragedy, a true tragedy." Professor Noble snagged his finger along the chain. He was so fidgety in his own skin he made everyone around him uncomfortable, probably why he was nicknamed: Crazy Kurt Noble. "You know, your father proposed research on earthen mounds in northern Louisiana long before anyone else and became the foremost expert on ancient mound-building cultures. His students loved him, and unlike most scholars, he was a pleasure to work with. He will be wholeheartedly missed."

No one said anything. A fresh ache surrounded us. Then Professor Noble noted the book in Brett's hand. "His recent discoveries would have made his name a household word. His research on human bones found at the site is safe with me."

Without missing a beat, Brett dropped the book into a box at his feet. Professor Noble thumbed the chain stretched over his stomach in a detached way. His vision glazed. He frowned as if struggling to gather his thoughts.

"Essentially, we must know about any of your father's proposals. This recent earthen mound has some exceptionally old bones and pottery. It will change how the world thinks about man and his origins. All recorded field notes, forms, drawings, and photos are stored here at the college, but he always kept his own file with his theories and thoughts. No one kept more thorough research notes." Professor Noble chewed his bottom lip. "If only your father hadn't been so depressed. Sadly, his death is a terrible blot on a good man's name."

I shoved more books into a box while my brother pulled down pictures, awards, and diplomas. We left the shadow boxes for last. They'd have to be wrapped to protect the glass.

Professor Noble only made this worse. However, one thing was certain. Dad's research folder was missing, and we weren't the only ones looking for it.

Professor Noble stood mute at the door, watching us. His thumb twisted into his watch chain. "I should be heading to the excavation site. There's work to be done." He looked out the window, but quickly shifted his gaze back to us. "I wish your father... Well, I wish he'd come to me first."

With that, his lip trembled, and he pivoted out the door, leaving behind the sickly sweet smell of pomade. Professor Noble was such a pompous man. I pressed more books into the box and then said in a low voice, "He didn't waste any time implying Dad's death was a suicide. Why would he say such a thing? He worked with Dad and knew him better than most people."

"People believe what they want to believe." Brett punched down the flaps of the last box.

"Even members of his own family." Incredible. Why did Brett believe the worst? I had doubts too, but I wasn't about to let anyone know.

"What do you mean?"

"You're more worried about what everyone's saying than defending Dad." There, I'd said it.

"Look. Get off my back." He folded the cardboard edges together and lifted the box to leave. "I loved Dad, too."

Sun streamed through the window and shimmered across the campus. The day was like any other warm spring day, but my insides were cold.

Brett picked up a box. "There's no point to all this talking. I'll carry this to the car. You take down the butterflies."

"Fine." I wanted space between us.

I moved to the shadow boxes. But sunlight hit a slick, shiny spot on the wooden floor near Dad's desk. I tilted my head to see it better. I knelt down and touched the surface. Something sticky formed a half-moon shape. I traced it, but couldn't make it out well. Suddenly, I remembered the alum on the shelf. We hadn't packed it away, yet.

I grabbed the jar of alum and a brush. Then I knelt again and sniffed the floor. It smelled like coffee. I dipped the brush in the jar and carefully shook the powdered alum over the print. Helping Dad at an excavation site had its benefits. Like learning how to dust something ancient so you didn't disturb it. The surface was nice and sticky and the alum stuck instantly. A partial-heel-print appeared, as if someone spilled super sweet coffee and stepped in it. I couldn't determine whether the print was male or female, but it was from a right shoe, and a line ran down the middle, a crack or two pieces glued together. Letters made an arc on the heel, divided by the split. Obviously a word or name, with several letters smudged, but two were clearly visible: **N** and **E**.

The heel print didn't belong to Dad. He wore a basic oxford shoe with no numbers or lettering on the heel. So whose shoeprint was this?

VI

I remembered Dad kept packing tape in the bottom file drawer. I tore off two pieces, creating a section about four inches by four inches, then stretched it over the mark, making a perfect print. Then I slipped the tape inside a manila envelope.

How did Dad miss this? He was such a neat freak; he would have cleaned up a coffee spill. Even if he were preoccupied, he would have straightened the shadow boxes on the wall. I'd seen him do it a thousand times: just reach out and straighten a photo or picture.

He was afraid of heights so I wasn't buying the accident. I wasn't convinced he'd commit suicide, either, especially now when he was on the verge of a new discovery. His office was always orderly, so why would he leave tins and specimen jars out of order, and his file drawer unlocked? Nothing made sense, and I wanted to get to the bottom of this. I had to find out what really happened to my Dad.

I was dying to tell Brett about the heel print, but he'd say drop it or accept the inevitable, and I couldn't deal with him right now.

When I arrived home, I raced to the study, searching for a place to hide the heel print. I slipped it into the bottom drawer of Dad's desk. Awards and personal mementos lined the shelves with his books. The room reminded me how much I missed him, but right now I had to concentrate on finding his research folder, and to do that I had to remember where I'd last seen it.

Sometimes I could let a memory in without falling into a total hyper-kinetic mode, but I had to focus the way a pilot focuses on a runway, and the conditions had to be just right. The study was quiet and once I closed the curtains, the room was muted with only a hint of light. I sat in his desk chair and relaxed, breathing slowly in and out. In my head I clasped a memory tightly between my hands, warming it before I released it. I let it go, and it unfurled like a flag.

Dad sat in his office, making hasty notes on a typed page. The brown folder was half hidden beneath the white typing paper. Dad was unusually distracted and didn't hear me until I stood in front of his desk. He flipped over the page, and I couldn't see what he'd written. I caught a glimpse when he tucked the paper inside the folder, but I couldn't make out a single word. I wasn't close enough. I wanted to reach out and touch Dad. The ditto copier clanked rhythmically across the hall, making purple inked papers for the students. Dad's spicy aftershave was overpowered by the chemical smell coming from the copy machine. He blinked. "What do you want, son?"

His image dissipated on the last word. My throat clenched, strangled with the fruity alcoholic odor from ditto pages. I missed Dad so much I could hardly think. Sadness gripped me, but I couldn't let it drive me over the edge. I pushed down my emotions, swallowed them down. What *did* I want? I wanted to prove Dad didn't kill himself. I wanted to prove it was an accident. Had to be. But to do that I had to find his research folder. It had to be here in the study.

I pulled out books and looked behind photos, opened every drawer, looked under every chair, and practically dismantled his desk. Nothing. I searched through all his papers stacked inside a lower cabinet. Again nothing. Then another thought hit me. Maybe the folder was with his diary. Maybe he hid them together.

I plodded up the stairs to search his bedroom. His drawers and closet were perfectly neat, as if he were in military school, waiting for inspection. What was I missing?

I threw up my hands and shuffled to my room then flopped on the bed and stared at the ceiling. Nothing. No hints, nothing. He always left his diary either on his bedside table or in the barrister's cabinet. It wasn't coincidence that Dad's folder and diary were both missing. But if he did hide them… why? And why was Professor Noble so worried about finding Dad's research folder? He had access to all the site maps and files Dad collected and recorded from the excavation. And what about the shadowy figure watching the house? Was all this connected? It had to be, but I couldn't figure it out.

My mind jumped all over. Crap! I was getting nowhere but depressed and confused. What if I divided my search and looked for the diary? Focus on one thing at a time? That's what I needed to do; too many thoughts cluttered my head like too many typewriter keys punched at one time, glommed together, forming one big messy splotch.

My Big Ben alarm clock clicked the time. I unconsciously ticked along the seconds. What time was it? I groaned. Midafternoon. Priss waited for me at Sweet Magnolia. I really wanted to stay and look for Dad's diary. If only the new girl, Sara, weren't there. She was pretty, but she was also stuck up. I didn't know if I liked her.

I rolled off the bed and checked out my bedroom window. The sun filtered through the trees and shadows filled the yard, but no one was there. The dark figure had been watching the house from the drive, but there was no evidence anyone had ever been there, a true phantom.

I wasn't in the mood to deal with Priss, but better to leave now than suffer the consequences later. Maybe Mom had a point. Some fresh air might clear my mind. Then I could come back and concentrate on finding Dad's diary. Maybe then I could start connecting the dots.

Sweet Magnolia came into view just off the road. An ancient single lane bridge spanned Cane River, less than a mile from Priss's drive. Shell Beach was just the other side. Sunlight skipped across two acres of blinding-white seashells, looked like a chipped, sparkling snowdrift refusing to melt into the river.

I parked in the Duprees' drive and heard giggling and shouting coming from the beach. About twenty or so girls were already sunning themselves on jumbo-sized beach towels. They smeared on baby oil mixed with Mercurochrome as if they were basting turkeys. I didn't see Priss or Sara.

A screen door slammed shut, and I set out for the big house to check it out. Priss and Sara stepped from the porch's shady side into the sharp summer light. Sara twisted the cap on a brown bottle of Coppertone and tossed it into Priss's picnic basket. Before she was even two feet from me, I smelled the very thing that reminded of summer and vacations: liquid coconut.

"Where've you been? We've been waiting all day," said Priss. A smile slipped across her face. She wasn't really angry.

"You said afternoon, right?" I lifted the basket off her arm, resting it against my cut-off jeans. I glanced over at Sara and nodded a hello. She nodded back as she looked into the sky, a habit I noticed before when she wanted to put a little distance between us. I, on the other hand, didn't want to say anything she might—and would—use against me later.

We angled through the glass bottle garden leading to the road. One of Priss's ancestors had planted the garden before the Civil War. Heavy green, amber, and crystal wine bottles were half buried along a gravel trail. Periwinkles grew over the bottles, ghosting blue and white in the foggy glass.

The girls' flip-flops slapped against their heels, just thin red rubber, barely enough to protect their feet from the hot pavement. We crossed the ancient trestle bridge to reach Shell Beach. Priss picked up speed and leaned over the railing first. Sara's fingers grasped the lichen-encrusted railing with uncertainty. She inched to the edge and peered over the side. Beneath us, Cane River moseyed past. Soft waves rippled through the steel-colored water.

"I wonder who'll take the plunge this year?" Priss asked, her question pointed at me.

I shrugged. "Whoever's fool enough."

"Come on. Don't tell me you've never wanted to jump over the rail and dive in the water. You could be first this year. Show the rest of us." Priss pressed her back against the railing. I didn't mistake the challenge.

"Why would I say yes to such an asinine risk?"

"Oh, I don't know. Just for the fun of it. Don't you ever want to throw caution to the wind? Maybe like Professor McKnight and Penny, your dad's secretary?"

"What are you talking about?"

"Mom said they eloped."

"How does she know?" My mom hadn't said a word about it, but then again, she wasn't talking about much. Knowing him, he probably took his new wife to some exotic island. Explained why no one could reach him.

"Everyone knows. Isn't it romantic?"

I didn't answer. Instead, hefting the basket close to my body, I turned my back to them and walked toward the beach. Hushed voices followed me. I knew Priss was dying for me to overhear, but I'd learned long ago she hated it when I ignored her.

A black transistor radio no larger than a shoebox flung music into the air. Brenda Lee's miserable song, "I'm Sorry" stung my ears. I grimaced. I'd never heard Priss say I'm sorry. Those words never left her lips.

The shells shifted under my shoes, and I heard Priss greeting everyone before she stepped foot on the so-called beach. I dropped the picnic basket to the ground and slogged my way to the river's edge through the bleached shells. I turned around. Sara crashed into me. A full body slam, and I hadn't even planned it. She was on my heels the entire time. Something I needed to remember. This girl could sneak up without a sound.

She blinked. "Sorry. It's hard to walk on this stuff. Shell crumbs get stuck between your toes."

"That's because you call those little pieces of rubber 'shoes.' I think it might be easier without them. Here let me help."

I slipped my arm around her waist so she could lean against me and slide her shoes off. She tipped her head and gazed at me through her lashes.

Her heart beat against my ribs. I couldn't help but notice the rapid rate. She didn't seem to like me, so why the racing heart?

"Much better." She backed away and unfurled a towel.

Her terrycloth cover lifted, revealing her swimsuit covered in black and yellow sunflowers. It cupped her rounded butt perfectly. The best view I'd had in a long time.

"I saw a snake near Priss's house yesterday." Sara shivered despite a warm breeze. "It coiled into a circle with its tongue darting at me. Priss said not to run, or it would chase after me. They're so evil looking. Tell me snakes don't come to the river."

"Statistically more people die from bee stings than snake bites." Sara thought she was so smart, but she obviously didn't know everything. "Do you hear how much noise everyone's making? Snakes hate humans. Believe me, they're long gone."

"Good…. " Sara's expression went from relief to thoughtful. "What about all the stories where hundreds of them coil into a big ball and stir up the water? You know, where someone falls in and they're bitten to death before they surface."

"Don't believe everything you hear. Just a myth. Snakes don't travel in packs."

"Are you making fun of me? You probably think I'm afraid because I'm from the city." Sara looked at me. "I read about snakes in a nature magazine."

I snorted. "Doesn't mean it's true."

She plopped on a towel and ignored me.

Priss meandered over and sank onto another towel. With a flourish, she pulled her cover over her head. Her platinum hair stuck up near the crown, making her look like a newborn chicken. She wore a pink two-piece with ruffles that showed off her smooth, flat stomach, but within two minutes a cloud of tiny gray gnats swarmed around her. She sprang up, swatting and spitting, then rushed to the river.

The little swarm was determined though and drifted to the other girls wading in the shallows. They dogged the girls until they were shoulder deep in the river. Priss dipped under the water. I knew something was up by the smirk on her face before she disappeared. A few local guys showed up and were horsing around, splashing the girls just to hear them screech and fuss. Sara stood beside me. For some reason the gnats didn't bother her. She held a coppery strand of hair to her mouth.

Since Priss hadn't surfaced yet, I knew it wouldn't be long before someone fell victim. She was worse than an underwater serpent. Two girls jerked, losing their balance, their arms flailing. Something snagged them. Their screams gurgled as their heads sank beneath the surface. In a snap Cane River roiled with arms and legs. It reminded me of scary movies where the piranhas eat human flesh with abandon, and the river becomes murky with body parts and blood.

I raced for the river. As soon as my feet hit the water, I remembered Sara and turned around. She unbuttoned her cover and let it fall to her towel. Whoa. Her flowered swimsuit stuck to her body like wet skin. Her hands settled on either side of her narrow waist, and she stretched out her lean legs. I couldn't move.

Sara looked at me. "Take a picture, it'll last longer."

I gulped and jumped into the river. The water was tepid at best. It lapped around my ears, and did nothing to cool my burning face. What was I thinking? She must have thought I was the most white bread guy she'd ever met.

I floated on my back. *Let it go.* She wasn't interested, anyway. I regulated my breathing and floated downstream. I let images of Dad float with me and prepared for a full blown hyperkinetic memory. His bedroom came to mind. *The barrister's bookcase opened. I smelled the dusty diaries and reached out...*

Fingers raked along my back and flipped me facedown into the river. Dirty water gushed into my mouth and up my nose. I kicked out, contacting nothing but water, then spun upward until my head crashed to the surface. Priss slapped my shoulder and laughed so much she could barely tread water.

"Did you think getting in last would save you?" She arched one brow.

"No. Had temporary insanity." I fanned the water. "Too much to hope for."

"You're no fun. Dare you to swim to the other side on one breath? I'll give you a head start." She looked over at Sara and winked.

Not waiting for an answer, Priss dove into the water. I swam fast, a swift freestyle, and darted past her within seconds, then dove deeper. With my ears fully underwater, I heard a distinct whizzing. I zipped to the surface. A sleek wooden Chris Craft skipped toward us. Its polished hull split a path in the river, and white waves crested with each bounce. Brett skied behind the boat's wake, shooting his middle finger at the kids on the beach.

Priss was still underwater. I dashed ahead to the shallows and stood up with the water lapping my knees. Frantic, I signaled for the driver to slow down, pointing to the last spot Priss submerged. Either he didn't see me or didn't care and continued to barrel toward the beach. Everyone shouted and leapt in the air, trying to get the driver's attention. The speedboat howled toward us, now only feet away. Panic zinged up my backbone as I desperately searched the river for Priss.

VII

The boat plowed toward Shell Beach. I dipped below the surface, but couldn't see a thing through the silt kicked up around me. Surely she could hear the motor–it's distinctive electrical saw sound permeated the water. I resurfaced. A hand grabbed my leg, and Priss rose beside me. A smile lit her face.

I grabbed her and lunged toward the beach. The boat jackknifed, spraying us with water before the driver turned off the engine. Brett bobbed past us on twin skis, barely missing us. He flew over the shells, coming to a smooth stop.

I yelled out, "Stupid trick. You could have killed someone."

I glanced back at the boat's driver, Jackson "Jack" Crawford. He laughed like Woody Woodpecker. Jerk.

"Not cool, Jack," I said.

He pulled a face and saluted. "Sure thing, Sergeant Safety."

I knew better. He lived to mock me. Priss jerked her arm away and waded to the beach. I followed her, determined to say a thing or two.

"Priss, didn't you hear the boat? That's the dumbest thing you've ever done. Why didn't you surface so they could see you?" She came close to being sliced into little pieces. Why did she do such foolish things? I didn't need her taking risks right now. I had too much on my mind trying to find clues about Dad's death.

"Good grief. You worry too much. I was beside you the whole time." She glanced at me. "It wasn't that big a deal. You don't have to get so bent out of shape."

"Priss…" I shook my head. She thought it was just about her. I wished I could tell her what was bothering me about the rumors, but she'd probably heard them anyway. No one really understood the need to find out how Dad died. It was more than insurance money. More than worry about where we'd live or what would happen to us. This was my father's reputation. He was a good man, a responsible man. He deserved better. The need to find answers was always with me. It occupied my mind and invaded my dreams.

A few people watched us from the beach, Sara among them. She stood apart from the others. I couldn't read her expression. Did she think I was Sergeant Safety? Was I too cautious? Brett sometimes accused me of overthinking everything. Was that the same thing?

The boat drifted into the shallows, grounding its hull in the mud. Jack helped Austin, his twin brother, coil up the ski rope. They were more mischievous than Brett and worked hard on their reputations. Fortunately for them, the entire town knew they weren't intentionally dangerous and turned a blind eye to most of their shenanigans.

The twins were on the beach in no time. They weren't identical, but they were the tallest kids I knew, at least six-three, and sported crew cuts so stiff you could pluck a hair and use it for a toothpick. Brett heaved down onto my towel before I had a chance to get there, positioning himself close to Sara. But Priss dropped on the towel between them, successfully blocking half his view. I stood to the side, dripping wet, not sure what to do. The Crawfords came up and wolfishly stared at Sara.

"Water's great," Brett said as he shook his head, shedding spray like a wet dog.

"We know," said Priss. She ran her hand seductively down her side and over her hip, eyeing the boys to make sure they watched her.

Austin whistled between his teeth before elbowing Jack. They grinned wickedly; trouble wasn't far behind. They gave Brett a tight nod.

"Water looks deep enough for a leap from the bridge," said Austin.

"Who's up for it?" asked Jack. He nudged Sara with his foot. "How about you new girl?"

"Leave Sara alone," said Brett. Then addressing her, he said, "Don't pay any attention to them. They're just dumbasses."

This was new. I'd never known Brett to come to anyone's rescue. Priss noticed too because she cocked her head and noted Sara's reaction. Sara just ignored them and looked at the sky.

Austin bent toward Brett. "Who you calling a dumbass? You know you want to be the first."

"No way, man. The last time somebody jumped off the bridge they broke both their legs. You won't catch me jumping off that thing," said Brett.

"Chicken shit! Come on. Jumpin's a blast." Austin pretended to dive from a standing position.

"Maybe later." Brett swatted at the brothers. Austin slapped Jack's back, and they made their way to another group of kids along the water's edge.

"Did someone really break their legs jumping off the bridge?" asked Sara.

Brett spoke like the voice of authority. "Not only did the guy break his legs, he broke his neck. So now you've been warned."

"Not true. Don't listen to him. No one broke their neck," said Priss. "He just wants you to think he's *so* brave. He'll change his mind in a minute and jump from the bridge. He does it every year."

Pointing at the bridge, I said, "It can be dangerous. Depends on the time of the year. In late summer the river can be down as much as five to ten feet. A few peabrained people have been stupid enough to jump. Once a guy even died."

"Julian, that's a big, fat lie. Something our parents made up so we wouldn't jump. As long as I've lived here, no one has ever been hurt." Priss pinched a ripe strawberry from the picnic basket and kissed the tip end. Then she seductively opened her mouth and sucked it onto her tongue. *Oh, brother.*

"All right. I'll go," I said

"You go. I go." Brett piped up, looking at Priss.

Priss sprang up. "What's the big deal? Let's go ski instead. Y'all think jumping from the bridge is so cool."

"You were the one who said our parents made up all those stories so we wouldn't jump." I threw it back at her. "Or have you changed you mind?"

Austin threw out the gauntlet. "No girl's cool enough to do it. Not even you, Priss Pot."

Not missing a beat, Priss put her hands on her hips and considered Austin. "Ready when you are, Mister."

Sara leapt to her feet and pushed through the guys to Priss's side. "You aren't really jumping off the bridge? Are you?"

"Why not? If they can, I can." Priss squared her shoulders and marched up the beach to the dirt road.

I followed her, but someone tugged on my arm, pulled me back. Sara. Her eyes were wide with fear.

"Why does Priss always have to be such a showoff?" she asked. "Do you think she'll really do it?"

"The million dollar question. Who knows with Priss?"

"Would you stay here with me? I don't want to stand on that rickety old bridge any longer than I have to. It scares me." She picked up the towel from the ground and held it to her chest.

Me? Why me? I wasn't sure she even liked me. But how could I say no? The last thing I wanted to do was jump off some ole bridge anyway. Just the same, I didn't want her to think I was a massive coward, along with already thinking I was a backward hick. But she did ask me to stay, no one else: not Brett or Jack or Austin. In the end staying, with her trumped possible injury.

"Don't worry. They'll be okay." Clearly, she needed reassurance. I moved to wrap my arm around her waist, but she slipped her hand into the crook of my arm instead, brushing bits of shell against me. Warmth entered my blood and swam through my entire body. I'd definitely made the right choice. We watched the sun begin its descent, and the bridge took on a pink hue in the flat light. Her fingers tightened as Priss tracked across the bridge.

"I wish I were more like her, to just be bold and do it." Her hand tightened around my forearm. "If my father could see her now, he'd have a stroke. When he visited our school for Parents' Weekend, Priss talked liked she'd just walked off the set of *Gone With the Wind* and gave him the impression Natchitoches was safe and, to be honest, a little boring."

"You're really lucky, you know." A sudden sadness crept into my voice. *Damn.* I hoped she didn't notice. I'd worked so hard to push away my thoughts about Dad. That's all I wanted, just a few hours without worrying about money, clues, or missing research information.

"Sorry. I forgot about your dad. I'm an only child and my father is overprotective. In fact, this is the first time he's allowed me to stay with anyone other than the nuns at Sacred Heart. Makes it hard to get close to anyone, but that's life, isn't it?" She gave a small shrug.

Why Sara chose to talk to me was a mystery. Maybe she wasn't such a snob, after all. Her nails dug into my skin, and I followed her gaze to the bridge.

Priss slipped through the metal trusses and clung to the rusted vertical bars framing the bridge. Silhouettes strutted behind her, coaxing her closer to the lip of the bridge. Her toes gripped the corroded edge. She looked down at the river before giving us a thumbs up.

"Geronimo!" She stepped off the railing, and fell with lightning speed. Her arms went straight to her side, forming an unbendable, unbreakable pike. Her hair fluttered in the wind.

Sara clutched my arm, nearly cutting off the circulation. She held her breath. Priss glided through the air with her fists glued to her thighs, and her eyes squeezed shut. She plunged straight to the river.

I glanced up at the bridge where Brett, Jack, and Austin peered over the railing. They whistled as if Priss were a falling bomb. When she hit the water, they made a noise like an explosion. Then they cheered and clapped.

We waited. Someone yelled from above, "You did it, Priss!"

Ripples dissipated and drifted down the river, but Priss didn't surface. Sara leaned toward the water. I swear, anxiety zipped through her fingers straight up my arm.

Priss's head shot out, and she pumped her fist high in the air. I sagged with relief. Why did she do it? What was she trying to prove? As much as I cared for Priss, she made me mad. She took too many chances. Which one would be the last? But I wasn't her guardian angel, something she'd reminded me at least once a week. Times like these I couldn't fathom why we remained friends.

Sara held out a wrinkled towel for Priss. I heard snickers coming from the road. The guys tramped to the beach and made their way to Priss as she waded out of the river. Her legs trembled so badly she could hardly stand. Sara slipped the towel around Priss's shoulders, but Priss quickly wrapped it around her waist, covering her quivering legs.

"I did it. Who's next?" she asked, a little breathless.

"No one." Jack winked at Priss. "Who'd a thought you'd really do it. Who'd a thought you'd have the nerve. Not me. Never in a million years. You cost me ten bucks."

"You bet against me?" Priss's mouth tightened, and her face turned an ugly scarlet. "Oh, you're jumping, you little squid. And you're doing it today before the sun sets."

"Yeah. Who's gonna make me? You and who else?" He retorted, moving within inches of her face.

"If you don't do it, I'll get you back," she said, each word clipped to perfection.

By this time Brett and Austin joined Jack. They flapped their arms like boneless scarecrows. "Ooo… We're scared."

They'd gone too far. Priss scooped up a handful of shells and hurled them, pelting all three. One glanced off Jack's face, but he ignored it and laughed. In no rush, they lazily waded to the boat and scrambled inside.

"Oh, please stop," yelled Jack, in a high pitched voice. "You're hurting us. We might have to tell your Mama."

Austin cracked up. "Come on Priss. You'll never make it to the major league throwing like some *little girl.*"

Jack cranked the engine, and they were halfway down the river before Priss stopped screaming and throwing shells. Brett sat back and waved.

She stamped her foot. Then shaking her fist in the air she yelled. "I'll get you, Jackson Crawford, if it's the last thing I do."

She turned away from the river. Between gritted teeth, she said, "One day, I'll marry him out of pure spite. Then he'll never get away from me. I'll make his every waking moment a living hell."

VIII

The sky was clear, and Mars flicked red as I walked home from the clinic, my first full week of summer colds, swimmer's ear, and the little things Dr. Pasquier passed my way, like splinters, sunburns, and diaper rash. I was pretty beat, between my job and looking for my Dad's missing folder and diary. I'd searched everywhere I could think, even checked the attic and garage. I came up with a big fat zero.

When I came to the front yard, I automatically searched the shadows. Since that first night, I hadn't seen anything or anyone near the house, but I was still uneasy. The side of the house near the drive was pitch black, a good place for an ambush. Was it just my imagination or the result of a reoccurring memory?

I pushed open the screen door and walked into the kitchen. Light framed Brett's massive shoulders as he rooted around the refrigerator shelves.

"Hey. What're you doing home? You're normally out on Friday night."

"The twins are eating supper at Cross Lake Inn. Jackson invited me, but I didn't really feel like wearing a suit. I hope I never have to wear another stinking tie or starched collar." Brett mumbled something about being hungry enough to eat a bear. When he stood up, his arms were full of jars, and he gripped a platter of left over roast beef. "You want a sandwich?"

"Sure." I went to the cabinet and took down a plate. "Do you ever think maybe Dad's death wasn't an accident?"

Brett sighed. "This again."

"Hear me out. I know he'd never leave us. He wouldn't. Not on purpose anyway." I held a knife tipped with a glob of mayo in my hand, zeroing it on an imaginary target I emphasized my point. "There are too many strange things, things only we'd notice. Like crooked shadow boxes. Or what about his mug? It wasn't on his desk, and I haven't seen it since we came home. Have you?"

Brett shook his head.

"Also, I didn't tell you the other day, but I found a heel print in Dad's office. It was next to his desk, and it definitely wasn't his. I brought it home and put it in a drawer in the study. Someone was in his office the day he died."

"Are you *sure* it wasn't Dad's?"

"This was a shoe with lettering on the heel, like someone had a special heel or a tap put on it."

Brett looked at me like he wanted to believe me, but something, maybe apprehension stopped him.

"What if his research folder has something to do with it? Professor Noble and Miss Sharp asked about it. I know you don't believe I saw someone on our front lawn, but what if the window was open in Dad's study because someone was looking for his research notes?"

Brett set his sandwich, an entire corner missing, down on his plate. I had his attention.

"I've been thinking. Where would Dad hide a folder? He usually kept them at the college, locked in the file cabinet. But the cabinet was unlocked when we went through it. And I didn't find anything. I checked his study, and they weren't there either. I don't know where else to look."

"Would you put the knife down?" Brett lowered my hand. "Getting awfully close to my face. Wouldn't want to mess up God's gift... would you?"

"Don't get me sidetracked." I plunked the knife on my plate and sat down. "Remember the calendar, and the date circled in red. Maybe it didn't have anything to do with his death or me coming home. Maybe he had something else planned that day. Another thing. Don't you think it's weird Dr. McKnight and Penny disappeared around the same time Dad died?" Something teetered on the edge of my brain. Something I could almost grasp, but it just wouldn't come together.

"Everyone knows they ran off and got married. Stop imagining things." Brett bit off the other corner of his sandwich. Luckily, I'd grown up with Brett and understood mumbling mush mouth. "Why would anyone try to steal Dad's research, anyway? It isn't like they were digging for gold. The most interesting things they ever unearthed were pottery and old bones."

I held two slices of bread, finishing my sandwich. "The only other thing that might help is Dad's diary. He wrote in it every day of his life. Maybe he wrote something in there to help. But that's the other weird thing. He always left it on his nightstand, but not the day he died. If I didn't know better, I'd say he hid it."

"Hid his diary?" Brett swallowed and stared at his sandwich, thinking.

"I think it's strange his research folder wasn't in his office, but someone could have stolen it. His diary is totally different. His room isn't the public library. He always left his diary next to the bed, in the same spot. So where is it?"

"Yeah, I see where you're going. You could be right. Maybe something's going on."

It made sense. Dad wrote his deepest thoughts, things he didn't want to share with anyone in his diary. How do I know? He caught me reading it once when I was about nine, and he grounded me to my room for the rest of my life.

"Are you sure you searched his whole room? How about under the bed?" Brett shoved the last of his sandwich into his mouth, then mumbled, "You know, I just thought of something. Do you remember him talking about making a secret drawer?"

"Barely. Do you think he actually made a false drawer?" My mind raced ahead. Pictures formed and flashed behind my eyelids. I quickly recalled searching Dad's room. Coldness ran through my brain like a finger through fog. I let the memory in.

First, I went to his closet… nothing unusual there, just his clothes, shoes, and some old coats. Next I opened his chest of drawers, socks and t-shirts were all neatly folded, everything easy to take out and put back… nothing. Then I looked under the bed, just dust. I checked his side table. Only two or three paperbacks were in it, but they filled the drawer all the way to the top. That was it! The drawer was too shallow.

I bit my lip, and I zipped back to present day. "Brett, you're a genius."

"Dad's room, right?" He raced behind me. I took the stairs two at a time to my parents' room and slid over the bed, landing in front of Dad's bedside table. I jerked open the bottom drawer and tossed two paperbacks, along with *The American Revolutionary War* and Dad's glasses, on the bed.

A slender navy blue ribbon rested along the bottom edge of the empty drawer.

"I'll be damned." Brett reached over my shoulder and ran his hand over the thin wood.

I grasped the ribbon and pulled. The false bottom lifted easily. A diary, matching the others in the barrister case, rested in a small recess. I grasped the black leather book. The idea that he went to all the trouble to construct a false drawer and then hid his diary in it frightened me. He wasn't hiding his daily thoughts from his family, but from someone else. Was it the figure hiding in the shadows outside? Why else would he go to such lengths?

"Start at the back," said Brett.

I thumbed through the diary. What I found astonished me. My father wrote most of his diary in a conversational style, except for three pages. They were written in code. Brett grabbed the book and rifled through it.

"I told you. I told you Dad would never do anything to himself," I said. "This is proof. Why else would he hide his diary?"

"Hold your horses. We don't know anything yet." He sat on the bed and slowly compared the three pages. "All three codes are different. And they aren't simple."

Dad wrote it the day before he died. I touched the last page, the last code, hoping I might feel a twinge of lingering energy. The page wasn't special in any way, just plain old paper, no energy, nothing. Brett was right though. We hadn't proved anything by finding the diary. He flipped to the first code written in February:

Tzyrfhz rpxykcqk hsfaf by kzdfbcunup tnzg. Izsco gupfx lqvsj ko rofejt nbdkt kdi cqukcs frvfwkf. Tjtfjsm ubrvnfx zq Ew Rgbpka gtx cofratny.

Then the second code written in March:

Rewa rdks edni deck oldu arff oecn ediv edna hcra eser noit avac xegn inia tnoc redl oF.t hgin tsal dehc raes ecif fO

Then the third code written in May:

Op Isahsy raiiso. Vspfbfso clksq aps klt jlps teak bsw ysapq lio. Aqhso Jrhkfdet tl pstpfsvs tesj. Wfii rlkbplkt Pscsrra Qeapm tljlpplw. Quqmsrt qes eaq arrljmifrs.

To anyone else the lines looked like gibberish, but Dad had written codes for as long as I could remember. Brett thumbed back and forth through the pages, comparing the three codes. They were obviously different.

I studied the codes looking for similarities. Maybe he used an easy substitution code. The first thing was to check for repeat letters, common letters like E at the end of a word. The first code was broken into word groups, but the second code was divided into equal sets of four. So trying to find reoccurring letters was out, especially in the second entry since it was impossible to tell where one word ended and another began. This wasn't going to be easy.

Surely Dad wouldn't use codes so difficult we couldn't figure them out. Yet, he'd always said a code shouldn't be too obvious. Well, he'd achieved his goal.

"We'll have to take them one at a time. They could be simple shift ciphers or he could have used a keyword or a combination. Looks like a different method for each one," said Brett.

"Since the first code is in word groups, and the words look like some alien language, he probably used a substitution cipher. Finding the substitution will be the problem."

Brett left the diary open on the first code, his finger on the first letter. "We probably should give the diary to Chief Hendricks."

"No way. He won't understand the codes, so what good would it do?" I pointed to the nightstand. "Dad left this in a hidden drawer on purpose for us to find. Not just *anyone* can solve them. He knew we'd decipher all three codes. We shouldn't turn it over to the Chief until we know what's in the diary."

"Yeah, you're probably right."

"You don't think he committed suicide anymore, do you?"

"I didn't want to believe it to begin with, but finding this..." Brett touched the diary. "Well, let's just say nothing surprises me anymore. But don't get too excited, J. J. It may amount to nothing."

I pressed the false bottom back in the drawer. Then I shoved the paperbacks and *The American Revolutionary War* on top, before grabbing a few small books off Dad's barrister shelf. I dropped them haphazardly in with the other books, not into neat little stacks the way Dad would have left them.

Obviously, he was hiding something important, possibly the reason behind his accident, which looked less like an accident with each passing moment. His diary proved that to me even if it didn't to anyone else.

The front door opened and closed. Mom's voice rose to the second floor. "Boys, Tudy? Anyone home?"

Brett flipped the diary closed and whispered. "I'll hide it in my room. No one'll ever look there."

When I stepped off the last stair, Mom wasn't in the entry. I started for the kitchen and was about to push the swinging door when I heard Mom talking to Tudy in a very low voice. "She told me she saw someone watching our house the other night when she let her dog out. She said he was just standing across the street staring at the house."

"Two women in the house alone with two teenaged boys." Tudy stopped. "I ain't seen nobody. She sees things, though. Member the ghost in her attic last year."

"That's right. I don't want the boys to know. I'm sure there's no need to worry. I'll call the Chief, and he can check things out."

I'd heard enough. I walked in and Mom turned. Her face was frozen in a false smile these days. She took off her scarf and shook it lightly. "Winds kicking up. Think a storms coming up."

Tudy frowned. "Best make sure the screens are on good and tight. Don't want none coming off if a storms brewing."

Mom looked at me. "Can you and Brett make sure the screens are secure?"

So the man watching the house wasn't some figment of my imagination. But Tudy just said she hadn't seen anyone. Brett would let me have it if I stirred them up without more proof.

"Sure." I held onto the swinging door since I'd be leaving soon. "We'll take care of it right away."

I jetted up the stairs to Brett's room. When I opened the door, I nearly tripped over a jumbled pile of dirty clothes. His room was the polar opposite of mine. If Tudy didn't hound him to clean it once a month, the stench would pervade the house. He'd shoved all the papers off his desk and opened Dad's diary to the first coded page. He scribbled furiously.

"Listen. Our neighbor saw someone watching the house, but Mom doesn't want us to know. I told you it wasn't my memory kicking up."

"Why doesn't she want us to know?" He leaned back on two legs of an old kitchen chair.

"She doesn't want to frighten us, I guess." But I was already creeped out about it. "I don't think we should give her the diary, either."

"She might be able to help."

"She might. But she's calling the Chief right now about somebody watching the house, and she's deliberately keeping the info from us. If she gives the diary to Chief Hendricks, we'll never see it again."

"This doesn't sound good. Maybe there's more to Dad's death. But you know we might be trying to solve these codes for weeks. You want it? Give it a shot?"

"Sure."

Brett handed me the diary. I'd expected as much. He didn't call me a know-it-all for nothing. "What about someone finding it in my room?"

"Who'd look? Besides, you have hiding places in that neat-nick room of yours." He nodded like he'd been in my room a few times. Why was I not surprised?

"Oh, Mom wants us downstairs to check the window screens. Seems there's a storm coming."

Brett rubbed his arms like he was cold and wanted to build up some heat. Clearly, I wasn't the only one creeped out by someone watching the house.

Dad hid his diary, wrote in code for God's sake, so something wasn't right. I wondered what Chief Hendricks knew. It wasn't as if he was sharing any information. Even though Mom was calling him, I needed to talk to the Chief myself, and I knew just the time to do it.

IX

Everyone in town knew Chief Hendricks went to the shooting range at dawn on Saturdays. He was a crack shot and massacred an entire flock of skeet before most people were awake. I drove Woody to the range. Wind blew through the windows like a small cyclone, picking up paper scraps off the floor and spinning them all over the car.

I drove past a chain link fence with an open gate. The range was little more than a waist-high tabletop stacked with rifles and a bare alley ending in an earthen dam about as high as two buses stacked one on top of the other. Chief Hendricks and his buddies blasted paper targets tacked to wooden easels. In between shots, one person loaded all the guns while the others set up new targets, a slow process. Not like the modern shooting ranges Brett and I watched on Dragnet. Wish I could hear Joe Friday say, "Just that facts, Ma'am." I'd feel better knowing Dad's case was in his hands. Just a silly wish, though, not real.

A slim deputy, dressed in jeans and a white t-shirt, shot at a long-range target as I drove up. Woody shuddered to a stop, and I waited until the deputy finished before opening the car door.

"Hey, son. You musta gotten up with the chickens." Chief waved as he ambled over. "How'd you know where to find me?"

I assumed this was a rhetorical question. I stroked Woody's hood and propped my hip against the car for support. "I wanted to talk to you about my Dad's accident."

Chief tugged his hat down, shielding his eyes from the rising sun. "Julian, we're still looking into it. I've been talking to some of the people he works with and all. Not gonna leave a stone unturned, you understand."

"My mom says you think it might *not* have been an accident. Is that true?" I wanted to hear it from him.

He cleared his throat, then pulled a new toothpick out of his shirt pocket. "No bones about it. A lot of people loved your dad, so I'm taking particular care to determine exactly what happened to him. After you told me he was afraid of heights, and when some of the people he worked with told me he'd been depressed, I decided to check out his death with a fine toothcomb. All in a day's work, you know."

I swear he tried to see how many idioms he could cram into a sentence. Most of the time this was annoying, but today it was maddening. He'd known my father for years. How could he even think it?

"My dad wouldn't have committed suicide." My voice didn't waiver.

"I know this is hard to take, but I'm not finished interviewing everybody, checking under every leaf, so to speak. One of your dad's fellow workers, Dr. McKnight and one of the secretaries flew the coop after the end of the semester. One of the other secretaries is trying to contact them, but so far she hasn't had any luck. I need to talk to him. See if he can add anything." He twirled the toothpick in his mouth. "I don't want you frettin over this."

I didn't like being talked down to as if I were some runny nosed kid. However, I didn't want my feelings in the way. Finding out what happened to Dad was more important. So I tried a different tactic.

"Dad's research folder is missing. We've looked everywhere, and Professor Noble and Miss Sharp have been searching for it, too." I wanted so badly to tell him about Dad having hid his diary.

"There are some strange things about this case, but let's not get the cart before the horse. I never said for certain your father committed suicide. There's not enough evidence to say for sure."

"Then why wouldn't the priest let us bury him in the Catholic Cemetery?" my voice rose an entire octave.

Chief scratched his head with the side of his hat. "I have to tell the priest when there's a doubt. And in your father's case, Professor Noble and Miss Rebecca both reported him acting real strange. Kinda depressed like. I can't let that go by without looking into it."

"Chief, I saw someone watching our house."

"When was that, son?"

"The night my dad died."

"I see." Chief wiggled his toothpick like he was thinking, and it was an extension of his brain. "But nothing since then?"

"No, sir."

"I see. We'll check this out. Yes siree, Bob. We'll check it out."

"I'm glad to hear you're checking out everything 'cause somehow my dad's missing research is connected to his death."

"What kind of research was he doing?"

"It's the research from the recent mound excavation. They've discovered some old bones and pottery, I think."

"Hmm. More than likely his folder's gonna turn up someplace right in front of you. I want your dad to get a fair shake. I really do, son. If all goes as planned, I'm hoping to have this whole investigation wrapped up in less than a week."

Chief Hendricks had his own theories. It didn't seem to matter we'd seen someone hanging around our house late at night. He wasn't fazed by it. Shots rang out, followed by a group cheer. Chief Hendricks's deputy shot a perfect bull's eye. The Chief grinned at his buddies and clapped my back.

"This'll all be over soon, and you'll go back to school. Everything will be fine. You'll see." The Chief smiled. "You need to take a deep breath and leave everything to the adults. We'll handle it."

Was he kidding? Leave everything to the adults? That's what I'd been doing. Antsy to return to his buddies, he walked away. The conversation ended. I couldn't help it. I checked his heels as he walked away. Cowboy boots. Thick heels, no cracks.

Dad's diary held the sole clues to his death, and I wasn't about to give it to the Chief. He discounted everything I said. And after what he just revealed, I had only a week to break the codes.

A lone, field weary tractor chugged down Highway One at fifteen miles per hour. I was trapped behind him. I went over my conversation with Chief Hendricks, trying to think of other ways to approach him. But what I desperately needed was more proof, something to convince him, beyond a shadow of a doubt, there was something or someone else involved.

Woody burped and shuddered. Driving was so boring, especially when all I could see was the back end of a muddy tractor. Finally, the crusty thing turned off the road, and I pushed Woody into a stuttering charge. Before long I pulled into our drive. Brett bounced a basketball on the pavement beside the garage. No sooner had I closed Woody's door, than he tossed me the ball.

Without so much as a word, Brett crouched down and guarded the goal bolted to the garage. He waved his arms over his head, daring me to aim for the net. He was taller and more muscular than me, but he wasn't as wiry. I faked a move to the left. He followed. I bounced the ball to the right and zipped past him. I tossed the ball toward the goal, but it hit the rim and deflected straight into Brett's hands. He popped it into the hoop.

I retrieved the ball and aimed at the metal ring, then flipped it into the basket. Score! We dribbled and shot over and over again. Soon sweat trickled down our faces, and wet patches formed under our arms. Throw in a few swear words, and we were in therapy. After a while Brett tucked the ball under his arm.

"Did you talk to Chief Hendricks?" he asked.

"Yeah."

"What did he say?" Brett bounced the ball and then tossed it me.

"Same old thing. Big fat nothing." I bounced the basketball hard. A knot burned in the back of my throat. "I told him about the missing folder. He wasn't impressed. I told him about the stranger watching the house, and he acted like it was nothing. We made the right decision not telling him about the diary. We only have a week before he writes his report."

"Obviously you didn't get anywhere on the code last night."

"No. I went through all the common letters, but no words formed. The solution isn't mathematical, either. I tried all kinds of formulas before I went to bed. No luck." I aimed at the hoop and let go. It hit the backboard with a TWACK! "I hate this."

The ball rolled to my feet. My throat muscles clinched under the tightening knot. I really needed to calm down.

"Shitty, right?" Brett kicked the ball to the side. "I'd help with the code, but… if you can't do it, I sure can't."

"We can work on it later. Dr. Pasquier assigned me to work extra hours. He's open for a half-day clinic. Something about summer flu."

I walked away then turned around. "The other night, at Priss's. You gave Sara our phone number. Why?"

"What's it to you?" Brett pushed his hands into his pockets.

"She's not the same as the other girls around here." I looked at the basketball goal, then at Brett. "She's pretty. Don't you think?"

"Wait. Are you telling me you like her?" Brett stepped closer.

"Look. I might ask her out. That's all."

"You've never said anything about girls before." His brows met, curious. "What you're saying is… you don't want *me* to date her."

"I just want to know if you're asking her out, that's all. I doubt she's interested in small town guys anyway."

"J. J., you never talk about girls. Priss is the only one you've ever hung around. I wondered if you even liked them. If you weren't, well you know… a twink. Jeez." Brett raised his hands in front of his body, thinking I might hit him.

"I've gone out before. I just don't go around bragging about it like you and your buddies." I shifted my weight from one foot to the other.

"Okay. I get it. You want to ask Sara out." Brett pinched his chin as if deep in thought. "I tell you what. You ask her out. If she says no, then she's fair game, and I get a stab at her."

"Man, she's not some animal to hunt." I bristled.

"Don't worry. I won't get in your way. At least, not until she says no." He grinned his stupid self-assured grin. Why was everything a competition?

I looked at my watch, keeping my emotions in check. "Great, now I'm late."

I darted for the house. As I reached the door, Brett swooped past. The door squealed closed behind him, and Tudy moved to the side, a silly smile on her face. Heat flared up my neck.

The clinic bustled with crying, sick kids and pasty adults. I took vital signs and shuttled patients into rooms. By noon we'd examined over thirty patients, pretty busy for a half-day office. After the patients left, Doc brought out a matchbox and two strands of black silk suture. Then he showed me how to tie a surgeon's knot inside the box. He said this would teach me to work in tight spaces, but I'd have to practice. He'd check in a few weeks, and if I could easily tie a knot inside the matchbox, then he'd teach me how to stitch… on real patients.

I slipped the box into my lab coat and set out for Rexall's. On weekends, they offered a special on hamburgers, two for the price of one. Not my favorite cafe, but it beat nothing.

I found a seat at the confetti-speckled Formica counter near the front window. My head was aching just thinking about the codes. I'd start on them as soon as I got home. I wanted to try a substitution code I'd read about where the letters of the alphabet were reversed. Maybe see if it worked on any of the codes.

After I ordered, I spun around on the plastic seat and saw Priss dressed in a pink and white striped uniform. She stood like Lady Justice in the candy aisle, weighing a pack of Juicy Fruit in one hand and a roll of Lifesavers in the other. In the end, she decided on both and swished down the aisle.

When she walked past the counter, I stuck out my foot.

"Oh, hi, Julian. How was work today?" she asked, clearly distracted. Who knew choosing candy was so challenging.

"Fine. How come you're in town so early on a Saturday?"

"Candy-striper training day at the hospital." She fluffed her bangs. "Racking up the service hours for school before graduation... I ducked out and had my hair cut. Like it?"

I couldn't tell the difference. Still looked like Audrey Hepburn's. Short was short. She eyed me expectantly, and I knew I'd better say something fast. "Suits you."

"Suits me? Well I guess that's a compliment."

A waitress leaned over the counter with her breasts straining against her uniform. She winked. "Here ya go, Hon." She waved a greasy white bag in my direction.

Priss sidled next to me. Her head swiveled to the plate glass window painted with large beach umbrellas, advertising summer specials, but her gaze traveled down the street.

"Have you seen Jack today? Sometimes he eats lunch here." I swear, she sounded disappointed.

"I didn't think you liked him. In fact, if I remember correctly you said you would, and I quote, 'make his life miserable.'" I made air quotes.

"Who says I'm not good for my word?" She opened the Lifesavers and slipped out a yellow pineapple disk. "Men are so easily led. Silly, stupid sheep."

I couldn't help myself. I cleared my throat to keep from laughing because she was so unbelievably serious. She slid her eyes toward me.

"I talked to Jack on the phone last night. He's meeting me at the riverfront around sunset. Willingly coming to the slaughter." Priss slipped a candy on her tongue and arched a brow, channeling Scarlett O'Hara. "Why don't you meet us later? I'll bring Sara. She's been asking a lot of questions about you."

Priss threw it out: the bait. Jack wasn't the only one being prepped for slaughter. I wanted to believe Sara liked me. Yet she was a distraction, and I had to solve Dad's codes. However, girls like Sara don't grow on trees, not in Natchitoches, Louisiana, anyway.

"Sure. I'll meet y'all." I said this against my own better judgment.

I creased a handle into the greasy bag, then opened the glass door.

Priss slid past me and walked in the opposite direction. She sashayed down the street with her hips swaying, her purse bumping her side with each beat. I shook my head and glanced down at her heels. Neither was split or imprinted with the letters **N** or **E**. Heel checks were a habit now even with my best friends. I couldn't help myself. The crazy part was the shoes had to be unusual to have a crack in them, however rubber cracked if overheated, and wood cracked if weathered. I was definitely having trouble figuring it out, but I couldn't let anyone know about this little obsession; they'd think I'd lost my mind for sure.

X

Brett didn't meet me after work. Tudy said he took off after I left and hadn't been home all day. No telling what held him up, most likely a girl. I wasn't any closer to solving the codes. Couldn't get a break. The reverse substitution cipher hadn't worked on any of the codes, so I'd tried a simple shift cipher. I put the original alphabet on the bottom and then on the line above it; I brought up the last letter, Z and put in front of the A. This made a new alphabet beginning with Z and ending with Y.

To solve the message, I then found the letter in the top line and substituted it for the real letter below it. I made twenty-five new alphabets, shifting every letter of the alphabet to the front, but none of them worked. It was exhausting. My brain pushed against my skull like it might blow up any second. I rubbed the back of my neck and let my head drop. Then I remembered I'd told Priss I'd meet her at the river. I was late, of course.

Mom and Tudy were at the church lighting candles. I checked across the street and made sure no one was hiding behind the Three Columns at the college. Then I checked the perimeter of the yard. Everything looked fine, but I couldn't shake the feeling that someone was watching me. I sprinted to the river, but the crazy feeling followed me.

Priss and Jack Crawford stood beside a weathered bench with their backs to me, whispering into each other's ear. Sara stood beside a Willow tree, its tapered branches ruffling the river. She looked at me, then to the sky. She wasn't interested. Then she glanced back and smiled.

She wore a white sundress with spaghetti straps tied on her shoulders. Once she moved closer, I could see blue bell-shaped dots on the dress, shifting into geometric shapes like optical illusions. I'd never paid much attention to what women wore unless it was tight or short but somehow everything Sara wore emphasized her body. God, she was beautiful. Her tanned shoulders contrasted with the white material, and her scent shoved everything else out of my head.

About the time I reached her, Priss and Jack strolled over. The sun dipped behind the trees and the temperature with it. Not really refreshing, just warm instead of hot.

"Priss and I are going to Rexall's for ice cream. Do you want any?" asked Jack.

Sara's arm brushed against mine, running her hand along the bench. No more than a feather's touch, but heat tracked along my arm.

"Ouch!" Sara grabbed her hand, holding out her middle finger. A thick splinter, at least an inch long, poked through the skin and blood was already pooling beneath it. She attempted to pull it out, but the crumbly wood broke off under the skin. "Oh my God!"

I grabbed her hand and applied pressure to the base of her finger. Priss and Jack hovered over her, but they were more in the way than anything.

"Let's go to the clinic. I'll take care of it." I held her hand, continuing to hold mild pressure while guiding her toward the street. Thank goodness, the clinic was just around the corner.

"Do you need any help?" Jack walked behind us.

"No." I gave a hasty response, maneuvering to the brick sidewalk.

"Are you sure there's nothing we can do?" Priss asked.

"Seriously, I'll have it out in a jiff. Then we'll meet y'all back at the riverfront."

"He's gonna be a doc one day. You're in good hands or I wouldn't leave." Priss tilted her head, taking Jack's arm, then they started in the opposite direction toward downtown.

Sara dipped a little closer to me, and I put my arm around her shoulder. When we reached the clinic, I pulled out a key and opened the back door.

"You have a key?"

"Sure, the nice thing about small towns. Everyone who works here has a key." I shoved the key into my pocket and turned on the lights.

Once we were in one of the exam rooms, I lifted Sara onto the exam table.

"Now if you'll just remove your clothes and put on one of these gowns." I held up a blue cloth gown I removed from a shelf underneath the table.

"What?" Sara was holding her finger, and her brows nearly met her hairline.

"Just kidding." I gave a laugh. "A little medical humor."

Sara smiled and relaxed. "Wasn't sure for a minute there. The doctor won't mind if you're here... with me, alone?"

"Believe me, he'll be glad he didn't have to meet us here." I pulled gauze and a small sterile instrument tray from the cabinet along with some latex gloves.

"This may sting a bit." I cleaned the skin around the splinter with Mercurochrome.

Sara blew short breaths and crossed her legs at the ankles, but she never let go of her hand. Then she watched as I opened the tray of sterile instruments, she tracked my every move.

"I've done this before. This is the kind of thing Dr. Pasquier lets me do while he handles the big stuff, like delivering babies." I popped a glove for emphasis.

She let go of her hand and pushed it toward me. I pulled an eleven blade out of the tray along with some tweezers and a stat. "This will hurt, but it would probably hurt more to inject it with anesthetic. Ready?"

She had gone back to biting her lip, but she nodded anyway. I made a quick slit with the blade, exposing the splinter and some nasty bruising. Then using the tweezers, I plucked the splinter out with one quick tug. I held it up for her to see.

A single tear clung to her lower lashes. Here I was thinking how great a hero I was, how impressed she would be, and all along she was crying. I had tried to be so careful not to hurt her.

"I'm sorry." I pressed the cut with gauze, trying not to look at her.

"Oh no, it's not you. You were great." Sara sniffed. Her voice shook when she spoke. "Mom was the best at removing splinters. It just made me miss her."

"Oh yeah, I forgot. You've been at boarding school." I checked the cut for any particles left behind, then wrapped her finger in Iodoform gauze.

A new tear formed and dripped down the side of her face. "No. You don't understand. You see, the reason I'm at boarding school is because my mother died four years ago."

"Oh. I'm so sorry." My heart actually felt as if someone squeezed it. I didn't know what to say, wasn't sure how to make it better. I secured a few pieces of tape around Sara's finger. Then I looked back up. She was staring at me, her eyes soft with moisture. Something tender pushed me, the desire to comfort her. I leaned in... so did she. She kept staring into my eyes, until they blurred deep amber. I pulled her closer and kissed her lips. They were smooth and plump, tasted like vanilla. We didn't move, held on to the moment, then I backed away, still holding her hand.

"I'm sorry I got so emotional."

"It's fine." Losing a parent was the worst, finding someone who understood, truly understood was nearly impossible. "What happened?"

"She had a brain tumor. It was so hard losing her, watching her become a lump on a pillow. The only thing I have left from her is a long rambling letter she wrote. It's nonsense, gibberish. I wish I knew what she was trying to say."

"I understand."

In one slight movement, Sara pulled her hand to her chest, putting some distance between us. "Your father died in a accident. My mother lost her mind little by little. It would have meant so much to me to know what she was trying to say."

Dad's diary immediately came to mind. I knew what it was like to find something left behind that makes no sense.

"Are you sure it was gibberish. Maybe it was written in code or something?"

Sara rubbed the bandage on her finger, studying me. "Funny, no one else ever said anything like that, but I thought about it." She gave an embarrassed giggle. "I earned a merit badge in Girl Scouts for codes and code breaking. I actually tried to decipher the letter. Silly, huh?"

I touched her hand, lightly. I could hardly believe it. She knew how to decipher codes. I needed help with codes. But the bigger question: could I trust her? If she told Priss, it would be all over Natchitoches in no time flat. Other than Brett, I hadn't trusted anyone. I swallowed hard.

"I don't think Dad's death was an accident. There're some strange things about it."

"Really? Like what?"

"If I tell you, you can't say anything to anyone, especially Priss."

Sara placed a hand over her heart. "Cross my heart and hope to die."

I started with the beginning, my first suspicions and told her everything, all the way to the diary. She turned her good hand over and laced her fingers through mine. "You don't think this is coincidence?"

"No. Especially since he hid his diary. Why else would he write it in code?"

"You're telling me this for a reason. Do you want me to help?"

I squeezed her hand. "I can't solve it. I've tried everything I know."

"And you don't think the police can help?"

"They would just think it's another crazy thing my dad did. If we give the Chief the diary, we'll never find out the message."

"So where is it now?"

"I hid it in my room."

Sara released my hand. "What are we waiting for?"

Relief spread through me and for the first time in days, I felt like things might turn out. I cleaned the exam room and was just about to hit the lights when Sara stopped at the door.

"Wait. What about Priss and Jack?"

I smirked. "Believe me. They aren't eating ice cream."

By the time we reached the house, I'd explained all the methods I'd applied to the first code. She seemed familiar with them and asked a couple of questions. The house was dark, and we crept up to my room without any lights, only turning the lamp on in my room. I glanced out the window, a habit now, but everything looked normal.

I'd hidden the diary between my mattresses, something I knew for sure Brett couldn't do without a ton of girly magazines falling out. I found the page with the first code.

Tzyrfhz rpxykcqk hsfaf by kzdfbcunup tnzg. Izsco gupfx lqvsj ko rofejt nbdkt kdi cqukcs frvfwkf. Tjtfjsm ubrvnfx zq Ew Rgbpka gtx cofratny.

Before Sara sat at my desk, she pulled a crinkled yellow package of peanut M & M's from her pocket and poured a few on the desk. *Snap!* A new image passed through my brain.

"Chocolate helps me think." She gave a nervous chuckle and bit a red candy into two pieces, then slid both halves into her mouth. It was the way she bit into the candy, slowly as if she'd done this a hundred times and had perfected it. Quirky. I liked it.

I pulled up a stool and sat beside her, pointing to another tablet and explaining the codes I'd tried. She started with a replacement code using numbers. After a while I was more than a little deflated. Apparently, she couldn't solve it either. She skimmed the diary, stopping on a few pages, not really reading it, but tracing the top of each page. Then slowly, a little hesitantly, she added numbers above the first two sets of letters. I looked over her shoulder.

A series of letters appeared and then two words. *Suspect possible...* *Suspect possible....* I couldn't believe it. She'd cracked the cipher. I threw my hands up. Excitement and relief rushed through me all at once. She'd solved the cipher, making me the thickest–smart person who ever lived. Maybe she was right. Maybe I wasn't as smart as I thought.

"Oh, my God. I think I have it." She scribbled the same series of numbers, converted the letters, and more words appeared. She looked up at me. "Is this right?"

"Yeah." I whispered the words with awe. She'd done it. "How did you figure it out?"

"You said you'd tried all the things you knew: keywords, birthdays, his anniversary, even the date he wrote it. He had a dash at the top of the page, and it caught my eye. I flipped through the diary and found the only other page with a dash above the date, 1-5-62. Thought I'd try it. I just lucked out on going left in the alphabet instead of right."

I didn't dwell on my hurt pride for long. Dad used an earlier date, 1-5-62. Nothing spectacular happened on that day. So why did he use it? I glanced back at the diary page. How did I miss the dash? Using the date, 1-5-62, and removing the dashes, the numbers ran together 1562, forming a long strand… I wrote 156215621562 above the letters of the message. I ran my finger over the message and the numbers, memorizing it.

I could work this out without putting it on paper, and shifted each letter left the exact number of spaces written above it. Using this method, the T floated left one space and became S, the Z hopped left five spaces and became U, the Y moved back six spaces and became S, and so on.

Tzyrfhz rpxykcqk hsfaf by kzdfbcunup tnzg. Izsco gupfx lqvsj ko rofejt nbdkt–KDI cqukcs frvfwkf. Tjtfjsm ubrvnfx zq Ew Rgbpka gtx cofratny.

So *Tzyrfhz* with 1562156 above it became *Suspect*, continuing with the numerical sequence 21562156 above *rpxykcqk* became *possible*. I relaxed and let my mind take over. A neon red alphabet burned brightly in my brain. Gold numbers 1562, repeated over and over above each letter in the message:

1 5 6 2 1 5 6 2 1 5 6 2 1 5 6 2 1 5 6 2
SUSPECT POSSIBLE FRAUD…

I found a focal point on my wall and concentrated on the message. Each time I solved a new word, I shifted it beneath the alphabet until several sentences formed. From the corner of my eye, I saw Sara watching me. She solved the code, but I rearranged things faster in my head.

When I finished, I wrote down the message before reading it out loud:

Suspect possible fraud at excavation site. Human bones found in midden layer-JYC appear altered. Sending samples to Dr. Leakey for analysis.

I sat back, dumbfounded. The proof I'd been looking for. It might not be enough to persuade the Chief, but it was enough for me. Dad was convinced the bones were fakes, or he wouldn't have sent them all the way to Africa. After all, Dr. Leakey was the most respected bone expert in the world.

"In the archeology world, these are serious charges. If Dad's right, then one of the soil layers at the site had bones planted in it. Fraud or the hint of it can ruin someone's career. They'd never work again. If someone planted false bones in the mound, the whole team would be implicated. This must be why Dad wrote it in code."

"If you're right, something may have happened to your father." Sara's face paled when she stepped back and dropped onto my bed. "Do you honestly think someone would hurt your father over some old bones?"

"People kill over less." I said. "But it doesn't prove someone murdered him."

We were talking about my dad's friends as well as colleagues, and I couldn't imagine any of them wanting him dead. However, one person's image kept coming back to me: Professor Noble's. He must have known about Dad's suspicions. He kept asking about Dad's research. Maybe he thought Dad shared his work and theories with us. I needed more proof. But exactly how did I go about getting it?

"Do you think we should try the code on the other pages?" Sara stood next to me. I wasn't even aware she'd gotten up.

"All three codes are different. But we can look." I turned to the next coded page. The minute I saw alphabetical letters divided into groups containing four characters, I knew the date wouldn't work.

"Not the same cipher." I slid the diary over to Sara.

She ran her finger over the letters. "You said some codes used key-words. Do you think he did that with this code?"

"Maybe." I said. "But to solve the next code it'll take two steps. First, I'll have to figure out if it's a substitution cipher like the first code or a shift cipher where the letters of the alphabet are shifted, could even be a keyword or transposition cipher. But after I figure out what kind of cipher, I'll have to make words out of the four letter groups."

Tudy bellowed out "Bringing in the Sheaves", slamming kitchen cabi-nets and making more racket than a blind squirrel trapped in an attic. When did she come in? Great, if she knew I was up here with Sara, I'd never hear the end of it.

"Tudy's home. She'll be up here in a minute. I'll work on the code later. We'd better get back to the river before Priss and Jack send out a search party," I said.

Sara stood between my bed and me. She rumpled my burgundy plaid bedspread and winked. "Give Tudy something to wonder about."

I closed the space between us, wanting to hold her, but Sara slipped to the door, leaving honeysuckle and heat to fill the space. She flicked the light switch. "If we don't want Priss in on our secret, we'd better go."

I wasn't sure how she maneuvered to the door so quickly. But one thing I was positive about. Sara was the smartest, coolest, prettiest girl I'd ever known.

We navigated the river slope, bumping into cypress and oak branches in the dark. Suddenly, Priss and Jack jumped in front of us. Priss waved her arms over her head, yelling at the top of her lungs. Sara shrieked and fell back into me.

Sara gasped. Her fingers clutched my shirt. Even after she recognized Priss, she didn't move away.

"I could ask you the same. Where have you been?" Priss asked.

"We went walking. After Julian took out the splinter, he wanted to show me the town at night." Sara held up her injured finger.

Jack cracked up laughing and slapped me in between my shoulder blades. "Wow, didn't know you had it in you."

I almost responded, but one look at Priss and my brain choked…. She stood with her hands on her hips, wearing her blouse inside-out, the buttons and buttonholes mismatched so her blouse gapped at her breasts.

Sara's gaze followed mine. She pressed her lips to together, but a small laugh sputtered in the back of her throat. "Priss, did you get ice cream?"

"Of course, we did, but since you weren't here to eat it, Jack and I shared it." Priss gave a sniff, and when she did, Sara pushed her head into my chest and lost it. Her laughter shook through my shirt, moist heat traveled over my skin, and I smoothed my hand over the top of her head.

"That's not all you shared," I said.

Jack looked confused until he glanced over at Priss. Then he chuckled. "Uh… Hon, maybe you should turn your blouse right-side-out before you go home."

Priss looked down and threw her hands over her body like she was naked. The shock passed, and she snickered. "Oh my. Thank goodness Mr. King waited on us. He can't see a thing through those coke bottle glasses."

She rested her hand on Jack's arm like some delicate debutante, and in a flash, waved the whole thing off. "Ah well, another Southern belle down the drain." She fixed her gaze on Sara then on me. "Luckily, I'm not the only one with secrets."

XI

I walked back home, dodging sidewalk cracks and smiling to myself. Jackson drove the girls home in a rusty Chevrolet and offered to drop me off, but I wanted some time alone. What did Priss mean: She wasn't the only one with secrets? Sara did her usual searching the sky thing. Was she talking about Sara?

Mist snaked around the college campus, making the buildings look haunted. More than mist moved. Someone sat on a bench near the Three Columns, watching my house. I slowed down. I couldn't make out who it was, but the figure was dressed totally in black with a knit cap pulled down to meet his collar... the Shadow Man from the night before. Electricity zipped up my spine. I froze.

The moon went behind a cloud, and when it came back, the seat was empty. Nothing moved that fast. But, I didn't stick around. I barreled across a few yards, shooting a straight line to the house.

I hid behind the white oleander hedge near the front porch, scanning the Three Columns. Mist continued to swirl, but I didn't see anything else move. Was it a memory like Brett suggested? I didn't think so. I hadn't had an aura or any kind of break. This was too real. My shoulders ached from the tension. A car backfired, and I looked down the street. Headlights shimmied my way. Austin Crawford's old army jeep bucked into the driveway.

I couldn't wait to tell Brett about the Shadow Man, but from the moment the jeep stopped, I knew something was wrong. Brett grasped the passenger doorframe and unfolded his legs with difficulty before dropping to the ground. He looked like liquid rope weaving to the house, his fingers hooked into his belt loops for support. Austin tooted his horn and drove away. Brett stumbled to the first step, and light struck his face.

"What the hell?" I rushed toward him, my hand stretched toward his face.

"Nothing." Brett slurred and batted my hand away. He gritted his teeth, sucking air between them. His lower lip looked like an overstuffed blood sausage, and a purple bruise stretched across his right cheek. His right eye hid behind a swollen lid.

"What happened?" I asked, shoving my hands in my pockets so I couldn't touch his face.

"You should see the other guy." He chuckled. "Not a scratch."

"You're hurt."

He bent over and clasped his ribs, a groan spilling out before he could stop it. "Look. It was nothing, just some guys from school. Everything was fine, except for this one smartass. He made a crack about Dad."

"You don't look fine to me. You can hardly walk." I held him under the shoulder to maintain his balance. He didn't shrug me off this time.

"We were at Zestos having burgers when these two rednecks pulled up. I've seen them at school before. Nothing but pasture pucks—you could smell the cow shit on their boots." Brett plopped down on the step. "The biggest shit-kicker said he'd heard about Dad. At first, I thought he'd be like everybody else and tell me how sorry he was."

Brett touched his cheek and grimaced. It sobered him up. "He said Dad was a sorry excuse for a man. That's why he killed himself." He shifted and flinched, bracing the flat of his hand against his ribs. "I exploded. Took a jab at his face. He was ready, though. He banged my face into Austin's hood. I hit the dirt. He kicked me in the ribs. I got in a few good punches before he backed off like a damned coward."

He leaned his head into the shadows. "Course the girls squealed and carried on. A few came over afterwards... put ice on my face. Best part of the night. Later, Austin and I drove to the river. Drank a few beers."

I didn't say anything. Everyone liked my brother. He had a temper, but he'd never gotten into a real fight before. He could talk his way out of anything. He had his share of tussles, but out and out fighting wasn't like Brett.

I sat down next to him. "Sometimes I hate living in a small town. Gossip starts, and everyone believes it, good or bad."

An owl hooted from a distant tree. "I brought Sara over tonight and showed her Dad's diary."

With his good eye, Brett squinted at me. "Why? Why her?"

"She broke the code."

"She didn't."

"Yeah. She did. And it didn't take her long either." I hated admitting it.

"What did it say?"

I cleared my throat. "Dad was suspicious of the bones dug up at the new excavation. He thinks someone tampered with them."

Brett winced and examined his hands. The knuckles on his right hand were scraped and bruised.

"That's not all. He shipped a few bones to Dr. Leakey." I watched Brett catch his breath when he moved and wished he'd let me check his ribs.

"Wow. Dr. Leakey, huh? Do you think we should give the diary to the Chief?"

"No. It's too risky. Besides, the Chief won't see it our way. At least, now we know we're on the right track."

Brett stood and favored his injured ribs. "What about Sara? Can we trust her?"

"She said she'd go to her grave… and I believe her." I supported Brett's arm.

"I don't know. Trusting her is a big risk. If she tells Priss or Mrs. Dupree, it's your head."

"Fine. Come on. Your face looks like shit. Give me your shirt so Mom doesn't spaz over all the blood." I picked up the water hose coiled in a heap beside the front porch and eased the water on. "Don't make any noise. Last night, I heard Mom tell Tudy the air was too thick to breathe in her room anymore. She's on the sleeping porch."

Wincing from the effort, Brett slipped his shirt off. He wadded it into a sticky ball before tossing it to me. Water trickled from the hose, and he washed his face and neck, scrubbing his hands as an afterthought. We crept around to the back door, and Brett opened it slowly so it wouldn't squeak. I unintentionally prepared for the sound, but it glided open easily. Someone had oiled the hinges. Who? Either Mom or Tudy, had to be.

Small day-to-day reminders made Dad's absence unbearable. He purposely never oiled the back door hinges, knowing the exact time his boys came home because of the drawn-out squeak. The thought made my heart clench. The day was too much: Sara, Dad's diary, Brett's fight.

I buried Brett's shirt beneath some old newspapers in the aluminum garbage can while he stood in the doorway in his stocking feet. He held the door open, but I did an about-face on the steps.

"Where you going?" he whispered.

"Out. Need to clear my head." I heard him shuffle into the kitchen, closing the door behind him.

I had no idea where I was headed, but I wanted to be far away from the house right now. I slumped into the driver's seat, pushed Woody into reverse, and rolled down the sloping drive into the street.

These days Mom either popped a sleeping pill or downed a glass of gin before bed so she could sleep. At least half our town had summer sleeping porches attached to the back of their houses, and believe me they heard every bark, every hoot, every backfire. I swear, some people heard bats fly.

I rolled down the windows and let the air blast around me. It wasn't the least bit cool rising off the molten concrete, but somehow it numbed my mind. I didn't want to think about anything... my dad, my brother, or my mother.

Heat rolled off the pavement like an eerie ground-hugging vapor. I pressed the gas pedal and roared down the road. The speedometer shook around ninety, and Woody rattled so badly I thought the windows might shatter. I slowed and made a left onto the gravel road leading to Sweet Magnolia.

Shell Beach Bridge was straight ahead. I wanted nothing more than to stand at the railing and watch Cane River drift lazily by. I turned off the lights, slowed Woody to a snail's pace and shut off the engine. The Duprees slept on screened porches this time of year like everyone else, except they had industrial-sized fans blowing across them, but I still didn't chance them hearing me. The last thing I needed was Mrs. Dupree in my business.

Gravel crunched beneath my shoes, but other than that, I left the car without a sound. If I'd been in a better mood, I might have compared myself to some cool super sleuth, combing my hair back and smirking on my way to the bridge. But I wasn't in that kind of mood. I wanted the summer to start all over again, before any codes or broken mug pieces, or ridiculous heel prints. My dad would be home now, and I wouldn't be here. I dug my hands into my pockets and took my time walking to the bridge.

The iron railing still radiated heat leftover from the day, and I leaned against the metal, staring into the water. A family of beavers swam below. Thwack! Thwack! Their tails slapped the water.

Laughter rang out, pinging off the bridge's metal struts. What? I looked again.

Two shimmering forms dove into the river from a floating raft, cleaving through the black liquid. Moonlight painted a bright stripe down the river's dark center, broken from time to time by a hand or leg reflected in the light. Two young women skinny-dipped in the water below, and their bodies glowed like silver embers. I recognized the laughter immediately. Priss and Sara.

Obviously they'd sneaked away from the main house using the trap door in Priss's bedroom. It had been there since antebellum times, and no telling how many Dupree women had slipped out that door. Priss's aunts probably taught her how to oil the hinges. She'd been sneaking out since she was a little girl, doing who knows what.

When I bent over, my belt buckle scraped the railing, zinging against the metal. Shit! I dropped to my knees, sharp gravel and shell bits crunched into the tender space between bone and tendon. I craned my head close to the bridge's edge so my ear faced the river and listened. Hushed voices peppered the air. The girls hadn't heard me; they didn't call my name or start for the bridge. My muscles relaxed.

I crouched and peered between the peeling struts. Sara and Priss splashed furiously, raced to the raft, then Priss spewed a stream of water at Sara. She batted it away with her palm. Priss called out a challenge, and they raced to the riverbank. Two white gleaming buttocks ducked and bobbed, appearing and disappearing on the smooth dark surface. After a while they wound down and glided side by side like shimmering minnows.

When they rose from the water, neither was timid as they waded to shore. I watched Sara, her waist-length hair streaming water down her back and legs. She grasped a towel and wrapped it around her hips. Shell Beach reflected stippled silvery moonlight, haloing their bodies. I was completely transfixed, fire pooled in my groin.

Priss picked up something. She flicked the lid and blue light reflected on her face. She lit a cigarette and blew smoke into a thin ghost flying over the water. I smelled honeysuckle masked by tobacco scent, curling to the bridge. Jeez, how could I be such a bonehead? If they watched the smoke drift upward, they'd see me. Yet, how could I leave? After all, two girls completely naked, uninhibited sat just beneath me. I'd be more than an idiot to leave.

Sara made a tower with her fingers and pressed it to her chin, as if thinking of something far away. Priss hugged her knees, facing Sara. Their conversation turned serious with small tight gestures. Oh man, if only I could be down there.

Sara was close to perfect. She wasn't goofy or silly like other girls, and she was clever. I liked talking to her. But right now, what I craved was her soft small body, the round curve of her hips, the way her breasts swayed when she moved. I could watch her forever. A groan nearly slipped from my mouth.

Something primal took over my body without warning. A feeling so strong I fought to control it. I wanted her. I'd wade through glass slivers to be with Sara. I couldn't get enough of her.

I looked down. Priss stubbed out her cigarette. Wouldn't be long before they left. An owl hooted and flapped its wings. Its claws scraped the beam above my head. Sara and Priss shot a look at the bridge. I flattened myself against the pavement. My breath blew red dust over the edge of the bridge. I closed my mouth, straining to take air through my nose.

Did they see me? I listened. I didn't hear anything. I waited.

Giggling.

I had to get out of here.

I crouched again and hastily moved to the other side of the bridge, then heard them laughing once more. Once on the road, I straightened up and hustled toward Woody. Their laughter sounded closer, but I didn't dare look back. I made it to Woody, shifted into neutral, and rolled down the gravel road. As soon as I hit pavement, I turned the key and Woody's engine stammered to life.

Sweat trickled down my back. What if they'd caught me? Priss would demand revenge, probably buy an ad in the Natchitoches Daily and accuse me of being a Peeping Tom. Nothing was beyond her.

I stared out the windshield as Woody's headlights plowed over the pavement, telling myself to think about something else. I stomped on the gas, hurrying to tomorrow. The codes had been simmering, waiting, and immediately entered my consciousness, knocking the girls aside. Right, I had to decode the last two messages in the diary, and soon. I needed to come up with something other than hunches to change Chief Hendricks's mind.

XII

Rain tapped the roof and woke me from a sound sleep. The house was stuffy from too much moisture. My fingers stuck together where they touched, and my sheets were damp, as if they'd been removed from the washing machine before a completed spin cycle. I hated Louisiana when it rained.

I had memorized the remaining codes before I slept. Maybe before bed wasn't the best time. The two unsolved codes invaded my dreams, reoccurring sequences spinning over and over. Sleep deprived and irritated, I pushed back the clammy sheets.

Mom had gone to Our Lady of Sorrows with Rebecca Sharp. Mom lit candles for Dad's soul daily and laid fresh flowers on his grave before the new ones wilted. She remarked that Miss Sharp was a comfort, but I don't think Mrs. Dupree saw it that way. She claimed Mom as her best friend, and Miss Sharp was currently occupying her seat.

I vaguely remembered the phone ringing earlier in the morning. Mom told Lila Dupree she was eating at Guy's Creole Restaurant right after church with Miss Sharp. Mom listened for a few minutes. Then she said, "Don't be silly, you can come with us. Of course, she likes you."

As Mom walked out the door I heard Miss Sharp say, "I don't want to cause trouble."

And Mom's voice faded away. "Lila's just being Lila."

Good Lord. They sounded like they were in junior high. Anyway, Mom left, and the house was quiet, except for Tudy singing *Bringing in the Sheaves*. She'd achieved the haughty position of Twelfth Deaconess at All Saints Baptist Church, and though she left right after Mom, she wouldn't return until sundown.

I slid from the bed and pulled a yawn. Tudy paced in the foyer, still singing her favorite hymn. The hands on my Big Ben sat right on eleven o'clock, too late for Sunday service. What kept her here? I padded to the top of the stairs. She wore her Sunday best, dressed in starched white from head to toe. She stopped at the foyer mirror and adjusted her hat ringed with pale roses before bobbing out the front door. I watched her through the window, tapping her foot, waiting on her ride. Eventually, she left the porch.

I had today, or what was left of it, all to myself, and I needed to tackle the remaining codes in Dad's diary. I'd examined the entries in order. The second code was written in March almost exactly a month after the first code, and the third code was written the night before Dad died. He had clearly written them to hide the possible fraud, but what else? What was he hiding?

I brushed my teeth and splashed cool water over my face, racking my brain for answers. The reasons didn't matter if I couldn't crack the codes. They were the keys to solving whatever happened to my father. Deep in my brain, a timer clicked off minutes, reducing my chances to convince Chief Hendricks that foul play was involved.

No one was home except Brett and me so I slid down the banister. A silly kid thing to do, but it felt great. I walked into the kitchen. Brett sat on the kitchen counter, drinking a steaming cup of coffee.

"Whoa… what're you doing up?" I rubbed my eyes. He never woke up before me.

"Couldn't sleep." The swelling in his lip had gone down, but his eye looked like he'd gone a few rounds with a heavy-weight-boxing champ.

"What did Mom say about your face? I can't imagine Tudy let you by without a lecture."

"Mom left before I came downstairs. She hasn't seen it. But Tudy gave me an earful." Brett smirked. "Then she said she hoped I beat the other guy to a pulp, and if I didn't, I should be ashamed of myself."

"Sounds like Tudy." I grabbed the glass milk bottle from the refrigerator and swiped my finger around the inner rim. Cream stuck to my finger, and I licked it off. I'd be a dead man if Mom or Tudy saw me. "Hey, do you want to help me with the codes?"

"Why?" Brett said. "You're doing fine without me."

"I don't get it. He was your dad, too. You fought over him last night. Why don't you want to help?"

"What good would it do?" Brett stared into his coffee cup. "No one listens to us anyway. They think we're just kids."

"We have to try." I swallowed my frustration. "Look. If someone killed Dad, we have to find out who. No one knew Dad's habits better than you and me. It isn't just the codes... I know you'll resist doing this, but I kinda need to see where you found Dad."

"I'm not going back there." Brett huffed.

"Come on. Don't be like this. We need more clues to build a theory with. Maybe we'll find something. Hell, we could even come up with a solution." I opened the refrigerator and pulled out the last piece of pecan pie. I had the feeling Brett wasn't helping because he was more afraid of finding out the truth than I was. He covered his doubts with indifference, but if he were faced with the certainty of suicide, could he contend with it? With everything in limbo, he could skate along, act as if he were doing fine. But I couldn't leave it alone. "If you don't want to do it, I'll figure it out."

"I want to help, but I'm no good at solving riddles. You know that better than anyone." Brett set his cup on the counter. "You and Dad deciphered all the codes. I'm not sure why ya'll included me. I never really solved anything."

"No problem. I'll just figure it out by myself." I stabbed the pie like it might jump off the plate.

"All right. All right. I'll help." Brett said. "Besides, if you find proof, I don't want you getting all the credit." He pulled a huge serving spoon from the drawer and scooped out half my pie.

"Hey. That's mine." I covered the pie plate with my body. "Breakfast of Champions."

"Come on, Champion Goofball, let's get to work on Dad's diary before Mom comes home." Brett poured another cup of coffee and dumped about six tablespoons of sugar in it, then stalked to the stairs. "Besides, you aren't the only one with a job."

"What?"

"Priss's dad is harvesting hay. He needs some extra hands. It's not glamorous like wearing a white lab coat, but the money will help."

We'd felt the pinch. Mom hadn't said anything, but money was tight. All the worry over Dad's insurance policy was never far away; I saw it in her face every time she opened the mail and placed another bill on a growing pile.

We'd just opened the diary when the doorbell rang. I halfway expected a key to scrape against the lock. Sometimes Mom rang the bell before she opened the door. I don't know why she did it, just one of those quirky things. I glanced over at Brett. He slapped the diary shut.

"Shh. I'll get it." I lifted my mattress, and Brett shoved the diary beneath it.

"See if you can get rid of them fast so we can finish the code." Brett dropped onto my bed. He wasn't coming down. No way was he letting anyone see his face.

I slid down the banister and opened the front door. Priss stood next to Sara. They stepped inside. Both wore their Sunday best, but Priss wore more ribbon than a War World II general. A cherry red ribbon was wound into a bow near the crown of Priss's head, and the buttons on her dress were covered with pearl white bows.

"Hey." Priss crossed her arms and pushed out her hip. "We were thinking of heading over to Zestos for Sunday lunch. Do you and Brett want to come?"

Before I could respond, a car door slammed and Tudy flapped past the girls. Then she stood in the middle of the entry, mopping her brow with a lacy white handkerchief, working her jaw, but nothing came out.

"Tudy?" I edged around the girls. "Are you all right?"

"Lordy… I gots to sit down." She fanned herself with the handkerchief as she made her way into the living room. "Oh, My Lord, I don't know what I'm gonna do."

With a slight gulp, she dropped to the couch, and her mostly white purse plunked to the ground, landing on top of her feet. Priss, Sara, and I stood around her. In all the years I'd known Tudy, she'd never come home from church early unless she was deathly ill. She didn't look sick.

"Tudy are you okay? Do you want some aspirin or a glass of water?" I sat down beside her, taking her birdlike wrist into my hand, checking her pulse.

She yanked her arm away. "What in heaven's name are you doing? I'm not sick, just overly excited."

"Did something happen at church?" Priss asked. She motioned to Sara, and they sat in the chairs opposite the couch.

"Didn't go to church." Tudy rocked, putting her head in her hands.

"But you were waiting for your ride. I saw you." I patted her back, thinking it might help calm her down. I'd never seen her in such a state.

Tudy stopped rocking and folded her hands in her lap. Her fingers twisted the poor handkerchief until it was one giant knot. "My ride was late picking me up this morning. When I finally got to church, Bessie Mae Johnson stood on the steps, waiting. She saw Big Red on her way to the church house. He was walking down the road, carrying two chickens, one striped black and one spotted red. She done decided it was a sign. Why she done decided it was a sign for me, I don't know. But, she said we needed to pay him a visit."

"You went to see Big Red?" Priss drew in a breath. "I've heard of him. Did you have your fortunes told? Does he use a crystal ball?"

Tudy's head snapped toward the girls. "He ain't no gypsy, Miss Priss. No ma'am. He's a true seer."

I couldn't believe my ears. "Tudy, don't tell me you believe in such nonsense. He's just a con man playing on your emotions."

"You don't know what you're talking about, Julian James. Big Red's respectable. He ain't never conned a soul. Now you apologize to me right now." Tudy huffed and gave me the stink eye.

"Hush up, Julian." Priss scooted to the chair's edge. "What happened? Tell us what he said. Every word."

"Can't repeat every word. Some things are only for the hearer." Tudy licked her lips. "Well, Bessie Mae went in first. She said his words was the gospel. He told her something she ain't never breathed to another living soul. Otherwise, I wouldn't have given him my hand."

"Your hand? Did he read your palm?" Priss almost fell off her chair she tipped so far forward. I looked at Sara. She swallowed a giggle.

"Lord no. I done told you. He ain't no palm reader. He's the real thing." Tudy cradled one hand inside the other, palms up. "Like this. He's got to touch you to feel the vibrations you put out. Then, real quiet like, he tells you something nobody knows, something from your past. So you know he's the solid thing. Then he tells you something real and true. Sometimes it's good, and sometimes it's bad."

Tudy mopped her upper lip and continued. "First thing, he told me something from my past so I'd trust him. He says I'd been married a long time ago to a no good, cheating man. True."

She nodded and dabbed her lips once more. "Then he says my money situation's gonna get real bad. It's gonna get worse before it gets better, and there ain't nothing I can do about it." She shook her head.

"Only means one thing." She looked right at me. "Your mama ain't get-tin' no life insurance money. Then what we gonna do? Y'all gonna have to live in Lake Charles with you mama's people, and I'll go back to the home place so far down Cane River nobody'll ever find me."

"You don't know what he meant. It could mean anything or nothing." I fiddled with the seams inside my pockets. "See. What did I tell you? He got you all upset for no good reason."

Tudy's gaped. "You call what he knowed about me and my old hang dog husband nothing? That's your problem. You don't believe in nothing, Julian James. I don't wanna upset your mama. But she needs to know."

"Please don't say anything to Mom. She's almost set fire to the church lighting candles for Dad already."

Tudy huffed again. "I won't say nothing to your mama if'n you go see Big Red. See what he says to you, I promise ain't nothing passing my lips."

Before I had a chance to answer, Priss jumped in. "You heard her. You have to see Big Red. I've never been to a fortu... a seer before. Sara and I'll go with you. Tudy can tell us how to get there. Come on. Don't be such a sour puss. It'll be fun."

I just wanted to finish the code. Brett conveniently stayed upstairs, using his battered face as an excuse. He could probably hear the entire conversation and was having himself a good laugh. Killing him could wait. If I didn't go, Tudy would worry me to death and worry Mom about the money. On the other hand, Brett would never let me live it down if I went to see Big Red. I watched Priss from the corner of my eye.

"Come on, Julian. What could he tell you, you don't already know?" Priss edged next to me. Sara moved closer. I was definitely being herded.

"If you promise not to say a word to Mom, I'll go," I looked straight at Tudy.

"I promise. Not a single word." She made a big X over her heart with her white handkerchief fluttering. It reminded me of a flag of surrender. I was such a chump.

Big Red's farm was right off Highway 6 close to Robeline. Why he came into Natchitoches early on a Sunday morning was anyone's guess. Tudy drew us a map, and Priss folded it away.

I started Woody, and the girls piled in. It took about twenty minutes to find the little dirt road leading to Big Red's. We passed it twice because there was no sign, no mailbox. I didn't know what to expect. We pulled in front of a neat white house with a wide cement stoop painted Charleston green. No bones or crucifixes hung from the trees, no sticks braided with animal hair or hexes along the fence, nothing spooky or crazy, just a normal house. A tall, bulky man came around the corner of a squat, smelly chicken coop.

He stretched upwards nearly seven feet tall. His overalls hitched on one side, and he wore a T-shirt striped with sweat underneath. He scratched the skin in front of his ear as if deep in thought and scanned us with cool black eyes. A little part of me wondered if he had x-ray vision.

"Is there something I can help you with?" His voice sounded low and smooth.

I cleared my throat. After all, he was an enormous black man, and here I was a lily-white kid with two teenage girls standing on his property. He could easily tell us to get lost. "We're looking for Big Red."

"Looks to me like you found him." He fished a small paper square from the top pocket of his overalls. "What can I do for you?"

Priss threw her shoulders back and stepped up first. "We wondered if we could have our fortunes told."

His scrutinized us, while he pulled a Prince Albert tobacco tin from his pocket. With slow precision he tapped the can, and the perfect amount of tobacco spilled into a paper rectangle. He pushed the tin back in his pocket, licked the paper, and rolled it into a cigarette. "I don't know. It's the Lord's Day. Not a good day for it."

For a moment, we all just stood around like dummies, watching him chew on the end of his fresh cigarette. What could we do anyway? What could we say? If it were up to me, we'd just pile back into Woody and go home.

"Things don't usually come ta me on Sunday." Big Red removed a tobacco speck from his tongue. "But since you're here, I'll try."

Priss thumped my shoulder as she moved past and whispered. "Me first."

Big Red loped toward his house. Priss practically stepped on his heels, and Sara and I followed her, which was fine by me. Priss was itching to learn about her future. I couldn't believe they'd talked me into this. I wanted to laugh, but the girls were into it.

He passed the house's painted green stoop. Priss and Sara trooped behind him as breezily as kindergarteners tied together on a rope. I was antsy to leave. Where were we going, anyway? On the other side of his house, away from the road, a narrow path led to a split-log building with a bright orange door. He unlocked the door and propped it open with a moldy brick. A red velvet curtain blazed out the opening. *Snap!* A flashbulb popped in my head. No choice. My brain was going to save this memory until the day I died. Served me right for coming. It would rank as the craziest thing I'd ever done.

Big Red walked in, held the curtain aside, and motioned for Priss. She almost jumped inside. At the opening, she turned and squeezed her shoulders together then silently clapped like an excited little girl. Then the curtain drifted down, and she disappeared.

"I'm the biggest idiot. Letting y'all talk me into this," I said.

"I don't know. Coming to see Big Red is kind of exciting. To know the future can be a powerful thing." Sara snapped open a small pink purse with a daisy on the front. A yellow bag of peanut M & M's rested on top. She pulled it out and dangled the package in front of me. "Want some?"

"Sure." I held out my palm, and she poured several into my hand. "Need some help thinking?"

"No. I'm hungry," she said. "We came to see if you wanted to have lunch with us, remember?"

"Oh yeah." I crammed a few candies into my mouth. "I can't believe we're doing this."

"Don't tell me you've never wanted to have your fortune told. Everyone has a secret desire to know what's ahead of them." Sara bit a green M & M in two, and nibbled the half with the peanut first.

"Not me. I don't believe in it. Just idiotic mumbo jumbo. There's nothing to it." I looked down at my palm. It was streaked with red, yellow, and green, the result of a hot hand and chocolate candy. I rubbed my hand on my jeans.

"But what if he's really and truly a seer?"

I shook my head. "Not possible."

"You're being a little cynical. Don't you think?" Sara bit into another candy.

How could I answer? I wasn't really a cynic, more a realist. And being a realist, I gathered we would be alone for a few minutes. Brett probably was lying comfortably in his bed, and Priss sat on the other side of Big Red's curtain and couldn't hear anything. Sara popped a candy in her mouth, watching me with a tiny smile. This was as good a time as any to ask Sara on a date. I stiffened my spine and said, "Sara…"

The curtain brushed open, and Priss stepped out. She looked a little dazed. Sara ran up to her. "What'd he say? What'd he say?"

Before Priss answered, Big Red stooped at the door and motioned for Sara. She hesitated, handed me the bag of candy, and then stepped inside. Just before the curtain fell, she looked back at me. Her eyes brimmed with curiosity.

Priss stood in the same spot for a minute or two with the goofiest look on her face. Then she blinked as if returning from another planet. "My, my. I would have never thought."

"Thought what? What did he say?" I asked. I shoved the bag of M & M's in my pocket.

"I can't tell you." Priss walked away from the little building.

"Oh brother. Don't act like you don't want to tell me. What did he say?" Now what? I guess she wanted me to tease it out of her.

"Really. I can't say. He didn't tell me *not* to say anything. But I just have a feeling. No, I won't do it. I guess I'm more superstitious than I thought." Priss touched her hair and looked back at the little building. "Don't you want to know how he does it?"

"Yeah, I guess."

"Well, once you're inside, you sit down, and he takes your hand and turns it palm up. He tells you something about yourself, first. Something no one else knows about you, just like Tudy said." Priss looked past me, collecting her thoughts. "Then he puts your hand palm down on the table like this." She demonstrated. "Then he wraps two fingers around your wrist, almost like a nurse taking your pulse. He's real quiet like he's listening for something. Then he tells you what's in your future."

"So what did he tell you from your past?" I tried to keep the skepticism out of my voice. "What convinced you he was telling the truth?"

"Wouldn't you like to know?"

"Come on. I know *all* your secrets."

"This one you don't." She looked me in the eye and crossed her arms. "You think you know everything. But you aren't as smart as you think. You don't know I'm going to live somewhere far away from here, somewhere larger than life with more people than I can count in a day."

"Jeez, I could have told you that. Some magic. Everyone knows you want to live in New York." I shook my head. I couldn't believe she fell for this stuff.

"He didn't say New York. He told me something else. But I'm not telling."

"See. Just a con. He tells you something vague. You buy into it. Then you can't repeat it. Not because you're afraid it won't come true, but because your friends will laugh at you." Exasperation crept in. Why should I try to convince her of anything?

"You don't know what you're talking about. Just like Tudy said." She turned her back on me.

I tapped on her shoulder the same time the curtain drifted back. Sara slipped out from behind the curtain. She looked so different from Priss. She wasn't all glassy-eyed and dreamy-looking. Instead, an impish grin stretched across her face.

"Your turn." She squeezed my arm as I walked past her and stepped behind the crimson curtain.

XIII

My pupils adjusted to the darkness once the curtain fell past the door. Big Red stood in front of an uneven table covered with a midnight blue satin cloth. A lonely rusted oil lamp occupied the center of the table. A gunmetal gray folding chair like the kind they use for church socials was pulled out for me to sit in. The room smelled of moldy, damp earth.

Big Red shook his head. "Always the last one. The unbeliever. Afraid you're a traitor to your own way of thinking?"

"I'm here because Tudy and my friends wanted me to come." I reached for the chair.

"Go then. Nothing I can do for you." He stood over me, a great dark giant.

"But you have to. Tudy sent me."

"I don't haveta *do* anything. Nothing comes ta me when someone doesn't believe." He waved his hand toward the billowing curtain and the open door. "Now go. There's nothing here for you."

"Can't you just give me something, so I can go back to Tudy and say you told me my future?" I didn't want to argue, but if I came home and told her a lie, told her Big Red read my fortune and he didn't... she'd skin me alive, one skinny strip at a time.

He waved to the door a second time. He wasn't fooling around, and he scowled. He obviously had more pull with the fates than I did. If I kept resisting, the end result could be something terrible and treacherous.

"If you could just tell me something about myself, then I'd believe." My hand gripped the chair. What was happening to me? This was ridiculous. Here I was trying to persuade a con man to include me in his little deception. I couldn't trust myself any longer.

He breathed in, his chest rising like a balloon. "Sit down."

I sat down so quickly I almost folded the chair in on myself. The table came up to my chest, obviously the perfect height for Big Red. Without thinking, I positioned my hands on the table, palms up. He shook his head.

"Don't need your hands. You have strong vibrations."

Oh man, strong vibrations? Did he really think that would hook me? This business was getting to me. I wanted to jump up and call him a fraud. But then it was probably best to just get through it. It reminded me of taking some ghastly strong medicine. I just didn't want to choke on it.

He sank into an old oak chair reinforced with cables at the bottom to support his weight. Once seated, he crossed his hands one over the other and laid them on the table. They were larger than a catcher's mitt. He stared at me. Everything closed in on me except the light from the copper lantern.

"You've been happy most of your life. But you said and done things to others you regret. Things that can't be undone." Big Red tilted his head as if listening to a small voice. "But something happened and now you have the miseries. Something so bad, you'll carry it with you all your life."

All right, I popped off at the mouth sometimes, but most people said things they regret. And everyone in town knew about Dad. He would have to do better.

Big Red massaged each of his temples with two fingers. He squinted as if some thought or idea was squeezing into his brain. His fingers stopped moving. He stammered. "I... can't tell you anything else."

He stood. "You have to go. I see something bad."

"Go? Bad? But you haven't told me anything about my future." Okay, now I was intrigued. He'd sucked me in. "Please. You told my friends their futures."

He shook his head and sat back down. "More trouble."

He had my attention now.

"Your father left something behind. Something no one else knows about." His words were clear, no doubt in them.

I inched closer to the table.

He stared directly at me and asked. "Did he?"

I paused briefly before I answered. Was this how he did it? He asked me a question. My answer gave him all the information he needed. Well, I wouldn't tell him about the diary. I'd give him a simple answer. "Yes."

"He left it ta help you. He knew you'd find it." He stretched across the table. His eyes pinned on me. "But it can't help you by itself."

I stopped breathing. His gaze never wavered.

"You gotta be careful. You're gonna search for answers. But you're gonna dig too deep, and you won't like what you find. Your decisions will put others in danger."

My heart stopped along side my lungs. Was he trying to scare me? "What? What kind of decisions? What kind of danger?"

"I can't see more than what I just told you." He slid his hands into his lap. "I've got a bad feeling about you."

"Why are you being like this?"

"I only give you what I'm given." He sat back. "I'm not always blessed with good information. You take it or leave it. It's up to you."

"I think I'll leave it." I stood up. Anger rose in the back of my throat like acid. I stalked to the curtain then turned back with my hand in my pocket. "How much do I owe you?"

"You don't owe me nothing. Being a seer is a gift from God Almighty."

"Then why do you do it?" I asked.

"Use your ears. God gives, and he can take away. No money exchanges hands." He stayed in his chair. "Maybe you shouldn't have come on the Lord's Day."

I thrust out my chin. Did he really think he could scare me? But what if? What if something horrible was in my future? No. I refused to believe it. I would never put others danger. I had to get a hold of myself. This was totally insane.

I flipped back the curtain. Sara and Priss stood together, expecting me to say something. But I didn't feel like talking to them.

"Come on. Let's go." I shoved past them, heading for Woody.

They were on me before I knew it. Sara was right at my shoulder. "What did he say?"

"Nothing."

"Come on. Just a little hint." Priss used her singsong voice, making me madder.

I ground my foot into the dirt and spun around. "I said nothing. Don't ask me again."

We slipped into Woody for the ride back home. Sara looked at Priss and raised her brows. For the first ten minutes, we all rode in complete silence. Finally, Sara said, "Do you want to talk about it?"

"No." I didn't understand my reaction. He didn't know me. Didn't know everyone called me Sargent Safety. I would never put the other people in danger. Not purposely anyway. This stuff was pure bunk. Can't believe I fell for it.

Sara glanced back at Priss in the back seat, then looked at me. "I guess we shouldn't have dragged you to see Big Red."

"Like I said before, a whole bunch of shit." For some reason her lisp pricked me.

Priss caught my reaction. "Then why are you so angry? Evidently, he said something to get under your skin. What?"

"Nothing. He sizes people up and then uses their weaknesses to scare them. I don't want to talk about this anymore." I wanted to be alone. I fumbled with the radio. Crackling honky-tonk music blared into the stifling summer air, effectively shutting off our conversation. Woody rattled down the road, and I floored the gas pedal. We couldn't get home fast enough.

I hustled up to my room. I threw the pillows off my bed and shoved the magazines off my desk to the floor. Why did I let Tudy and Priss talk me into seeing a fortune-teller or seer or whatever he was? Oh yeah… I was a dumb shit. Priss had manipulated me into something… again.

I went to slam the bedroom door, but Brett caught it before it made contact.

"Whoa, J. J. What gives?" He smirked. "Sara turn you down or a bad fortune?"

"All that fortune business is just a joke. And no, I haven't asked Sara out yet." I didn't need this right now. If Brett didn't watch out I'd give him another fat lip.

"Clock's ticking. If you don't ask her by week's end, she's fair game." Brett winked. Huh? His eye looked almost normal. When I left, he couldn't even open it.

"Hey, what happened? Your eye's almost healed."

"Rebecca Sharp came back with Mom. She has three brothers who fought each other all the time. She said she knew just the trick and made some concoction to smear on my face. Then she pressed a box of frozen peas on the swollen part. In about an hour, it looked like this. Cool huh?"

"Yeah. Is she still here?" I asked. I had hidden Dad's diary, and I didn't want to risk anyone besides Brett and me seeing it.

"Nah. She and Mom went to the evening service. Probably to light more candles. But she did say something weird." Brett moved to the window in my room and looked out.

"What?"

"She and Mom were downstairs in the study, and she was helping Mom hang Dad's butterfly collection. You know the stuff from his office. I overheard them talking."

I wrinkled my brows. "Did she ask about Dad's missing research folder like Professor Noble?"

"No. But she said she thought someone would have found Professor McKnight by now."

"Yeah. Priss said he eloped with Dad's secretary. Didn't Chief mention some people were out of town he needed to interview before he finished his report?" I asked. "He must mean Professor McKnight."

"I wasn't with you the day you talked to him." Brett ran his fingertip along the window screen. "Did he say that?"

"Yeah. He did." I knelt beside the bed and pulled out Dad's diary from between the thin mattresses.

"Here's the weird part. Miss Sharp told Mom that Dad and Professor McKnight argued the Thursday before Dad died. She said they shouted so loud, she heard them all the way to her office."

I opened the diary and leafed through it. I found the entry and read it out loud. "McKnight came into my office today, and we argued. Things are at a boiling point, and I must do something. Just hard to know who to trust."

"What do you think he meant?" asked Brett.

"More cryptic stuff. Just like the first coded message. He must be referring to the fake bones. But he still doesn't say who's behind it." I grasped the diary's red ribbon and lifted it, opening to the second code.

"We've got to finish these codes. They're our only hope for really finding out what happened to Dad." I picked the magazines off the floor and stacked them back on my desk. I opened a drawer, pulling out a pad of paper and two pencils.

Brett picked up the chair across the room and brought it to the desk. "This is screwed up."

"I never thought we'd be doing this either. But he had faith in us. Big Red said Dad knew we'd find it."

"You said Big Red was a joke." Brett bit into the school bus-colored pencil, leaving teeth marks.

"I did. But, he claimed Dad left something behind for us to find, and it would help us." I moved Dad's diary where we could both see it. "But everything else he said was just bullcrap. He said I caused trouble."

Brett shook his head. "You? Trouble? Some fortune-teller."

"Yeah... some fortune-teller." I wrote down the code. It was divided into four letter groups:

Rewa rdks edni deck oldu arff oecn ediv
edna hcra eser noit avac xegn inia tnoc redl
oF.t hgin tsal dehc raes ecif fO

This didn't look like a shift or substitution cipher, but to be sure we still looked at repeated letters first, then Brett and I split all the keywords and dates we could think of between us. Big Red's words distracted me every so often, making the process slower than necessary. What decisions would put someone in danger? How did he know Dad left something behind, something to help me? Just made it more difficult to ignore the rest.

One thing was certain. According to Dad's diary, he and Professor McKnight argued before he died, just like Rebecca Sharp told Mom. She thought this was odd, too. The fact that no one knew where he went was even stranger.

XIV

Brett and I worked for hours on the code. We unpacked the little black codebook we found in Dad's office and used every example in it. Nothing worked.

Why did he create such an impossible code? I dropped my head on my desk and closed my eyes, completely exhausted. Cold fingers enveloped my head, and a memory drifted in.

Dad's face came into view as if I were looking through a camera lens. He laughed. The image panned out, and Brett entered the picture. The three of us were standing in the kitchen near the oven. Heat from the open door buffed my knees.

"Be ready. The moment you see the letters appear, remove it from the oven." Dad stood behind us, his hands on our shoulders.

Brett was eleven, which made me ten. I knew because Brett wore the New York Yankees baseball cap he'd gotten for Christmas. I reached up and touched the hat. The brim felt stiff and smelled like starched cotton. He loved the Yankees, and since he did, I did, too. To me, Brett hung the moon.

We doubled over, looking inside the oven at a paper strip. It turned from white to beige, soon three printed words appeared in sepia brown. I held my breath, watching the thin page curl and char at the edges. Brett grabbed a woven potholder and pulled the paper from the oven. Heat wafted off the page and blew into my face. I waved it away.

"Real words. Look, Dad." I said. "It's magic."

"No magic to it, son." Dad words trickled over one breath. "I wrote the words with lemon juice. The letters fade away as the paper dries, and reappear with a little heat."

"Move... move out of the way." Brett dropped the paper on the kitchen table and fanned it with the potholder.

Dad's laughed. "It should be cool by now. It doesn't take long."

Brett and I hovered over the table. Soon these letters appeared:

EZI RPK CAJ REK CARC

The words were meaningless. I looked up at Dad. "Where should we start?"

*I tapped the letters with my fingernail, landing last on the letter **Z**. "Here, here. Cause in the book is says to start with letters like **Q**, **X**, and **Z**."*

"Good." Dad ruffled my hair. "Take your time. And remember it might be written right to left instead of left to right. You'll figure it out."

Brett and I smirked at each other. We didn't need the hint. Dad reversed the letters sometimes. Soon we had the word Prize.

"What?" Brett's brows came together.

"Which word should you unscramble next?" asked Dad.

I raised my hand as if I were in school. Brett snorted. "We're at home, you know. Dad isn't the teacher. Dum-dum."

"Brett...." Dad cautioned. "What do you think, Julian?"

"The middle word. It has a "J" in it."

"Good." He smiled and gave Brett a pat. "Do you see the word? Move the letters around in your head. It'll come to you."

"Just like Scrabble," Brett said under his breath.

*Before he said another word, I ran out of the kitchen and opened the game closet, pulled down Scrabble, and raced back to the kitchen. I plopped the box on the table and removed the wooden tile stamped with a big black **J**.*

"Good idea, J.J." Brett helped me pick out the tiles until we had all the letters we needed to unscramble the word.

Brett stared at it. I stared at it, rearranging the letters in my head. I had it! "Jack!"

"Jack, that's a boy's name. Why Jack Prize? That's stupid."

Dad leaned over us and smoothed the page. "Combine the remaining letters and you'll have it."

We pushed the remaining letters together over the Formica tabletop. Pretty soon, we spelled the last word, Cracker.

"Cracker Jack Prize," Brett and I said in unison. We looked at each other, puzzled. Our heads swiveled to Dad. A broad smile stretched across his face, one of those smiles like he's enjoying the game more than my brother and me.

"Where would you get a Cracker Jack Prize?" he asked.

"In a box of Cracker Jacks, of course. Everyone knows that." Brett answered.

"And where would you eat Cracker Jacks?" Dad grinned, again.

Did I even hope? I bit my lip. I didn't dare say it, but it popped out of my mouth anyway. "At Yankee Stadium!"

Brett looked to Dad. He nodded. "I have a meeting in New York and thought you boys might want to tag along. Ride the train. A real guys' trip. We can take in a game while we're there."

Brett jumped up and down, waving his arms. "I'll get to see Whitey Ford, Mickey Mantle... and Yogi Berra?"

"Yes." Dad didn't try to calm us down, just grinned and nodded his head. We jumped all over the kitchen, bumping the table. Wooden tiles bounced on the floor.

"Take me out to the ball game...." I sang. Brett joined in.

The image faded. I didn't want it to fade. I tried to hang on to it. I gritted my teeth, but only orange spots danced beneath my lids.

For a few minutes I was ten again, and Dad was alive. A mild tingle still ran along the part in my hair, and I touched the spot where Dad's fingers had been. But the image meant more than a cherished recollection. The memory was the second code's solution.

My head eased off my arm. Imaginary ants scurried through my hand. I opened and closed my hand pumping blood back into veins, and the stinging diminished. Such a simple solution. I'd forgotten Dad liked to write out the codes from right to left. Why didn't I think of it before?

Brett lay on my bed with his back to the window. He'd fallen asleep. I scooted my chair, and he opened one eye.

"Any luck?" he asked.

"Be right back. We need the Scrabble Game."

He frowned. "What are you talking about?"

I shot downstairs to the game closet and pulled out a worn, frayed box. Brett hadn't moved.

"I can't believe I didn't figure this out sooner." I motioned for Brett to get off the bed.

"Nope. Not 'til you tell me what's up."

"Do you remember the first message Dad gave us?"

"Sure… How could I forget? Dad made invisible ink with lemon juice, and we heated paper in the oven." Brett looked so sad with his semi-bruised eye. "Yankee Stadium… the best trip we ever went on. No digging, no bones, or anything. A great trip."

"Remember the letters were divided into groups of three. This code's the same except there are four letters to a section." I shook my head. It was so simple. "I bet Dad wrote it right to left. We need to reverse the code first."

I rubbed the tattered box's frail edge. "God, I miss him Brett." I removed the top. "We owe it to him to find who did this, even if no one *ever* believes us."

Brett looked at me hard. Something changed. Memories did that. They reminded us of the good times. I think he missed Dad more than he let on.

He sat up and tucked his legs. "Yeah."

I chucked all one hundred Scrabble tiles onto the bed. "Let's go."

Brett propped the diary on a pillow, and we picked out all the tiles we needed for the code, flipping them face up until they were a chain of letters. I glanced down once memorizing the sequence.

*Rewardksednideckolduarffoecnedived
nahcraesernoitavacxegninia tnocredloF.
thgintsaldehcraeseciffO*

We rearranged them from left to right in the same groups of four.

*Of fice sear ched last nigh t.Fo lder cont aini ngex
cava tion rese arch ande vide nceo ffra
udlo cked inde skdr awer.*

Some words were clear right from the beginning. Words like office, last, and night didn't need much effort. Also, a period was in the middle of one group with a capitalized letter, a sentence break. It didn't take us long once we started separating some letters and pushing others together. I read it out loud:

*Office searched last night. Folder containing
excavation research and evidence of
fraud locked in desk drawer.*

After we decoded the message, Brett threw a tile against the wall. "Damn. We've known all along someone had the research folder. We've wasted all this time solving this idiotic message."

"We didn't waste our time. Before, we thought Dad's research folder might have been misplaced. Now we know for certain he hid it someplace other than his desk." I picked up a few tiles and tossed them in the Scrabble box. "Not only that, but someone tried to steal it from him. If they tried it once, they probably tried again. Someone may have found it. Four main people worked with Dad: Professor Noble, Rebecca Sharp, Professor McKnight, and Miss Penny."

Brett scratched the side of his head with his chewed pencil. "Professor Noble could have the folder. He might be purposely throwing us off base."

"Yeah." I said. "But, Dad would have smelled his pomade and known it was him right away. That stuff reeks after he leaves a room."

"He's crazy, but I don't see him stealing anything. But sometimes it's the person you least expect. Remember. He's the one who told Chief Hendricks Dad was depressed and acting strange." Brett scooped up the tile he'd thrown earlier and dropped it in the box.

"What about Rebecca Sharp? She's been more helpful than anyone since Dad's death. She's driven Mom to church and the cemetery a million times." I replaced the box top and scooted it under the bed. Never know if we might need it for the next code.

"Guilty conscience?"

"Maybe, but she seems like the last person to tamper with the site. Besides, she hasn't shown that much interest in Dad's research, and she's had plenty of opportunity to search Dad's study while helping Mom."

Brett shrugged.

I combined hints and clues together, moving them around in my brain, but nothing made a whole picture. We didn't even have enough for a good theory. It was possible Dad found out about the altered bones, and it had nothing to do with him falling out the window. The idea didn't sit well with me, but it was possible.

"Only leaves Professor McKnight. He's the most suspicious. Maybe they're in this together. Maybe he has the research folder with him."

Brett edged close to the bedroom window and stared out into the night. He listened to me, but he didn't respond. I couldn't tell if he was even listening.

"And he argued with Dad a few days before Dad died. Odd no one mentioned it before now." I picked up the diary off the bed and skimmed through it while we talked, looking for Professor McKnight's name. "You know what else is weird? Professor McKnight eloping with Miss Penny. No one knows where they went or how to contact them. Two people who saw Dad everyday, two people who knew Dad's schedule, and one of them had a key to Dad's office."

Then I remembered something Mom said the day Dad died. "Brett, I know you don't believe me about the man watching the house, but Mom said Dad found a screen off his study window, and the window was open the day he died. What if it wasn't the wind? What if the Shadow Man is the one looking for Dad's research?"

"I don't know… could be, but why would anyone want Dad's research? Who else would be interested? I think it has to be someone he worked with."

Brett dropped to the floor. He lowered his voice and pointed outside. "Whoa, too bizarre…. Crazy Kurt Noble just walked up. He's on the sidewalk out front."

I scrambled over the bed, dropping the diary and clicking off the lights. Being my usual stealthy self, I slammed my knee into the bedpost on my way to the window and bit my inner cheek to keep from howling. I knelt down, rubbing the sting out of my knee, and looked through the screen.

Sure enough, Professor Noble paced up and down the sidewalk, plucking his watch chain off his beach ball stomach. His black hair stuck out in a hundred directions and glistened like spikes under the streetlight. He clicked his heels three times like *Dorothy in the Wizard of Oz* and mumbled something.

"What's he doing?" Brett said.

"He acts deranged. It has to be after one o'clock. Do you think he knows where he is?"

I shifted closer to the window screen, looking past the ledge. I watched him for a good five minutes. It looked like he argued with himself.

"Oh no, he stopped. Holy smokes, he's looking up at our room," I whispered a little louder. I ducked beneath the sill.

"Get up. He can't see us with the lights off."

"Are you sure?"

"See for yourself." Brett moved to the side so I could see. "He's still pacing."

"Man, this just keeps getting weirder and weirder." I peered over the sill. Professor Noble walked up and down the sidewalk, pulling at his hair, talking to some invisible person. Then he paused and stared into space. "He stopped, again. Boy, his watch chain sure gets a workout. He's looking at the house again."

"I don't need a blow-by-blow. I can see," murmured Brett.

"He's coming up the front walk." I couldn't imagine why he was coming up our walk this late at night. Had Professor Noble finally cracked?

The doorbell rang. Brett and I looked at each other. We raced for the stairs, reaching them the same minute Mom appeared from her room, tying her robe. She gave us a blurry look. Brett and I pounded down ahead of her.

"Who in the world could it be at this hour?" Mom asked.

"It's Professor Noble." I answered.

She missed a step and careened into us. Brett caught her at the waist. I noticed then how thin she was; her hips protruded against the fabric. She wasn't eating. About the time we made it to the front door, Tudy tore around the corner, swinging a baseball bat.

"Lord, who's calling this time a night?" Bobby pins and lozenge-shaped tissues stuck out of her hair at the most impossible angles. Well, not impossible. A page from my geometry book flashed in my mind. The pins became intersecting lines and perpendicular lines. I shook my head to clear the image.

"Kurt Noble?" said Mom.

"This time a night?" Tudy shook the bat. "Let me at him first. Didn't his mama teach him no manners?"

Mom smoothed her hair. "Whatever he wants, it must be important. Now, everyone be nice."

Brett and I moved to either side of Mom. Tudy sidled next to me while Mom opened the door. It dawned on me he might have been the person watching the house all along, but tonight he just wasn't dressed in black. An eerie feeling caused me to shudder. I reached for the door, but it was too late. Mom opened it.

"I'm so sorry to bother you, but it just couldn't wait." Professor Noble barged into the entry. He smoothed his hair on either side of his face while the rest prickled up into pomade peaks. Dark rings pooled underneath his eyes, and his mouth twitched when he talked. Without a doubt, he owned his nickname, Crazy Kurt. I tensed and looked at his hands, checking for a weapon. He tugged on his watch chain. I relaxed, but stayed alert.

Mom gestured to the great room. "Have a seat, Professor Noble."

Tudy, Brett, and I trailed behind them. Once Noble crossed the great room, Tudy inched over next to him, stroking the bat with her hand. She wasn't about to let him discombobulate the whole family without a show of defiance.

Professor Noble didn't sit. He paced and jabbered all at once. "I didn't want to do this, but… Uh, I need to confer with you before I turn everything over to the college's financial office."

He stroked his face, then dropped his hands, searching for his watch chain. Was he having a nervous breakdown right in front of us? Mom sat down and motioned for the rest of us to do the same. "Now, Dr. Noble, please tell us what's so important it can't wait until morning."

"I, uh… I received a call yesterday from the Mr. Coker, president of Natchitoches Central Bank. He was examining a special checking account set up for the new excavation when uh, when uh… he found something suspicious." He rolled the watch chain between his fingers. "A check for an unusually large sum cleared the bank this month."

"I don't see why this couldn't wait until morning." My mom smoothed her robe and studied Professor Noble. "What does this has to do with us?"

Crazy Kurt toed the fire irons by the mantel, clearly stalling for time. He reached into his inside coat pocket and unfolded several ragged mint-green papers that looked like they'd been ripped from an oversized checkbook. "Since your husband's death, I was given all the financial information for the archeology department. I checked over the accounts. The excavation account had the usual withdrawals associated with an excavation until last month. Uh, uh… a check was written for a thousand dollars. That's a lot of money. I could buy a new car for a thousand dollars."

"Again, I don't see why this couldn't wait until morning. And I certainly don't see why this concerns us." Mom voice sounded stern. She wanted him to get to the point.

Tudy prodded me with her elbow. I stood, and so did Brett. Sweat beaded Dr. Noble's upper lip. He swiped his lip with the back of his hand.

"As I was saying... A thousand dollars is a lot of money, and I didn't see a receipt for a major purchase. Your husband wrote the check for cash."

"What are you saying, Kurt?" Mom asked.

"With a non-profit account, each check has to have two signatures." Professor Noble pulled his watch from his vest pocket and twisted the chain around his index finger. A soiled white bandage covered the same finger. "This check had Professor James and Professor McKnight's signatures on it. Uh... their names are on the pages I ripped from the register. You can see for yourself."

Dr. Noble handed Mom the pages, and she examined them before handing them back.

"I still don't understand. You've worked with my husband and Professor McKnight for years." Mom rose, but her hand remained on the couch's arm. "Can't you ask Professor McKnight about all this? Surely, you have some way to reach him."

"No. He never leaves an address or anything after term. The only person who might have known was your husband, but he didn't leave behind any information. A rumor is circulating Professor McKnight eloped with Penny. I have nothing to base that on other than gossip, didn't even know they were dating." Professor Noble closed his hand around the watch, clutching it close to his body. "No one's heard from them since the day before your husband's death. It's as if they disappeared."

XV

Mom's face turned sickly white. What was going on? Every time we turned around, something new popped up. Was my father part of some conspiracy? Had Professor McKnight been blackmailing Dad? None of this made any sense.

In one stride, my mom stood in front of Professor Noble and crossed her arms firmly over her thin chest. "We've been friends for a long time. You've hinted at some wrongdoing since you first walked in. Exactly what are you getting at?"

Brett's breathing changed. Tudy glared and stood near the end of the mantel, the bat a heavy pendulum in her hand. We waited for Professor Noble to answer.

"This hasn't been easy. The facts alone look as if he and Professor McKnight were doing something illegal, but I can't imagine it. Melton James was a good man, but something was bothering him when he died. Possibly McKnight forced him to do something... I don't know. I just don't know. They didn't share anything with me." Professor Noble tucked his watch back in his pocket. "When I turn the checkbook and account statements over to the chancellor, they'll institute a formal investigation. I wanted you to know first."

"I appreciate your concern, but my husband didn't do anything wrong." Mom pushed her fists into her hips. "I think you'd better leave now."

Tudy was at Mom's side in a flash. "What you boys waiting for? Walk Professor Noble to the door."

Brett hopped around the furniture and opened the front door. I walked with Professor Noble through the entry. He fiddled with his watch chain, tugging on it while he ambled to the door. Before he left, he faced Mom one last time. "I'm sorry about all this, but I do need to ask one more question."

"What else?" Mom glared at him.

Tudy scowled at Professor Noble, giving him one last chance before she came after him with the bat.

"You haven't found any money among the things you brought home from your husband's office?"

"You know he didn't take any money." Mom's eyes spit fire. "Do we look as if we've been living the high life since his death? How could you? We're doing all we can to make ends meet. You've insulted us enough for one evening. Now go."

"Sorry." Professor Noble bowed his head and didn't say another word.

When he turned to leave, I automatically checked the heel of his shoe. It had become a serious obsession. He wore brown moccasins with elaborate blue beading. I was totally unprepared for that. I'd never seen him wear anything but dress shoes. I couldn't rule out anyone, anymore. Was Professor Noble setting up Dad? If so, why?

Brett slammed the door behind him. Tudy and Mom dropped on the couch, stunned.

I padded across the entry floor. "Mom, what does this mean?"

She shook her head. "I don't know. Your father would never embezzle money from his department. He wasn't a thief. He never mentioned anything about Professor McKnight's needing money, either. I don't understand."

Tudy stood up, using the bat like a cane. "Well, I'm up for good. Expect I'll fix some coffee."

She cut me a look that said *I told you so*. Thankfully, she didn't say any-thing to Mom about Big Red. Maybe he had a gift. Maybe things would get worse before they got better.

"I'll be there in a minute." Mom stared into space, at nothing.

"What can we do?" I asked Mom.

"Nothing, boys. There's nothing we can do. We have to have faith and believe it will all work out. Your father was an honorable man. I'm sure there's a simple explanation for all this. Whatever happens, they can't pan for gold in a dry creek. We don't have any money, at least not until the Chief finalizes his report." Tears dripped down her cheeks. Brett and I were by her side in an instant. She hugged us close.

"Your father was a wonderful man. I don't know why all this is hap-pening." She wiped her face with the back of her hands. "Always remember that…. No matter what anyone else says."

Mom settled deeper into the couch. "Boys, if you don't mind, I'd like to be by myself."

I nodded at Brett, and we tramped back to my room. Dad's diary lay on the bed next to the second code. How lame brained. We left it right out in the open. We'd gotten careless. I picked up the diary.

Brett stopped at the door. "Did you ever think maybe we really didn't know Dad? Maybe he was, you know, like a spy or something? A person who lives a double life."

First, the Chief accused Dad of killing himself. Now Professor Noble accused him of stealing money. If Brett and I hadn't found his diary, it would be easy to believe he was a different kind of man: someone who didn't care about his family and lied to everyone he met.

"You don't really believe what you just said, do you? Do you remember what Dad said about honor?" I asked Brett.

"You mean a man is nothing without honor?"

"Yeah." I ran my hand across Dad's diary. The leather felt cool and soft. "Doesn't sound like the same man the Chief and Professor Noble have been describing. *That* man would never give up on you if you were in trouble. You can't ride the fence forever. You're either in, or you're out. You have to believe in him or we'll never find the truth."

Who was I trying to bolster, Brett or me? I didn't want to lose the last bit of hope. I couldn't let this get me down, or Brett would completely give up. I couldn't act as if this were a setback. I had to push on.

Brett stepped into my room. "I just knew we were on target. Then, this money business comes up. Maybe we should give Mom the diary."

"No. If we tell her about the diary, and she turns it over to Chief Hendricks, he might think someone stole Dad's research, but nothing else. Right now, I feel powerless to do anything. Chief Hendricks doesn't listen, and Professor Noble thinks Dad's a thief."

"But you have to admit it's weird. Why would Dad hide money from the department or give it to another professor?" Brett said.

I picked up the top mattress and slid the diary under it. "You heard Professor Noble; he said no one told him anything. Could be a lie, though. Think about it. If Dad suspected Professor McKnight doctored human bones, why would he give him money?"

My mind was charged. An icy sensation crept along the outside my brain, and images popped up in random order: Dad's office, shimmering white shells, the codes, Tudy's hose wrinkled around her ankles. I tried to slow the images down, but they swirled into a thick tornado of colors, whirling and heating my brain. It was an information overload, and my brain couldn't process anything else.

"I've got to get some rest." I fell onto the bed.

"We need a break." Brett said. His voice sounded distant.

My mind fizzled like tired bubbles in stale seltzer water. I didn't want to dream or fall into a memory. I couldn't take it. My dad was a good man. I wasn't about to let this rest, but I craved sleep more than anything right now.

The next day, the clinic closed at noon. Fortunately, it couldn't have happened on a better day. I pushed my hands deep in my pockets and started home. I hadn't sleep well, tossed and turned all night, unable to keep the newest allegation against Dad out of my mind. I couldn't figure out how the hell everything fit together. I wanted to believe in him. I wanted evidence so clear all doubts would evaporate. When I walked through the back door, Tudy was slathering a triple-layer red velvet cake with thick creamy frosting.

"Thought your mom might eat a little a this. She's been eating less than a bird lately." Tudy spun a knife over the cake, making a deep swirly path. "Red velvet's her favorite."

"Tudy, you're the best." I draped my arm around her and dipped my finger into the bowl of icing. I stuck my finger in my mouth and moaned. She was the best cook God ever made.

She slapped my hand with the knife, splattering white frosting all over me. "Getcha hand outta there. You know better."

I licked my hand. "More for me."

Tudy chuckled and spread another dollop. She'd removed the pins from the night before and combed her hair into smooth curls around her ears. A little corkscrew straggler hung down her collar above the knot of her stiff apron.

"Heard anything new today?" I held my hands under the faucet. Burning water, heated from noonday sun, shot from the tap. I jerked my hands from under the water, doing a little hop-hop dance, searching for a hand towel.

"Nothing I know of." Tudy was fixated on the cake. "When you was with Big Red, did he tell ya the same thing he done told me?"

"No." I wrung my hands on a cloth. "I don't believe him. He said—"

"Don't tell me. Lord, don't tell me. All I need is a yes or a no." The knife she held clanged to the floor. "If you tells all he says, it'll turn good luck to bad.

"But you rattled on about your future." I was thoroughly confused. After he told her future, she ran into the house confessing like a snitch under a white-hot lamp.

"Some. Not the whole thing." Tudy retrieved the knife and wiped her hands on her apron. "Now don't you go saying you don't believe. I just need to know if he done told you the same."

"No. He didn't tell me the same thing, Tudy." I wanted to break for my room, tired of this conversation and tired of nothing but bad news, but my room wasn't far enough. I needed to disappear. So I made for the back door. "All I know is… we'd better hope my fortune never comes true."

I pressed my spine into the base of an ancient Cypress tree, enjoying the cool canopy of limbs arched all the way over a dirt path. Striped bass slurped bugs from Cane River's rippling surface. I'd tried to stop thinking about Dad's diary, the codes, the heel print, and the missing file. Somehow all of this was connected, but no matter how hard I tried, nothing fell remotely into any order. Someone coughed.

When I looked up, the corners of Sara's mouth lifted. She dodged a branch and wended her way toward me, carrying a crinkled paper bag from Rexall that crunched with each step. She stepped carefully over the root-clogged path. Her legs were tanned, especially against pale blue shorts. She stopped in front of the tree.

"Hey… Have you eaten anything?"

"No. How'd you know I was here?"

"I stopped at your house, and Tudy said you sometimes come to the river to think."

"Did she tell you I was hungry too?" Acid crept into my voice.

"Do you want me to leave?" Sara frowned, and the paper bag slipped to her hip.

"No. No." I stood up. "I'm sorry. I don't know what's wrong with me."

"I brought pimento cheese sandwiches. Oh, and corn chips. You know what they say?" She dug in the bag and pulled out an open bag of chips. "You aren't truly Southern if you don't like corn chips." She giggled.

"I never heard that before."

I took the bag from her and emptied it on the grass. Two pimento cheese sandwiches wrapped in wax paper, a large yellow bag of M & M's, and two iced Coca-colas in thick green-glass bottles tumbled onto the thick grass. A white napkin fluttered out with something written diagonally across it. I caught the napkin and examined it.

A backwards message written in black ink seared into my brain, the image like white neon on black velvet.

.em htiw efas si terces ruoY

Reversing the words was easy. They simply floated into place and became:

Your secret is safe with me.

Sara had written her own code, using a mirror image, almost as if she'd known about Dad's second code. Not likely. Everything seemed to revolve around solving the message in Dad's diary these days. She sucked on a corn chip then flicked it into her mouth. Who was this girl? Not the stuck-up girl I met the first night. She was like a yo-yo, though. Sometimes she'd let me close, then she'd say something to push me away.

"Where's your sidekick?" I tried to sound nonchalant

Sara opened the waxed paper folded around a sandwich. "She told her mother we were going to the library. Then she ditched me at the library door as cool as you please. She instructed me to check out two books, one for me and one for her."

"Where *did* she go?" I pressed the crusty bread between my palms, flattening it. Cheese oozed over the edges.

"Where do you think? To find Jack." Sara sat back against the tree and wrinkled her nose, then she pulled off a bit of sandwich. She ate it like M&M's, one tiny piece at the time. "It's nice down here. Hard to believe it's the same river that flows past Shell Beach."

"Most people don't come down here in the heat, but there's a cool breeze off the water most days. The riverfront is my favorite place in the summer." I'd never told anyone before. She stopped chewing, and Brett's challenge filled my ears. I didn't want to think about Brett right now, didn't want to ruin being with Sara.

"Did you have any luck with the second code?" She lifted a frosted bottle to her lips, but the metal cap was still on. Her mouth crooked to the side. "Forgot the opener."

I grabbed our bottles. Taking one bottle at a time, I wedged the cap between two tree branches and jerked the bottle down with a flick of my wrist. Ping! The last cap bounced along the path. Stooping under one of the branches, I pulled a long draw. Ice chips slid down my throat, burning a trail all the way to my stomach.

"Brett and I broke the second code." I handed her back her bottle and watched for her response.

"Wow! How'd you do it?" She tilted her head to the side. She did this earlier when something perplexed her.

"Dad wrote the words backwards from the end to the beginning like you did on the napkin. But then he broke the words into groups of four letters so the message wasn't obvious. Such a simple code, don't know why I didn't catch it." I sat back down and held out my hand. Sara took it. Her hand was moist, but warm. She sat down on the paper bag. Her eyes were massive and intensely dark. Leafy shadows played across her face.

"How did you finally figure it out?"

"We played Scrabble with Dad from the time we could spell dog. Playing word games is the same thing as solving codes." I'd have to tell her about my memories at some point. I wondered if Priss ever mentioned it. It struck me now might be the right time to tell her, but before I said anything, she asked the next question.

"And the message?" Sara positioned her drink between us. The cold bottle rested against my leg.

"Someone broke into his office looking for the research files. So he locked them in his desk drawer. Problem is Brett and I cleaned his desk, and his research folder wasn't there." My throat ached. It was such a strain to talk about Dad. Discussing the codes with Sara made it all the more real.

"Julian, you'll prove your father didn't kill himself. I just know it." She looked at me, her gaze was kind, yet determined. Her confidence encouraged me.

Licking the salt off my lips, I screwed up my courage. "Sara…"

"Did you hear something?" Sara sat up, her back straight, alert.

"What?" My body tensed.

"Someone's crying."

XIV

Partially hidden behind the spindly limbs of a weeping willow, Priss hugged her knees close to her body. Her shoulders heaved, and she made a noise similar to a cat mewing. I'd never seen Priss cry. Scream, get mad, stomp her feet, shake her fist at the sky, curse like a farmer in a drought, but never cry.

Sara crept over and wrapped her arm around her friend.

Priss jumped, clearly startled. She rubbed her nose, sniffing.

"What are you doing here? Did you find Jack?" asked Sara.

"Oh I found him, coming out of Guillory's Restaurant. I wanted to surprise him, so I snuck up behind him. He was surprised all right. Almost hit me. Then he acted strange."

"What do you mean strange?" asked Sara.

"All funny. And not ha-ha funny." Priss pinched a tree branch. "He kept swallowing and looking around, tucking and untucking his hands in his pockets. Then, Miss Kathleen Dubois strutted out of Guillory's and walked right up to him. Being her usual spiteful self, she looked me right in the eye while she wrapped her arm through his. Like she owned him."

"What did you do?" Sara clutched her hands together.

Priss's voice shook. "I waited for Jack to do something. Instead, he just looked at me like all the other sheep around here. Kathleen couldn't wait to tell me they were invited to a party on Sibley Lake. I can't stand her. She tries way too hard to be the perfect Southern belle. Her and her ridiculous frilly dresses all covered with lace." Priss paused. "Well, she wound her arm a little tighter and said they would be late if they didn't leave right that minute. Jack just stood there like a dumb dodo. Of all people, Miss Goody-Two-Shoes. Right there in front of me."

Priss's face crumpled, and she looked like she might cry again. I didn't know what to do. I'd never seen her like this. It didn't matter we'd been friends forever or she'd seen me at my lowest. This was Priss Dupree.

"I hate them." Priss's shoulders drooped, and tears slid down her face. "He said he liked me. He said he'd never seen anyone take a dare like me. I impressed him."

"He doesn't know what he's missing. Everyone wants to be like you. I wish I had half the courage to do the things you do." Sara tucked a wisp of hair behind her ear.

"You're awfully quiet. What do you think? Why is he going out with Kathleen Dubois?" Priss stared at me.

"He has to." I shrugged. "Don't y'all keep up with anything? Did you forget the Plantation Ball is in a few weeks? He's pledged to escort Kathleen. Their moms planned it when they were in diapers. You know the first party is always at Sibley Lake. Besides, why do you care? You were the one who said you'd marry him and make his life miserable. Or don't you remember?"

Priss gave a mischievous smile, rose, squared her shoulders, and wiped her face. "I did say that. Forgot all about the ball. Besides, revenge is always best when it's unexpected." She scuttled up the grassy embankment. Over her shoulder she said, "Thanks for reminding me."

The sky darkened. A summer rain cloud drifted in just as thunder rumbled overhead. Sara and I went back to our picnic area. We quickly stuffed all the leftovers and trash into the Rexall bag.

My chances for asking her out were never better. She hadn't said anything since Priss scampered away. Was she waiting for me to say something? The air seemed tense and electric, and it wasn't from the coming storm. Now or never. I opened my mouth.

Priss drove her mom's car to the curb and honked. She gestured for Sara to hurry. The tension dissipated. I was jinxed. Brett would ask Sara on a date the next time he saw her, for sure.

She squeezed the bag of candy to her chest and ran toward the worn dirt trail. Rain sliced through the trees. I'd lost my chance. My heart floundered under my ribs. Sara turned at the top of the embankment.

"Wanna go for a burger at Zestos tomorrow night?" she yelled.

"Yeah!" I yelled back and gave the okay sign for good measure. My heart ticked up a beat, practically flapping in my chest.

She'd asked me! Me! I couldn't believe it. I waved as she drove away. A part of me wanted to jump in the air and click my heels, beat my chest, instead I walked up the embankment, playing the moment over and over in my mind. I pulled out specific details like when the rain made exclamation marks on Sara's pale blue shirt. I watched her face light up when I said yes. I've heard some moments stay with you forever. I hoped like heck this was one of them.

The rain turned out to be a typical summer shower, the devil beating his wife, over in a flash. But the afternoon was almost gone, and I had decided to take a detour. I turned on Church Street and walked along the steamy sidewalk to the next block, Fourth Street. On the corner, Professor McKnight's butter-colored craftsman house shared a drive with a mismatched red brick garage. The house looked abandoned. Weeds owned every sidewalk crack, and knee-high grass had taken over the lawn. Clearly, no one was home.

I looped around to the back of the house. An ancient 10-speed bike was tipped against a metal clothesline pole. A beige hunting shirt still pinned to a swaying line flapped in the breeze. The shirt had been there a while; bird poop streaked the back and shoulders.

Three steps connected a tiny porch to the house. I hopped up two steps and stopped. My mouth was dry. What the heck was I doing? Nothing wrong with checking on Professor McKnight, right? After all, he might be back. Just no one knew it yet. When I swallowed my Adam's apple caught, scraping down the center of my throat. Calm down. He would want me to check.

I tried the back door. It was unlocked. I twisted the knob, the door eased open. The house smelled like wet paper and moldy bread. An entire lumpy blue loaf wrapped in a red, white, and yellow Sunbeam wrapper sat next to the kitchen sink. Disgusting. I pinched my nose. Dirty dishes were stacked every which way in the sink. Greasy bicycle parts stuck to newspaper covered the kitchen table. Nothing was organized or neat. He was the complete opposite of my dad.

I left the kitchen and went into the living room. Open, dog-eared books were scattered across the coffee table, and typed pages slid off the table into hills and valleys. I walked down the hall, checking the first bedroom. Cardboard boxes and stuffed tan duffle bags occupied every space on the floor, leaving no room for furniture.

Across the hall his room was chaotic. Shirts and shorts were jumbled on the bed. In his closet a few shirts still hung on a wooden dowel, but most of the clothes had been dumped on the floor in front of the closet, hangers and all. Drawers were emptied, sweaters and shirts, socks and underwear flung all over the room, hanging off chairs and lamps, even the ceiling fan. Either he left in a hurry or someone ransacked his room. I didn't touch a thing.

I stepped into the closet. Since it was all but empty, it was easy to check out his shoes. Only two pair sat in the closet; dress shoes with thin heels, no visible cracks or splits, and muddy tennis shoes with rubber treads. This obsession with shoes might be a dead end. If someone had a crack or split in a shoe, wouldn't they throw them away? This was the part of my brain I wished I could shut off sometimes. But it was impossible to stop thinking about the shoe print left in Dad's office.

I looked around the room, again. Hiking boots with long black laces were partially visible behind the door. One shoe was turned on its side and on the base of the heel was stamped: TRAPPER, the boot brand. Not the same letters I found on the print in Dad's office, but it was a name stamped in the heel. For some reason, I kind of snickered. This was why my mind kept going back to the heel print. Some shoes were specialized either with a name, a tap, or a brad hammered into the rubber. Did Dr. McKnight own other shoes with specialized heels? Was he wearing them at this very moment?

Turning to give the room one last look, I snagged my foot on a dumbbell covered with clothes and fell. A pile of sweaters cushioned my fall. When I pushed off the carpet, I spied a small brass key taped underneath the metal bed frame. Good spot to hide a key. What did it unlock? I didn't have time to find out. Maybe another day.

I left his room and went back through the living room. The front door was painted black and flanked by carved wooden panels. It was locked, but no one could open it anyway, a mountain of letters banked the door. I pulled an envelope from the bottom of the pile. It was dated January 1962. The mail was nearly six months old.

After seeing his house, it made perfect sense that no one knew where he and Miss Penny were. He was the most disorganized person I'd ever seen. As baffling as his behavior was, it didn't explain why he argued with Dad or why he left his house in such a wreck.

I trailed back through the kitchen where the moldy odor made my stomach cramp and pitch. I raced through the back door and started to nudge it closed with my foot, but something caught my eye.

Dark clothes, folded into a neat pile, were behind the door. I carefully lifted black sweat pants and a black sweatshirt. A pair of black Keds rested on the bottom, white rubber soles blackened with a felt tip pen. I replaced the clothes, and a black knit hat slipped from between them. This couldn't be a coincidence. These were the same clothes as the man watching our house. My stomach contracted, my lunch roiled to back of my throat, and I choked. I banged out the door.

Overheated air hit me, and I grabbed the railing, pulling in the warm oxygen. I wanted to run, but I had to check one more thing. I swallowed hard. Dad had said Professor McKnight kept an extra key in the flowerpot on the top step. I fished under dried, brittle flower, my fingers sifting through clumps of peat. My breathing hitched. No key.

A stray dog, with scaly, bald patches all over, grumbled around the corner. He spotted me and started growling and snarling. I jumped from the top step and beat it out of the yard using a straight-legged fast walk. He chased me, barking and snapping, but I knew better than to run full out. He kept at my heels for a good block or two.

I stopped at the end of the block, next to a no parking sign. I turned to check on the dog. It was barking and lunging like crazy, but not at me.

Whoomf, something whisked down over my head.

XVII

I smelled oats and tasted crumbly bits on my lip. Before I could react, someone bound my hands behind me. My legs kicked furiously out in all directions, attempting to kick the shit out of somebody, but all I got was air. I fought back the best I could but having my hands tied behind me threw me off balance.

The next thing I knew, I was tossed into a car trunk, the stench of burnt oil swirled into the sack over my face. Choking, I rolled onto my back when I heard the trunk slam shut.

Over a bone-fracturing rumble, obviously caused by a broken muffler, I couldn't hear a thing.

I kicked the lid. "Help! Help me!" I shouted until my voice was hoarse, but the car never slowed. Shouting and pounding the lid wasn't getting me anywhere. I rolled back and forth. My knees had started cramping, folded half way under me. It was hard to judge how large a space I was in.

A memory snaked around in my brain. *Not now.* I had to calm down. Easier said than done when adrenaline careened through my body so hard I shook. The car sped over several bumps, and I tried to figure out where we were going. Occasionally, the muffler stopped rumbling, but all I heard was a droning engine and tires shushing along the pavement.

I took a breath and pressed my shoulders into the wool mat, bringing my knees up and curling into the tightest ball I could possibly make. A movie about Houdini showed how he escaped form a trunk–maybe I could do the same thing. The tips of my shoes scraped the trunk lid. I rocked up and pulled my arms over my butt. My arm sockets screamed, and pain seared all the way to my wrists. I had to swing my arms up and over my legs in the next motion or I was sunk. The rope bit into my wrists as my hands strained past my shoes. Once my fingers rested on my shins the pain subsided.

Frigid air blew over my brain, and a memory slipped in. I bit my lip hard, tasting oat powder on my lips. It retreated, leaving a grainy image. I lifted my hands and jerked the sack off my head. The air stank like stale oil, but I gulped it in. Once my pupils adjusted, I noted a metal tire jack near my feet and traces of light around the trunk's perimeter. I didn't have enough room to flip over with the lid only inches from my face or to move the jack so I concentrated on untying my hands, but they were wrapped three times, and I couldn't get the rope to nudge. *Damn.*

Twin taillights burned demon-eyed red in each corner of the trunk, blaring like fiery stars when the brakes were hit. If I could break one, maybe someone would notice. I pounded on the light closest to my foot, only cracking it. The car jostled over a cattle gap, tossing me into the air. My head crashed into the lid. It felt like someone poured cold alcohol over my brain, and a memory shoved its way in.

A man stood on a hill, a white silhouette against a gray sky. Wind whipped a cloak up and around his shoulders.

"It's the Grand Wizard!" Brett grabbed my hand, and we raced down the hill.

We ran so fast a searing pain stitched my side. I hung on to Brett's hand and looked back at the spooky, crumbling antebellum ruin. Why didn't we listen to Dad's warning?

The man saw us and yelled our way. "You boys, better run."

Our legs pumped harder, and we sprinted for the woods. Brett stumbled, tumbling down a sumac-covered slope, and I skidded after him, landing on his leg.

"Ahhh." He dropped to the ground, grabbing his leg. "Ahhh. I think it's broken."

I looked at his ankle already, swelling and blue. I pulled him up, he threw his arm over my shoulder, and we hobbled down to another cut in the hill, surrounded by scruff pines and a bramble thicket. Brett was wheezing by then.

"Let's look for a place to hide." Brett grunted and turned as best he could on one foot.

We spotted a burrow in the thicket. We glanced back and saw the man with the pointed hat, now joined by three other men dressed like ghosts, tramping down the hill. He carried a wooden staff and swung it high in the air. He whistled an eerie tune, and I trembled against Brett.

"Don't make a sound. We'll hide in the thorn bushes. He'll never find us."

We scudded over to the bushes, cold wind pushing against our backs. Brett crawled in first. "Ouch. Ahh." He stopped before he was completely hidden. "You can't come in this way. Too many thorns. You'll have to find another way."

"No. Let me in."

"There isn't enough room for two." Brett shoved me away.

I panicked and rushed around the bushes, looking for a spot. The bushes bunched together so tightly, I couldn't find an opening. I pulled a pine branch away, exposing a cleft just big enough for me. I pounced down on all fours and squirmed into the cleft. Hairy thorns pricked my socks and pants, scraped my arms, but I hardly felt them. I wedged myself farther into the cleft so only a toe stuck out and closed the hole with the dangling branch. My hands balled into fists, while I watched the hill, a thick haze bloomed around the bushes.

The men approached the thicket. One laughed. "Guess we could burn em out."

"Did anyone get a good look?" One of the men stopped right next to the cleft. His foot scraped against the fallen pine branch, moving it away from the opening. Soundlessly, I tucked my foot under a tangle of dried stems. The men reeked of soured white lightning.

"Nah... Just some kids." One man burped. And hit another guy, pushing him into the thorn bushes. His weight forced thorns into my neck, arms, and legs. I bit my fist to keep from yelling. Tears oozed down the side of my face.

"Get me outta here, you moron." The man thrashed around.

Each movement scraped a new thorn over my body. I was starting to shake; the leaves around me rustling. Someone grunted, lifting the drunken man off the bushes, a strip of white cloth fluttered through the branches and landed on my knee.

Somebody from farther up the hill. "Let it go, for now. We'll look later. Got bigger fish to fry tonight."

Feet shuffled through the leaves and underbrush. I sniffed and squeezed my eyes closed. Didn't want to look. Why did Brett and I come into the woods? Dad told us to say away from the rotted old plantation. He said nothing good goes on there, but we just had to find out for ourselves. If we could wait it out, maybe they'd forget us. Nothing else to do. I concentrated on one breath, slowly in, slowly out, then another, then another…

The trunk popped open. The Grand Wizard stood over me. I kicked at him and swung at him the best I could. My foot landed in the soft spot of his stomach, and he bent over.

I continued to kick. The muscles along my backbone spasmed, but I kept kicking. My name… I heard my name again.

"Julian… Julian, It's me." Brett. He sounded like he was in a well shouting down to me. "J. J., It's okay."

Confused, I lifted my hands to block the light. The man disintegrated like shifting sand and became Brett.

"Shit. Why'd you leave him in here?" Brett's face came into focus as he untied my hands; a chafed line ringed my wrists, and they stung when the air hit them. Colors swirled into place, and Austin peered into the trunk, outlined by a late afternoon sun.

"I thought you said wait until you got here."

"Shitty, shit, shit. I had a flat. You shoulda let him out." Brett practically lifted me out of the trunk. "He's coming out of it. Go get him some water."

I concentrated on the scowl running across his face. He knew the signs; he knew I'd fallen into a memory. Re-entry was the worst. My muscles pulled away from the bone, overworked, tense, and tired. I waved him off.

"Bad?" Brett placed his hand on my shoulder.

I nodded and whispered our code word for the Grand Wizard. "The boogeyman."

"The boogeyman?" Austin laughed. "It was us. We were playing a prank on you."

Brett shoved Austin. "Dumbass. You didn't take him out of the trunk in this heat, so he went into a memory. He doesn't think we're boogeymen. He could have died. Now go get the water."

I ran my hand over my head, the hollow space in my brain filling. "What? What are you talking about?"

Austin gulped. "It was Brett's idea. Jackson and I went to the turkey-ass party at Sibley Lake. Kathleen Dubois likes Jackson, but Mom didn't do such a good job with my date. I got stuck with Ginger Gardner. She hates me, showed up for ten minutes, and split. I left the Mickey Mouse party and ran into Brett."

Brett stood close, massaging my shoulder. "It's my fault. I knew you wouldn't come with us. I suggested we throw you into the trunk and come here."

The fuzz lifted from my brain. God save me from Brett and his lame-brained ideas. I looked around. We were at the Crawfords' camp. It didn't have a sophisticated name like Oak Alley or Sweet Magnolia because the camp wasn't much more than a musty dogtrot-style cabin on stilts. A mild headache sat on top of my brain. Woody was parked next to the twins' rusty Chevrolet, a sharp contrast to their cool WWII jeep.

"What were you thinking?" I leaned against the dusty car, eyeing Brett. I expected as much from Austin, but Brett and I were getting along so well, working on the codes and all.

Brett cleared his throat. "Austin, go get the water."

Austin grunted, but walked away. Brett brushed some dirt off my shirt and leaned in. "We're getting nowhere on the code. I've seen you work on science problems before, where you mind churns. Dad always made you take a break. I was just trying to help."

I sank onto the bumper, heat pressed on my butt. "Brett, you think I'm confusing the Shadow Man with Klan memories. It's what you think, isn't it?"

"You were in the trunk for a good hour. Your memories always come out when your guard's down." Brett sat beside me, and the car dipped beneath our weight. "The Klan Rally more than any other. With Dad gone, I think about that night, too. I'll never forget his face when we told him where we'd been."

"Yeah. We were lucky you ended up with just a sprained ankle. The Klan's nothing but criminals and white trash."

He slammed the car trunk closed. "All this business about Dad is making me crazy, but the idea of a Shadow Man, someone watching the house. That's scary shit."

"Talk about scary shit. I thought y'all were him. I found some black clothes, the same kind the Shadow Man wears at Professor McKnight's house." I massaged my wrists. "It could be him. They're built the same, but that's all I know. If only I had gotten a better look at him. But it didn't look like McKnight was home. In fact, it looked like someone had gone through his place. I can't get a handle on anything. Nothing makes sense. We're missing something, some clue. It's more than the codes. Maybe we need to start at the beginning. Where Dad fell. Can you show me? Show me where he landed?"

"Ah man.... I don't want to go back there." Brett looked out over the cow pasture surrounding the Crawfords' camp.

"You owe me." I looked straight at him.

"Not fair. You're gonna use being stuck in the trunk to twist my arm, aren't you? But I don't know if I can take it."

A hundred-year-old hound dog hobbled over from the dog-trot and nuzzled my hand. "Honestly, I don't know what we'll find, but we have to try. If we could just piece together that day, it might help."

Austin stood on the porch, holding a jelly jar full of water. "Come on."

Brett walked toward the log dog-trot, I reached for his arm. "I'll stay if you promise we'll go to Dad's building tomorrow."

"All right." His voice was firm. If he could find a way to retract his promise, he would. It would be hard for him.

We wrapped our arms around each other's shoulders and squeezed before stepping onto the porch. Brett dropped into a cane-bottom chair while I angled to the entry and took the water from Austin. Drinking, I looked through the bottom of the jar, through the dog-trot and saw a couple of pirogues pulled up next to Bayou Camitte, the perfect fishing spot, loaded with lily pads and jam-packed with alligators.

I heard the Jeep jostling over the pasture before I saw it. Jack flew over one berm after another, gathering speed over the flat dam between the camp and the swamp. His fly-boy sunglasses glinted snakeskin silver in the waning light. He was moving too fast. I scampered to the far edge of the porch, ready to jump, just as he stomped on the brake; the bumper just inches from the steps. He jumped to the ground, slamming the door behind him. "Damn Priss Dupree."

He was obviously in a sulfurous mood, a walking stick of dynamite. One match, and he'd burst into flames.

XVIII

Brett bit first. "What'd she do now?"

"Aww. She's mad. Won't talk to me. Her little sister come to the front door and told me Priss hadn't finished with me, yet. Then the little stinker stuck out her tongue and screamed, 'Suffer!'" He clomped up the steps.

In a little town, you couldn't hide anything. He had to have known Priss would learn about his date with Kathleen. Especially since their moms planned it from birth.

Jack noticed me standing near the breezeway. "Thought you'd hang with the big boys, did you?"

Night had closed in, and mosquitoes already lined up along my arm for an evening snack. I slapped my arm, missing most but killing two, and moved to the porch railing. Staying here was a mistake.

Jack grinned wickedly toward the bayou, then back to me. "So, chicken shit, you up for an alligator hunt?"

I was sick of his calling me chicken shit or a damned baby. Brett cleared his throat, and I glanced his way.

"I've heard there's a way to catch an alligator without getting in the water." Brett studied the sky as if some grand scheme was unfolding in the stars.

"What? Using your chicken shit brother as bait? And then bop the gators over the head when they swim up?" asked Jack with a snort.

"I'm not chicken shit." My hands ground into fists.

"Whoa." Jack smirked. "You wouldn't say that if your big brother wasn't here to protect you."

I jumped off the porch, so close to Jack I smelled him, sweat and beer. He didn't move a muscle. He was spoiling for a fight.

"Say it one more time." My fingers scraped my palm.

"I heard all you have to do is sneak up on a small gator and wrap your hand around its snout. With the other hand free, and you just flip the gator into the boat." Brett acted like some great safari hunter. He propped his leg on the lower railing and puffed out his chest. "All we have to do is slide the pirogues into the bayou and follow one. Then easy as catching a June bug, we reach down and grab it."

Jack sneered. "Do you honestly think J. J.'ll go out in the spooky ole water and bring back an alligator? Fat chance. I'll do it if he does."

"I'm in." I was sick to death of being called a coward.

Brett leapt off the porch and slapped my back. "You don't have to do this to prove anything to Jack."

"I'm not proving anything to Jack." I picked up a stick off the ground and whipped my leg for emphasis. But in reality, it was all about proving myself to Jack... and my brother.

Everyone looked at Austin. He sighed. "Oh man. How can I say no? If J. J. can do it, so can I."

Great, I was lowest common denominator. Obviously, if I could do it, anyone could. I pointed the stick at Jack. "If I catch a gator, I don't want to hear the words chicken shit come out of your mouth ever again."

"If you catch a gator, it's a deal." Jack pivoted toward the cabin door.

When he came back, he carried a bottle of Jack Daniels and a shot glass. He poured a shot and held it out to me.

I didn't hesitate. I needed all the Dutch courage I could muster. We drank two pops each before everyone was pumped and game. Like the fools we were, we made for the bayou with two flashlights, duct tape, and four lengths of rope.

Fog moved like a serpentine specter above the water. A cow moaned from the next field, sending chills up my spine. When we aimed our flashlights across the bayou, blood red eyes stared back. Long black shadows noiselessly slithered into the water one at a time. Alligators.

Brett and I pushed the pirogue into the water. He jumped in and tottered to the front, then adjusted the flashlight between holding prongs so that light skimmed the dark water. When the narrow end of the pirogue dipped into the bayou, I tried to hop in, but the boat was slippery. Water reached my thighs before I tossed my legs over the side, and flaccid duckweed clung to the hair on my legs. Not the greatest beginning. The twins' pirogue broke the water behind us with a splash.

Adrenaline surged through my body with each heartbeat. The alcohol thickened my blood, yet I knew what flowed through me was false courage. I had to do this though, had to. I was fed up with all the challenges thrown at me. Even Priss challenged me every chance she had. Why... because I let her. Never again.

Brett baited a hook and dropped a fishing line over the pirogue's side. It wasn't in the water more than a minute before the cane pole skittered across the boat. The fishing line stretched tight like a new string on a guitar. The next thing we knew, a four-foot alligator leapt out of the water, his long teeth gleaming in the foggy light. His tail thrashed boldly, slapping the water. Then the line snapped.

Brett flipped over the side and disappeared beneath the slimy water. The boat rocked back and forth in my brother's wake. Jack shot the light into the dark, fizzy water. The surface rippled, but nothing else moved.

I unclamped the light from our boat and spun it over the surface, looking for bubbles, anything. I stared into the water until my eyes stung. Panic set in, and I didn't know what to do next. Jump in? That's all we needed, a double drowning.

The water churned brown. An arm shot up. Water sprayed in all directions. The surge nearly tipped the boat. I held onto the pirogue, its sharp sides biting into my hand. Brett's head struck the pirogue with a loud *thunk* and glanced off. He sank beneath the water, and all was quiet again.

"Why didn't you grab him?" asked Jack, looking straight at me. "Chicken shit."

"He wasn't close enough." I didn't need this. I came out on this fool-hardy alligator hunt just like them. I might be a dumbass for letting them push me, but I wasn't a coward.

Brett exploded through the water a second time. Sucking in air, he grabbed the side of our pirogue. I held my breath and snagged his wrist.

"Are you okay?"

"No." he groaned. "The gator bit my leg. I'm losing... blood...."

His voice trailed off. His head dipped under the water again. I held on to his wrist. This was bad. I pulled, but he sank deeper. Jack paddled closer.

"I have his wrist. Can you help lift him?" I yelled.

Brett's wrist was slipping from my grasp. Jack and Austin looked at each other, then over to me. No one said a word. I struggled, hanging on to Brett's wrist, afraid to let go.

He shot up again, this time breaking free from my grip, laughing and slapping the water's surface. "Had y'all going for a minute there."

Brett flipped into the boat and leaned back, laughing so hard the pirogue quaked unsteadily. "You really thought the gator had me."

Austin flung his paddle into the pirogue with a clatter. No one else said a word. The mood changed. Instead of it being another good-ole-boy outing, everyone became silent and serious.

"Okay. Okay. Sorry. Let's get some gators." Brett tried to lighten the mood, but there were no takers. He lifted a paddle and let it slowly sink into the water. "You ready, J. J.?"

"As ready as I'll ever be." I heard the twins arguing about who would go first, but their voices sounded distant, echoing over the night water.

About twenty red eyes glinted from the opposite bank, half hidden in the clotted grass and reedy filaments. A few bobbed at the water's edge. One demonic pair skimmed the water just beyond the pirogue. I tried to estimate the distance between the eyes, but the gator was too far away. Brett surged after it, the pirogue gliding soundlessly across the surface.

I tried to ignore a slight headache and let a memory edge in. Again, I held it, warmed it, and released it. An encyclopedia page hovered behind my lids. I zeroed in on one of the paragraphs: *Due to the alligator's four-chambered heart, it recycles oxygen rich blood to the lungs. Thus the animal has the capacity to dive and stay beneath the water for long periods of time, killing its prey.* Shit. Sometimes it didn't pay to have a sensorial memory.

I inched to the pirogue's front section and repositioned the flashlight between the two metal prongs. Then I knelt so my chest rested against the pirogue's side. Sweat dribbled off my forehead, and my hand shook when I wiped it away, but I lowered my hand so it hung above the water. Moist heat rose off the surface. The boat surged forward, splitting a narrow ridge through the bayou.

"Go ahead. Put your hand in the water so you'll be ready to grab him." Brett said. "Don't overthink this. Just do it."

I screwed up every fiber of courage and pressed my palm to the waterline. Gritting my teeth, I pressed my entire hand beneath the surface. So far, so good. The bayou rushed past. Fishy-tasting spray splattered my nose and mouth. The paddle splashed faster and faster.

A ripple. I gaped into the water. An alligator swam directly beneath my hand. It jerked right, and I plunged my arm into the water all the way to the elbow. Rough skin ripped under and past my fingers. The gator sped up, but so did we. One last blind thrust deep into the dark water, and I grabbed the gator at the base of its muscular jaw.

He thrashed and jerked, trying to wrench from my grip, but I had him; he belonged to me. My fingers squeezed under its jaw into a trough of soft skin the same texture as a frog's belly. I wrapped my other hand around the gator's snout, tipping the pirogue completely on its side. Water gushed in, but I held on.

Brett clutched the pirogue's sides and kept it from flipping completely over. I wedged my feet under the seat struts so I wouldn't submerge and drown. My fingers tightened, pressing deeper into the gator's throat. Its tail hammered at me, but I dodged it despite my fingers going numb.

It was hard, but I managed to land back in the pirogue. It righted with a snap. At least two inches of slimy water covered the bottom seeping up my shirt, covering my back. I unhooked my feet and clung to the gator, bringing it alongside me. Its sickening claws clacked against the wooden bottom as it fought to find purchase. Then just like that, it stopped moving, went flaccid and surrendered.

Brett loomed above me with the gray duct tape stretched taut between his hands. He captured the gator's snout in one swoop and wound the tape snuggly around its jaws. Warm snot blew out of the alligator's nostrils, and thick, banded muscles bulged beneath the binding, but its mouth was secure. I'd never be called a chicken shit ever again.

Brett tipped the flashlight from the clamp, showering the alligator with light.

"Damn."

He yanked me up so fast I nearly fell out of the pirogue. I barely heard the twins whooping in the background. The gator's tail angrily slapped my ankles as I dropped into my seat.

My knees quaked so badly I could hardly stay seated. Another gator sent a distress signal, a cracked sound like a creaking door. A long hiss answered from the opposite bank.

I'd done it. Adrenaline overflow coursed through my body. Electricity zinged from one nerve to the next. Jittery, I rubbed my hands over my face. I'd done it. A smile spread until it hit my ears, and I slapped my knees, settling back in the boat letting my body catch up to my mind.

Brett paddled over to the twins. "Okay. J.J. showed you how to do it. Your turn."

Jack looked down into the pirogue. "Good Golly, Miss Molly!"

His light beam splayed over a young gator with a tail as long as my arm. A thrill raced up my spine. Thank God I didn't know its size when my hand hovered above it.

"That's no baby," said Austin. He looked at me with awe. "How'd you do it?"

I shrugged. Inside I was bursting, but I acted nonchalant. Besides, I never wanted to do anything like this again. It didn't pay to be the top gun slinger.

Jack whistled. "J. J., when you decide to do something, you do it right. I gotta hand it to ya."

The jitters subsided, and normally, I'd puff up with pride, but it was all I could do not to throw up. The gator scraped its claws once more for good measure. How did I do it? Didn't matter. There was a fine line between being unbelievably brave or incredibly stupid. The best part was when it was over.

Sometime after midnight, we returned to camp with two gators. The twins had been able to snare a small one. Sober from the experience and waning adrenaline rushes, we crashed into our beds. No one said a word; we were tangled in our own thoughts.

I once read that courage is about mastering fear—not the absence of fear. It made perfect sense. My greatest fear had been realized—losing my dad. Even now I feared the facts about his death, but the time had come to master my fear. No more delays. No matter what I discovered, even if it was bad, I had to know what happened to my father.

XIX

Sun slipped past the windows earlier than expected. I creaked out of bed stooped and sore like a rickety old man. Everyone met on the porch stretching still drowsy with sleep. Two sluggish alligators rested side by side, connected by one soggy rope. It slowly dawned on me last night wasn't some crazy dream, but today was a new day, and Brett promised to take me to the spot where he found Dad.

Jack's father sent over the camp caretaker. He brought fresh-baked cinnamon rolls and a king-sized pot of coffee. Breakfast smells drifted through the cabin, spicy cinnamon along with fried bacon and roasted chicory, making me hungrier than ever. We propped our feet against the railing, tipping our chairs back like the cool guys we thought we were, sipping coffee out of stained, chipped mugs. It was the breakfast of famed alligator hunters, or the remedy for the criminally insane depending on which of us you asked.

Alligators eyed us from the splintered floor, proof of our insanity, their mouths taped securely shut in case they decided to spill the beans about our plunge into midnight madness. The crotchety caretaker rounded the front porch and grunted at the animals, making sure he kept his fingers well out of chomping range.

"You boys are plumb crazy. Do you hear me? One of these days, one of them gators gonna rise up outta that water and eat you whole, skin and bones. And what ya gonna do then? Nothin', cause you'll be deader than spit in the desert. When your daddy hears about this, he's gonna have a conniption fit. He is… Austin, Jack, you hear my words?" He wagged his finger at the twins.

Austin flicked his crew cut and tossed back his coffee, ignoring the old man. "I guess we oughta let the gators go."

"You boys are up to no good. Don't listen to a blessed soul…" The caretaker drifted off, shaking his head as he slammed the door to the dingy camp truck and rattled away.

"We need to get back anyway. J. J. and I have some things to do." Brett didn't sound overly excited. He didn't want to do this, but he'd said yes, and I knew he wouldn't renege.

Jack stood up with his arms pulled high above his head and stretched his back until it cracked. "I'm gonna get a quick shower. Get the gator smell off me."

He sauntered into the cabin. Once he was out of earshot, Brett winked and let his chair drop to the floor. He rubbed his hands over his knees with a mischievous grin.

"Let's throw a gator in the shower. It'll scare the crap out of him."

Austin threw his remaining coffee over the rail and laughed. "You're on."

Any other time I might have talked Brett out of it, but not for Jack. He had it coming. Austin picked up the smaller gator, about the size of a yardstick. Brett bracketed the animal's jaws with both hands, and I removed the tape. The gator snarled at us in a foul temper and tried to bash us with its tail. Austin jammed the nervous tail under his arm, and we hurried into the cabin.

Steam billowed over the top of a pink-flowered shower curtain, hanging askew from four or five broken plastic rings. Jack sang "Summertime" from *Porgy and Bess* at the top of his lungs.

On the count of three, I ripped back the plastic curtain. Brett and Austin tossed in the gator. We snapped the curtain closed and leaped back into the hall, screaming with laughter.

Oh, your mama's good– Jack stopped mid sentence. A mile-long howl followed, a sound I thought only a beagle could make. His feet disappeared a good three feet above the shower tile.

Jack fought with the curtain. It clung to him when he flew out, clutching the plastic rings until they popped one by one and pinged to the floor, two bouncing off the gator's nose. Jack clutched a bar of soap, his eyes bugging out like golf balls. The alligator stayed planted in the corner, its mouth wide open. Hot water shot over its entire body and cascaded between his teeth in tiny rivulets.

Jack yelped all the way out the breezeway. He bolted past us straight into the pasture and didn't stop until he was on the fifty-yard line. His body glinted wet in the sun, and the three of us cackled, leaning against the cabin walls, laughing our guts out.

When we could finally breathe again, we strolled onto the porch, holding our sides. Jack pointed at us with the soap.

"I'll get you back. All three of you. Someday... some way..."

Jack's threat just didn't carry much weight with his man parts hanging out for all the world to see. We broke out into fresh guffaws, pinching our sides in sweet agony.

He stomped back up the steps and marched past us, but he couldn't resist throwing the soap at his brother before he went back into the cabin. Austin fell onto the porch, laughing and wiping away tears with the back of his hand. Hard to pull one on Jack, but we'd done it.

"Somebody better come get this gator before he ends up in a gumbo," Jack roared from the bathroom.

We rounded up the alligator and released it back into the bayou. It took us forever. Every time one of us looked at the other, we started laughing all over again. Eventually, we rounded up the other gators, cut the tape from their mouths, and dropped them next to the water. They weren't very friendly, and snapped at us before scuttling off the muddy bank. Angry hisses bubbled from breathing slits as they descended into the dank water. Their cracked, marble eyes slid along the waterline, staring at us. With a final defiant splash, they disappeared under the murky surface.

Brett and I made it home by midmorning. Woody bumped along the road, windows wide open with the radio blaring. We were silent, dreading our next search for clues. My knit shirt stuck to me, and when I pulled it away, sweat trickled down my backbone like snot from a runny nose. We turned onto Second Street and watched as Rebecca Sharp's car pulled away from our house.

We walked through the front door. Hushed voices came from the back of the house. It sounded like Tudy was talking to someone in the kitchen. Brett and I made our way through the dining room and pushed through the kitchen's swinging door.

The door flapped behind us. Tudy stood alone near the kitchen sink. The smell of starch filled the space around her. She looked as if she hadn't slept in eons.

"Who were you talking to?" Brett asked.

"The Lord. He's the only one'll listen these days." Tudy blinked. "Miss Sharp just left. She been by to check on your mama. Came straight from the excavation site, covered in dirt. She says your Mama called her. The Chief dropped by, and your mama been in a bad way ever since. She done swallowed one of those pills Dr. Pasquier gave her. She'll be sleeping for hours."

"What did Chief Hendricks want?" I asked.

"Your mama asked if he'd heard 'bout the missing money." Tudy shook her head and looked to the heavens through the ceiling. "Lord knows. She's all wound up. It woulda helped if he'd called her back yesterday instead of making her wait."

Brett came over and stood beside me. "She called him yesterday?"

"Sure 'nuff did." Tudy turned the water on. She squirted a milky stream of liquid soap into the steaming water. "But he didn't come by 'til just a while ago. She asked him again what he gonna do 'bout the missing money. He said nothing. Whatn't up to him."

"That should have been good news. Is that why she's so upset?" Brett asked.

"No. He says to her, he just about finished with the report for the insurance company. The coroner's report gonna be in his office first thing Monday morning." Tudy turned her back to us and swished her hands in the sudsy water. "She asked him what the report says. He says he couldn't tell her nothing until his report was official."

My lips curved into a frown. So what was new? Why would she be so upset? "What else did he say?"

Tudy lifted a dish dripping with suds and made small circles with a pink sponge. "He asked her if she knew anything else. Warned her if you boys came across anything, to turn it over to him. Said your Dad's case could use the help. That's when she got upset. It's the way he said it. Like he done decided your dad's death was a suicide."

Brett stepped to the swinging door, his jaw clenching. I didn't have to say anything to him. Mom had suffered enough. Clearly, no one would help us. Mom's friends had stopped dropping by, even Lila Dupree. She'd fallen into a major tiff over Rebecca Sharp and had no idea how hard all this was on Mom. Dad's friends weren't supportive, either, except Miss Sharp. She was the only person who seemed to care. The Chief's interviews went nowhere, and to use one of his clichés, he couldn't figure shit from Shinola.

Dad was so secretive about his work. He left loose ends he thought would easily lace together; instead they were fraying into separate, unrelated strands no one could tie together or figure out. For a while it seemed I was the only one interested in searching for clues, but things had changed. Now Brett wanted to find out what really happened to Dad, too.

I pounded up the stairs behind Brett. When I reached my room, I closed the door. I needed to be alone, some time to gather my thoughts. Monday was the deadline, and pressure to solve the next code or find any new clues built each time the second hand ticked over the face of my clock, the sound echoing from every surface in the room. Brett promised to show me where Dad fell. No matter how difficult, we had to do this. Time was our biggest enemy. Mom knew it. Tudy knew it. We all sensed it. My bedroom door flew open.

"Come on. We'd better get on it. I'll take you to Russell Hall." Brett looked more determined than I'd ever seen him.

I nodded and hurried out behind him, shoving a small notebook into my back pocket. "Right." Half way down the steps another thought occurred to me, and it had nothing to do with finding clues.

"I just need to get back early. I have date with Sara."

"Wait, you have a date with Sara?" Brett held his hand up like a stop sign, thumping me in the chest. "And you didn't say anything last night?"

"Didn't want you to think you pushed me into it." I shot back.

"And you tell me now?" Brett twisted the doorknob, then slapped me on the back as I walked past. "Guess I'll have to wait until she gets tired of you."

I didn't respond. We bounded down the steps. The air was so hot birds had ceased flying, preferring to chat on shadowy tree branches. Brett and I walked along the sidewalk, stepping on scarred roots reaching for the sun between the cracks in the concrete. We headed a few blocks down College Street until we hit Caspari and turned left. Russell Hall and all its glass windows materialized at the top of the hill.

XX

Burnt red bricks formed a thin ledge around the windows of Russell Hall. It was easy to see, at least from the outside, that Dad could fall from the third floor with nothing to grab on to, nothing to stop his fall.

I trailed behind Brett, giving him ample space. He eyeballed the distance from the window to where he stood, then he stepped out several feet and glanced back at the window. A few seconds later, he sidled a few spaces to his left, but he wasn't satisfied and moved maybe an inch or two to his right. He stood there for I don't know how long, staring at the window and then glancing at the ground in front of his feet. Finally, he turned.

"I'm pretty sure this is the spot." Sadness claimed his face.

The spot, as he called it, wasn't sunken in or outlined like a human body. The only difference between a few weeks ago and this week was the grass length. Someone had cut it shorter than usual. If I'd been walking past, I wouldn't have known my Dad's body had ever been here. The fact nothing remained, no blood, nothing, to say *Melton James died here*, was heartbreaking.

"Are you sure?" I stepped beside Brett.

"Hard to forget. I remember the exact spot because the window was open and from where I stood, those shingles..." he pointed to several gray crooked shingles above the dormer, "formed a straight line to Dad's body. See how we're at the bottom of the line."

"Yeah. So Dad was laying right here?" I asked.

Brett frowned, and for a minute, he looked like he might cry. Instead, he swallowed, and his Adam's apple bobbed up and down his throat. "Let's see. His head was near where you're standing."

I planted my feet and watched as Brett measured heel-toe, heel-toe until he stood a few feet away. "His feet were about here."

"You mentioned his legs were twisted under him."

This wasn't easy. Brett rubbed the space between his brows. I'd seen him do the same thing before when we worked on the codes. Some people eat chocolate, while others look up and to the right when they think. This was Brett's method. Somehow the pressure on his forehead drew his thoughts directly to the front of his brain.

"Yeah. His right leg bent at the knee, but twisted under him at an impossible angle. One arm jutted out over his head, and the other arm was broken at the wrist." Brett traced his jean's pockets with his thumb as he spoke.

"Odd." I studied the pale grass on either side of my sneakers.

"Why?"

"It's odd he fell so close to the building if he committed suicide." I scratched the inside of my thumb as Newton's laws scrawled on flash cards fluttered in my mind like paper rain in a parade. "If Dad had jumped, wouldn't he have landed farther out, not right next to the building?"

Brett looked up at the window, then to me. "I guess that's true."

"Ok. You said his arm was over his head. I'm not sure if I have it right. Can you show me?"

"Are you kidding me?"

"I just need the image. To help me figure this out."

"All right." Brett reluctantly dropped to the ground and duplicated the position the best he could.

His right knee was bent under him, and his left arm crooked at the elbow, resting just above his head. He faced upward, grimacing at me.

"So he landed face up." I scratched my head. "If he accidently fell, he might land face up. But if he committed suicide and jumped from the window, wouldn't he land face down?"

Brett rolled to his side, supporting himself with one arm. "Yeah. I see where you're going."

I fell to my knees and crouched on all fours like a dog. "But remember I'm just a kid. I don't know anything."

"What are you doing?" Brett asked.

"Checking to see if Dad dropped anything. He might have had something in his hand or pocket when he fell." I ran my palm over the grass. "You can help."

Brett squatted next to me. "Do you have any idea what you're looking for?"

"No. Not even a half-baked theory, but I have to do something." I went back to combing the grass. It was tedious work. My mind drifted and my imagination took over. Images popped up of Dad lying in the grass, a drizzle of blood at the corner of his mouth. My mind boomeranged, then skidded to a stop. I couldn't go there, couldn't stand it, and concentrated again on the ground in front of me.

"I found something." Brett sounded excited. He fingered a disc-shaped key chain with a Northwestern demon in the center. "Could be anyone's, though."

"Keep looking. Something may pop up." I ran my finger over a clear Bic pen. I started to pick it up, noticed there was no ink in it and figured it most likely belonged to a student.

We kept spreading the grass and peering into the dirt below. A campus cop walked over, a young guy wearing a beige uniform with Northwestern College embroidered in white over his chest pocket. His name badge spelled out: Sam. "Is there something I can help you boys with?"

When Brett and I looked up, he angled his head to the left to get a better look. "Aren't you Professor James's kids?"

"Yes." I answered.

He studied us for a moment. I didn't want him to suspect we were investigating on our own. I had to come up with something quick. It's a good bet he was on duty the day Dad died. More than likely he knew this is where they found Dad.

"Such a shame about your father." Cheering erupted, and he glanced toward south campus. Then he turned his head back in our direction. "Did y'all lose something?"

"Actually, I dropped something out of my pocket." I wasn't the best liar, but I had gotten better over the last month. Since Dad's death people stopped me on the street and asked how things were going; few really wanted to know. They wanted me to say fine so they could go about their business. It was the Southern way.

"Maybe I can help." He seemed eager. "What was it?"

"A pocket watch. It belonged to Dad." Brett was more convincing. He'd had more practice in the lying department.

"Man, too bad. Good thing you're looking today. New construction begins Monday, and this place'll be a mess."

"New Construction?" Brett asked.

"Sure. Didn't you see the sign? It's been up for months. Your dad served on the planning committee. Didn't you know?"

"He didn't talk much about the college." My shoulders drew together, tension bunching the muscles in my neck. If he'd talked more about his work, maybe we'd know about a lot of things, including his death.

Sam looked up at Dad's window. "The attic floor above your Father's old office is scheduled for reconstruction first. They're turning the whole building into a welcoming center. Supposed to move the professors out of the building next week. Gonna be a mess."

We heard more cheering coming from the back campus near the baseball field. Sam looked like he wanted to leave. He probably wanted to be anywhere except searching for some keepsake.

"We don't mind looking by ourselves."

"Are you sure?" He smiled. His two front teeth, overlarge Chiclets, made him look like an eager rabbit. I immediately felt guilty. He was just trying to be nice. "I had to check anyway after all the commotion this morning."

"What commotion?" I asked.

"You don't know? Ball gowns flew from every flagpole on campus this morning. All the lace had been ripped off and wrapped around the poles like some kinda weird maypole. About 50 yards of that stuff was thrown up in the trees like toilet paper. A mannequin was sitting on the Court House lawn in a red bra and petticoat. Caused quite a stir."

"Didn't hear about it. We were at the Crawfords' camp. Did y'all catch who did it?" I had my suspicions.

"Don't know. Apparently, someone snuck into the Dubois' house and stole their daughter's fancy ball dresses, along with the red bra and petticoat. But no signs of a break in."

"I bet she's mad," I said.

"Funny thing is their dogs didn't whine or bark or howl or nothing. They slept right through it. Whoever did it musta used a key. I heard someone say she's not going to the Plantation Ball anymore." He drew his hat off his head. "Well, I'll leave you to it. Let me know if there's anything we can do."

He gave a small wave and marched off across campus. Brett sat back. "I have a good idea who took those dresses."

Brett had a hunch, but I knew for certain. "Yeah, but I'm not talking."

"Same here." Brett stopped looking and rocked back on his heels. "If only we were looking for a watch. Probably a waste of time."

"Do you want to give up? We've been looking for a good twenty minutes." I moved closer to the building. My hand came down on something sharp. "Ah."

Pain shot up my arm. I swept my hand up and blood dribbled down my wrist. Without thinking, I crammed my hand in my mouth. The coppery taste of blood coated my tongue, and I rocked back.

"What the heck?" Brett pounced over on all fours like a huge dog.

"I cut myself on something." I pointed at the grass with my uninjured hand. Blood dripped off my elbow, making a silent dot on my pants.

Brett parted the grass. There on the ground, half buried, was a jagged piece of pottery. A blue stripe ran down either side. My brother cradled what looked like the bottom of a cup or mug. He rotated it so we could examine it thoroughly. This little pottery fragment was meaningless to anyone else, but Brett and I recognized it immediately. It was part of Dad's Scottish mug, the one he was given before he left Edinburgh. The students gave it to him while he was researching burial mounds. They couldn't believe how much coffee he drank. It was the same mug I had noticed missing from Dad's office when Brett and I cleaned it out.

"What's this doing out here?" Brett asked.

I closed my eyes and sucked on my hand. The afternoon before blasted into my mind, and a grainy image of the Shadow Man moving across the hill took hold. I bit my lip and resisted the memory. "Dad kept that on his desk."

"Do you think he had it with him when he fell from the window?"

"How else would it get out here? Let's see if we can find the rest."

Brett and I combed through the grass and bushes, searching for other pieces. No luck.

I studied the building, particularly the windows. Did Dad have his mug when he fell? Maybe he was just looking out the window and fell. But it didn't feel right. He hated heights. He would never have opened a window and stood so close. Maybe, someone threw the mug out the window or stole it and broke it out here, but where was the rest of it?

"What are you thinking?" Brett asked.

"Can't figure why a single piece is out here. If someone stole it and it broke, wouldn't the other pieces be here? And it doesn't make sense, at all, that Dad would throw his favorite cup out the window."

Brett nodded, looking to the window.

"Another thing, why would he hold a coffee cup and jump to his death? That's just ludicrous?"

Brett folded his fingers around the ceramic piece. "Where are you going with this?"

I pulled my hand out of my mouth. A jagged line, sealed with jelled blood, ran across the base of my palm. "I can't imagine Dad standing at the window calmly drinking coffee, jumping to his death, then twirling in the air so he'd land face up."

The image was so ridiculous I didn't consider it for a second. Brett passed me the broken piece and sat down with a thump. The sticky coffee-scented heel print came to mind. How did the coffee spill, the mug get in the grass? How is it related?

"Still doesn't prove anything."

"Goes back to Dad's death being an accident. I think we need to go over Dad's office again. Maybe we missed something." A tiny spark of hope blossomed in my chest.

Brett's stood up and brushed grass crumbs off his pants legs. He pulled me up, and we pounded under the stone arches to the front door. A thick chain was threaded through the door handles.

"What about the side door? The door the professors always use." I clipped down the steps.

We raced to a metal door tucked into a narrow alcove. I wiggled the ancient handle. Again, locked. My body sagged against the brick. "How do we get in?"

"We could find Barney Fife." Brett jerked his head toward the baseball field. "He could open it."

"All we'd have to do is ask if we could sit in Dad's office once more before they tear down the building. That might work?"

The sun had moved into the highest point in the sky. My brain was boiling. Heat prickled the skin on the back of my neck, and I reached up to loosen the back of my collar and scraped the cut on my hand. A dull pain remembered the path up my arm.

"It might if we were better liars. Besides he'd follow us in, and then we couldn't look around. I think we should just wait til tonight." Brett suggested. "Break in when it's dark."

"Break in? Who are you kidding?" I watched his expression. It never changed. "Why so eager to help?"

"Because you're on to something. What you said earlier sounds right. He didn't jump. I'm not sure what happened, but things don't add up, and we're the only ones who can clear Dad's name."

"Okay. So what do we do?"

The broken pottery piece, along with the diary and heel print, finally convinced Brett we were on to something. He had come around. We were partners, looking for the truth about our father. I didn't want to spoil what we had.

"We jimmy the door."

"You mean use a crow bar?" My hand throbbed. "Seriously?"

"We can meet back here after midnight. Get in without messing up the door, if we're careful." He mimed holding a crowbar and clicked his tongue. "We'll look around Dad's office. Should be pretty safe. Hardly anyone's on this side of campus that late."

"It might work." I mimicked James Cagney, my favorite Hollywood gangster, pretending to rotate a fat cigar between my fingers. "We'll pull off the job without a hitch."

Brett rolled his eyes. I'd make a laughable criminal, but I wasn't frightened. Maybe I should have been. However, I was fed up with being Mr. Boy Scout. I wanted to spit on the sidewalk and comb my hair into a greasy ducktail. I was more determined than ever to right some wrongs, and if it took a wrong to make it right, then I was all in.

"Meet ya at midnight." Brett nodded toward the side door, then beat it to the sidewalk.

"Hey. Where you going?" I called out.

"Anywhere but here." Brett hurried to the sidewalk.

He hated reliving the day he found Dad. I didn't blame him. He'd have to deal with the image of Dad lying on the ground forever. I was secretly glad it hadn't been me.

I pulled the spiral notebook out of my back pocket and drew a quick sketch of the broken mug. A scenario began to crystallize. Hopefully, I'd find more answers tonight.

I didn't think evening would ever come. I cleaned and polished Woody until I saw myself in the gleaming wood side panels. Tudy reminded me it was my week to mow the grass. Normally, I'd hate pushing that stubborn vibrating mass of nuts and bolts, but the constant whirling blade and gasoline smell was mind-numbing, just what I needed. As soon as I'd finished my chores and showered for the second time that day, the clock clicked to six-thirty. Time to pick up Sara.

I hadn't dated much, not like Brett or the Crawford twins, anyway. Nothing about me was cool, not James Dean cool, but if I could get through the night without Sara thinking I was a country bumpkin, I'd consider it a success. Sara was gorgeous and clever. Sometimes, she was standoffish, but ever since we solved the first code, she'd changed. I liked her, the smell of her skin, the way she spoke with a slight lisp, how her eyes changed color with her mood, and I wondered if she felt the same about me. She had asked me to Zestos, right? But, what if I screwed up this entire evening?

Then I remembered midnight, meeting Brett, and a tremor ran through me. Finding out the truth about my dad was such a part of me, an extra membrane on my soul; I could never leave it, no matter what else I was doing. Some motion, some word, some image always brought it back to me. But tonight, I didn't want anything to spoil my time with Sara.

If I could capture an alligator, I could damn well take Sara to Zestos and grab a burger. I had to think positive thoughts, let everything else slide away. I tapped the steering wheel three times for luck.

Sweet Magnolia appeared in the bend so I checked myself in the rear-view mirror for the fortieth time. Woody shimmied along with some country tune about lost love, a drippy nasal twang wailing out the windows.

When I parked near the glass bottle garden, Lila Dupree and her husband waved from the screened porch. She sipped on a Pink Lady while fanning herself with the flat of her hand.

"One hot evening, Mr. James." She smiled and stopped rocking. "How's your mother? I've been meaning to stop by, but I've been so busy."

I opened the screen door. "She's having a tough time. You should go by when you have a chance."

"Hurry. Close the door. The mosquitos are bad this year." She swirled the translucent pink liquid in her glass. I smelled the grapefruit juice from where I stood. Then she fluttered her hand at a mosquito making it look as if she were conducting an invisible symphony. "Hmm. Maybe I'll drop by if I'm not needed. Vacation Bible School is this week at First Methodist, and even though we aren't Methodist, they always ask me to help."

She took another sip, leaving a double lipstick print on the glass. Priss's dad rocked slowly with a sweaty beer clutched in his hand. A line ran horizontally across his forehead, dividing his face into two distinct colors, the top a sun-deprived sickly white, and the bottom an over-baked acorn-brown. He preferred farming to the continual drama his wife and four daughters dished out on a daily basis. He grunted in my direction.

Priss's younger sisters ran past, giggling, pointing, and whispering like silly little girls. They disappeared around the corner at the same moment Sara walked through the front door. I stopped right in the middle of the porch. She was a knockout in a sky blue sundress, her hair loose and hanging around her waist. She smiled at me. Heaven had come to Natchitoches. Then Priss stepped from behind her. She wore a black dress speckled with fireball-colored hearts and a wicked grin. My heart plummeted to the ground. *Hell's Bells.* She was going with us.

"If you could see your face," Priss laughed. "Don't worry. I'm not tagging along on your special little date."

Sara frowned. I slid between her and Priss, then whispered. "Good. Three's a crowd, especially one who sucks up all the air."

Priss flounced off the porch, turned around once when she hit the sidewalk, and stuck out her tongue. She probably would have flipped me the finger if Mrs. Dupree hadn't been there. Sara coiled a flimsy sea-foam green scarf around her neck, shaking her head as we walked to the screen door. I held open the door, touching her waist when she glided out. My throat constricted. This was it. An entire evening with her and no one else.

Lila Dupree cleared her throat. "Don't stay out too late, Sara. I promised your father you'd have the same rules as Priss."

Oh brother, was she serious? Everyone knew the Duprees passed out by ten. It was also common knowledge Priss snuck out through the trap door in her room more nights than not.

"I'll have Sara home by eleven." Even if I didn't have to meet Brett, I'd have her home by then. Natchitoches rolled up the sidewalks at ten. There was nowhere to go but Cane River.

"Y'all have a good time." Lila rocked back, sipping her little pink drink.

Priss clutched the keys to her mother's car. "What's Brett up to tonight? I called him earlier. He wasn't at home, and Tudy didn't know where he went."

"Somewhere in town, I imagine. He can't go too far since I have Woody for the night." I opened the passenger door, and Sara sank into the seat.

"Where're y'all going?" Priss pressed a magenta rabbit's foot into her lower lip. Brass keys dangled from the ring and made a slight tinkling noise.

"Maybe Zestos or a movie." I walked around the car. "I guess we'll see you later."

"I doubt it." Priss pranced to her mother's car, jammed the key in the ignition, and revved the engine. "I have my own plans."

XXI

Sara didn't say anything until we were on the highway. "Priss doesn't have any plans, unless you call 'finding Brett' plans. She must have called him five times this afternoon."

"She still mad at Jack?" I guided Woody with my left hand and slipped my right hand along the top of the seat, completely natural, until it rested next to her. My fingers fell lightly on her shoulder. She didn't move.

"He called this morning and this afternoon. He asked her to go out with him this evening, but she said she was too busy. She wants him to suffer. I'd hate to be Jack right now. I guess you heard about Kathleen Dubois's dresses."

Her hand rested on the seat with her fingers curled next to her leg. Her dress hitched up slightly and her thigh, smooth and tanned, showed. I wanted to run my finger up the rest of her leg and find out what was under that dress. I gulped and shook my head. *Stay in the moment.*

"Yeah. Sounds like a lot like Priss. Wonder why Chief hasn't talked to her about it?"

"She didn't do it. She was in bed. Whoever snuck into their house had a key. She accused Jack, but he swore he slept at the camp."

I didn't buy it. I knew about the trap door in Priss's room. Sara was either in on it or she slept through it. Priss was a pro when it came to sneaking out.

"She knows you went out to the camp last night. Jack told her all about it. How you caught a gator with your bare hands." Sara watched for my reaction. "Is that true?"

I was shocked. Jack told Priss I caught a gator? He only bragged about himself. He must have been impressed. It went without saying he left out the part about the shower. I chuckled.

"What?" Sara asked.

"Oh nothing." I chuckled, again. "Did he say anything about a gator in his shower?"

"If he did, Priss didn't mention it. Why? What's so funny?"

"We threw an alligator in the shower with Jack this morning, and you should have seen him. He jumped three feet off the ground before he bolted out the cabin." The image played in my head; I cracked up again.

Sara laughed with me. "He deserved it."

"I have to admit. It *was* a great prank, and I was doubly glad it wasn't me." I casually moved my arm off the seat and placed my hand over hers, letting my hand graze her naked thigh. She wrapped her fingers around mine. They were smooth and moist, like she'd just put on lotion. My heart picked up a beat.

"Is it true about the gator? Did you really catch one with your bare hands?"

"Is that so hard to believe?"

"You're not a risk taker." Sara angled her head toward me just as we pulled into Zestos parking lot. Here we go, again. Was she going to start insulting my lack of courage along with my intellect? "I don't really see you as the hero type."

I let go of her hand. Sure the guys were shocked I caught a gator, but did she have to go along with them? I wanted to be closer, but there was a part of me that was more afraid of being hurt than anything. I couldn't take another hit after losing Dad. I had to be careful. If I was worried about her getting too close, there was no need. Every time we seemed to be getting along, she threw in some zinger and pushed me away.

I held open the door to Zestos. The smell of French fries, batter-dipped onion rings, and grilled burgers blasted us, rich unadulterated restaurant exhaust. If I wasn't hungry before, I was now. A boxy harlequin-colored jukebox owned the back corner and spun a vinyl forty-five, a new group called Peter, Paul and Mary harmonized their hit, "Michael."

Sara cocked a brow, unimpressed. Overstuffed glittery booths that escaped from Oz's Emerald City lined the walls. We headed for the closest booth and slipped into the same seat. I wanted to say something, but I was still stuck on … *I don't really see you as the hero type.*

Doris, a fossilized waitress with hair the color of gunmetal, adjusted her blue cat-eyed glasses and shuffled to our table. The smell of cigarettes clung to her clothes with the strength of old mothballs. She slammed down water, spilling a wave onto our table. "Whatcha want dearies, a shake or a malted?"

Once I'd recovered enough to speak, I said, "Their chocolate malts are triple thick, but they have terrific summer shakes made with fresh strawberries."

"Strawberry sounds good." Sara made a steeple with her index fingers, then rested her chin on her fingertips.

"One shake, two straws?" The waitress rasped.

"Sure." I answered.

We placed our order. The waitress's rusty cigarette-stained fingers pushed a nubby pencil across a palm-sized notepad. She crept back to the kitchen, and I hoped she'd make it through the meal before keeling over.

Sara gave a little cough and swallowed some water. "Was it really necessary to take such a risk just to show your bravery? I mean, you've had to go through your father's funeral and defended him despite all the gossip about his death. You've never lost faith in him. That takes a pretty strong person, a brave person."

What? I'd never really thought of standing behind my dad as brave. It was true though; my belief in him had made me bolder. But believing in him didn't mean I didn't fear what I might find when I dug deeper into his death. I looked at Sara. Her head was tilted to the side. She knew I was thinking about what she just said. I liked that she gave me the time to process it.

Doris shuffled back to our table and poured a Pepto-Bismol colored concoction into a tall frosted glass. Sara dipped her straw in and sucked with all her might. The straw collapsed. She skimmed the top with a long handled spoon and lifted out a swirl of shake so thick it looked like ice cream bleeding strawberry chunks.

"If you had to show courage, why didn't you choose something a little less dangerous?" Sara dipped her spoon deeper into the glass, cleaving the shake down the middle. She let go, and the spoon stood straight up.

"I could have, but the time was right." I pulled a paper napkin out of a metal holder. "Chief Hendricks came by our house this morning. Through Tudy, he warned my brother and me to stay away from his investigation. I'm tired of being called chicken shit and told to stay out of the way. We're not giving up." I tapped my spoon against the glass.

Sara's gaze followed my spoon and up my hand. She reached across the table and stroked the fresh cut. "Did you get this hunting alligators?"

The one-hundred-year-old waitress shuffled back with our burgers and fries. She thumped the ketchup bottle on the table and left.

"No." I shoved the fries between us and Sara released my hand, leaving a warm trail beside the cut. "We went to the spot where Dad fell. We found the bottom piece of a broken mug when I cut my hand on it. It wasn't just any mug. It was Dad's missing mug."

"The mug from his desk?" She bit into an inch wide piping hot French fry.

"Yeah. Brett walked me through discovering Dad. Everything is confused, the broken mug, the way Dad landed face up. Here's the thing. If it was an accident, maybe he would have landed like that, but it doesn't make sense if he purposely jumped." I picked up a fry, but my appetite had fizzled away, and it tasted like wet paper.

"So where do you go from here?" Sara cut her hamburger in half and munched small birdlike bites around the edges, making a circle. It was if she invented new ways of eating regular food.

I wanted to tell her about my plans with Brett, but I didn't dare. It wasn't that I didn't trust her, but I wasn't sure how she'd use it later. One minute she was kind and concerned, then she struck out when my guard was down, when I least expected it. However, as far as I knew, she hadn't said anything to Priss.

Just then the door to Zestos banged open, and the jukebox shuddered out an Elvis number, "You're the Devil in Disguise." Priss stormed into the restaurant, her strappy sandals clacking like penny firecrackers over the floor.

Sara and I stopped chewing and gaped as Priss plowed toward us. Brett trudged several steps behind her, looking like he was about to puke. Priss shoved him into the seat across from us then slid in beside him. Her face was as red as the hearts on her dress.

"So you've been keeping secrets, I hear. Why am I the last to know? Aren't we friends?" She swiveled her head from me to Sara.

"What?" I asked.

"What are you talking about?" Sara replied.

Brett dropped his head in his hands and moaned. "She knows everything."

I looked at Priss. She crossed her arms over her chest while tapping her foot under the table. Sara swallowed. Brett raked his hands over his face, distorting his normally handsome appearance.

"Just exactly what do you think you know?" I didn't say anything. No telling what information Brett leaked.

Priss leaned into the table, her voice low but clear. "You're planning to break into Russell Hall."

I gaped at Brett. He held up his arms in surrender. "Couldn't help it. She wheedled it out of me."

Priss sat back. "Don't blame him." She looked at me under heavy lids. "I have my ways."

Sara hit the side of my leg with her fist. "Was this what you were about to tell me?"

I didn't answer. For once in my life, I was actually sorry for Brett. Priss was hard to resist. I'd seen her work her breathless magic on other guys. Besides, I almost confessed the same thing to Sara.

"Lower your voices. Have you lost your mind?" I glared at Brett. "Can't trust you with a thing."

"I'm telling you, I had no choice." He rubbed his neck. "I didn't blurt it out. She guessed most of it."

"That's hard to believe." How could she possibly guess about the codes? Maybe she thought she knew everything. Surely Brett had some sense and kept a few things to himself.

"He's telling the truth." Priss slapped the table for emphasis.

I looked around. A couple at another table was staring.

"Keep your voices down." I leaned into the table.

"Obviously, everyone here knows something I don't." Sara half turned to face me. "What's this about a break in?"

"Brett was carrying a burlap bag to the garage when I stopped at your house. He lied and tried to convince me he found the bag on the road, but I knew better. I got it out of him. He didn't crack as easily as you think, Julian." Priss's gave a smug smile. "I threatened to tell Chief Hendricks a thing or two. Blackmail is a beautiful thing. That's when he told me about the break in tonight. I can help, you know."

I glanced at Brett. How could he be so lame-brained? What if Tudy or Mom had caught him? This was a disaster.

"Brett told me you helped with the codes, Sara. So I know you're in on it." Priss stared at Sara for a full beat, then kicked my leg under the table. For a moment my mind blinked. Okay, so Brett didn't exaggerate. He'd told her everything. This was more than a disaster. We couldn't go through with the break in. Not now, not with Priss knowing all our business.

"Actually, I think it's pretty heroic to try and clear your father's name. I never believed all the gossip about your dad anyway. He was always so nice, in a nerdy kind of way. Why would anyone think he wanted to do himself in? It's your duty to find out what really happened, and seriously, I can help."

"Priss, you can't help. This isn't some game like hanging ball gowns from flag poles," I said.

"I didn't hang *any* gowns from *any* flag poles."

"Sure you did. You over did it with the lace." I ruffled my fingers around my neck, imitating a lacy collar. "You made a crack about Kathleen and her frilly dresses. An easy catch."

"Wow," said Sara.

Priss stomped my foot. "So what? She had it coming."

"This is different. This could be dangerous," I said.

Surely she'd figured out this wasn't some escapade. People could get hurt, and I didn't want to be responsible.

"Exactly why I want to help." Priss crossed her legs, her knee bumping the table. "Y'all are amateurs when it comes to this stuff. I've been sneaking out since before I could tie my own shoes."

"This isn't the same." Brett spoke up. "I've been trying to tell her, but she won't listen."

"Why do y'all want to break into your father's office?" Sara asked. She hadn't touched a bite of anything since Priss and Brett entered.

"I keep feeling we overlooked something." I answered.

"Why not just have campus security open the building for you?" Sara looked concerned, not intrigued like Priss.

"Because they'd keep anything we find just like Chief Hendricks. This is something we have to do ourselves. Besides, the Chief doesn't believe us. We have to have proof. There must be more evidence." I looked over at Brett, sucking in a breath. "Construction starts in Russell Hall on Monday. Afterwards, it'll be impossible to look around. We have to go tonight."

Priss looked at Brett. "Exactly how did you plan on getting in?"

"I showed you the crowbar. What did you think I was doing with it?"

"See. What did I say? Amateurs." Priss opened her purse and pulled out a metal nail file. She kissed the sharpened point and winked.

I couldn't believe she talked us into letting her come. All you could see was Priss's back as she worked on the side door to Russell Hall. Brett, Sara, and I pressed into the building's shadow, watching her. Priss calmly ran her nail file down the door seam, twisting the doorknob simultaneously. After a minute she sighed. The door clicked and silently opened.

Priss held up her nail file and mouthed, "Simple."

I grabbed Sara's hand. "Stay close."

Brett leapt up the step as Priss turned around. She grinned like some warped Cheshire cat, her teeth gleaming in the starlight. "See. I told you I could do it."

"How did you learn to do that exactly?" Brett's voice was husky and low.

"One bathroom in our house, four girls—remember?" Priss slunk inside, and we crowded behind her before closing the door. We were in a narrow hallway lit by soft light streaming through an upper floor window.

"You may have done this at home once or twice, but I think you've used your nail file on other doors." Brett whispered to Priss as Sara and I inched our way along a plaster chair rail.

Priss arched a brow. "Old town, old buildings."

I wasn't surprised; few things shocked me about Priss. Besides, how could I stomach being a major hypocrite? It wasn't her idea to break in. Speaking of stomachs, mine went ballistic once the door closed behind us. I appeared cool and collected on the outside, but my insides wiggled more than a bag of newborn worms.

We stuck tight to the wall, eventually ascending three flights of stairs. The stairwell was pitch black. I turned on the flashlight. We stood on a small landing. Cardboard boxes were stacked on a burgundy velvet bench, ready to move into temporary offices. Sara stepped left into the hallway and waited. Priss came up the stairs next. She moved down the opposite hallway followed by Brett.

We had discussed what each of us would do once inside. Sara and I would check Dad's office for any new evidence. Brett and Priss combed the other offices for anything unusual. Priss carried her own flashlight. Brett tried to take it, but she slapped his hand.

Sara glided next to me, and her dress fluttered against me without a sound. Her eyes shimmered black in the diminished light. She seemed calm for someone new to breaking and entering.

"We'll meet back here unless you find something." I nodded to Brett and Priss.

He flashed me the okay sign. A narrow cone of light echoed down the walls ahead of them as they started in the opposite direction. They disappeared into the first dark recess. I glanced down the hall and ran the light over Dad's office door. Brass winked at me with Dr. Melton James etched in the metal. No one had removed it.

Sara bumped into my elbow when I stopped at the door. Her breath was warm against my shoulder and smelled slightly of strawberries. For some reason, it reassured me, reminded me I was doing the right thing. I tried the knob, and it opened easily. We stepped inside.

Gold sparks flashed behind my lids, disorienting me. An icy memory pushed into my brain, warming as it expanded.

The room exploded into brilliant light and looked exactly as it did the day we removed Dad's things. His magnificent butterfly collection covered the wall next to the window. One shadow box filled with iridescent wings tilted to the right. The shelves behind his desk were filled with all his books, all in precise order. I reached out and moved the telephone next to the scratch pad on his desk, the empty wooden coaster was there, no mug. I glanced over at the medicine cabinet tucked behind his door and mentally scanned the interior, the red tin of ether, the specimen jars jumbled on the shelf. Searching the room, I spotted the heel print. I touched it, felt the sticky residue, and smelled old coffee. The print grew brighter, and I felt a sharp pain at the tip of my tongue. I was biting it—a reminder to come back. The colors in the room bled to a muddy brown.

I wanted to hold the image longer, my brain stuttered for less than a moment, unsure what to do, but I had to come back to the here and now. I felt close to Dad, as if he'd never really left. The memory dissipated, leaving the room dark, and deserted, and slightly cold.

The shelves were empty, and the walls were covered with anemic rectangles where pictures, diplomas, and mementos once hung. I shined the light beam over the desk, a scratched, cloudy waxed surface without family photos or mementos; only the basic black phone remained.

Sara cleared her throat. "I've seen you with that far away look before. Priss said you have a something called Hyperkinetic Memory. That you can walk into a room, walk right out, and remember everything down to the tiniest detail. She also said you can get lost in a memory."

I didn't want to talk about it right now, didn't want to explain how unpredictable it was. Didn't want her to feel sorry for me.

"Priss said you don't like people making a big deal out of it." Sara watched me for a response, then clasped my hand. "You shouldn't be embarrassed with me."

Then she smiled. A smile that shoves everything else out of your head, and only she exists.

"I have a friend from school with epilepsy. She has a funny taste in her mouth before she has a seizure. She calls it an aura. Do you have any warning?"

For the first time in my life, I felt like someone understood. She didn't look puzzled or shocked. She didn't glare at me like I was some kind of freak. "Yeah. I do. It comes on fast, like a brain-freeze from eating too much ice cream. But, it's not like I can do anything about it."

Sara moved closer and kissed my forehead. I wanted to hold her—instead I cleared my throat. We were in Dad's office after all. Seemed kinda weird to have feelings for Sara here. I let go of her hand and ran my fingers over Dad's desk. "A picture of my mother and a pad of paper used to be next to the phone. Almost any time he used the phone, he doodled. His mug normally sat on the other side. But the day we moved his things, there was only a wooden coaster."

Sara's watched my every move. I pointed to the bookshelves. "His books on archeology were on these sagging shelves. He owned hundreds of books."

Using the flashlight, I directed the light toward the abandoned wall. "Dad's butterfly collection was between the window and the bookshelves. The bottom shadow box was crooked, like someone ran into it. It caught my eye right off. Dad would never leave a picture like that; he'd have to straighten it. It was the first thing to catch my eye."

I moved to the medicine cabinet and opened the doors, tracing the area where he'd kept his specimen bottles, touching the bare shelf where the ether tin and the box of cotton had been. Without Dad, the office was just a shell with all the life scooped out. All the furniture left behind was just pieces of wood occupying space.

"Do you have any idea what we're looking for?" Sara whispered.

"None. Something bad happened here the day Dad died. I was just hoping we'd find a clue to tie it all together." I aimed the flashlight over to the windowsill. The beam skipped across the deep gouge in the wood.

Sara stepped behind me, and I handed her the light. "Can you hold this for a minute?"

"What are you doing?"

"This gouge is new. I noticed it the day we cleaned Dad's office, but I don't know what made it." I felt the groove and studied the path. I pointed to the inside of the groove. "See how the wood is light and unstained? It hasn't been exposed to air long enough to darken."

I pulled the piece of broken mug from my pocket. I slipped one edge along the groove, but it didn't fit. I turned the triangular-shaped piece until the sharpest point glowed in the light. I slid it into the groove. It fit, perfectly. I guided the fragment from one end to the other without a snag. I glanced up at Sara.

"Brett and I found this piece of Dad's mug outside. It fell with him."

"What does it mean?"

"I'm trying to figure that out."

She let the light drift downward. My eyes wandered with it, not thinking just letting my brain go blank for a minute. Something glinted along the baseboard. We both spotted it.

"What's that?" Sara held the light steady.

Without bothering to answer, I dashed to the opposite wall and dropped even with the floor. A pottery fragment was wedged between the floorboard and the wall. With a gentle tug, I loosened it.

Sara focused the light over the piece. It matched the ceramic from Dad's mug. I turned it over in my hand. A blue stripe ran down the middle, similar to the piece I'd found on the ground. When I joined the two pieces, one side formed the Scottish flag. The other side was stained with coffee. I gripped the fragments in my hand. A lump the size of Oklahoma stuck in my throat, and I could hardly speak.

"Dad's mug must have broken before he fell."

"How did a piece get outside?"

I walked back to the window. I ran my finger over the jagged piece we found outside and retraced it in the window gouge. "It must have fallen with him. Possibly made this track."

I looked out the window. The mug had dropped and shattered, coffee must have splattered along with it. Even if it had gotten on Dad's clothes, from the way Brett described him blood covered any coffee stains. Someone cleaned up the mess, but not the police. The Chief hadn't mentioned anything and hadn't noticed the ceramic chunk wedged in the baseboard. In fact, he hadn't mentioned any clues other than Dad's colleagues suggesting he was depressed. No, someone else picked up the fragments, but not all.

"Whoever was here with Dad must have stepped in the coffee. That would explain the sticky heel print. No one noticed. I didn't either, until the light hit it just right."

"Where did you find the heel print?"

"Here." I stepped next to the desk, pointing to the floor. Then I gestured along the windowsill, not more than two steps away. "It took pressure to make this long scrape in the wood. Dad could have stepped on it, but that would had ground the piece into the wood. It's almost as if the sharp piece had been dragged under something, something heavy." I turned to look at Sara.

I didn't want to make the next leap. What if I was wrong? But I could see it in Sara's face; she knew what I was thinking.

"Until now, I thought this was kind of a game. Solve the codes, find the clues. But this is real. What are we going to do?" She shuddered.

The door banged open and a beam of light rounded into the room. Brett and Priss skidded in. Her face was ashen.

"We found something." Priss held out a brass key.

"You have to come with us." Brett's words were rushed. "We found it in Professor Noble's office. But his office is… well… you need to see this.

XXII

Brett led the way past the stairs and the landing with the velvet bench. Bulletin Board messages fluttered as we sped down the hall. In the low light, we stumbled over a few packed boxes, a not too gentle reminder of imminent construction.

"The first door we came to was locked, but Priss used her handy-dandy nail file to open it. It's just a conference room, with nothing but a long table and cardboard boxes stacked to the ceiling. Professor Noble's office is this way," Brett said.

We came to the second door. The brass plate was inscribed: Dr. Kurt Noble. Brett pushed the door with his fingertips. It yawned open, and we stepped inside. No one said anything. I'd never been to his office before, but I had a good idea it didn't usually look like this.

"His office was open. I don't mean unlocked, either. Someone left the door halfway open." Priss ran her light over the room as she talked.

Unlike my father's office, Dr. Noble's office was unbearably narrow with brown metal bookshelves instead of built in wooden cabinets. Books were stuffed into every available shelf in the most helter-skelter manner. Stacks of periodicals leaned together like crumbling skyscrapers, drifting into the windowsills, and climbing the walls. Boxes littered a corner, but he hadn't started packing.

The room clamped around me, claustrophobia wasn't far behind. Army green file cabinets stood at attention behind his desk. All the drawers were jerked open, and files were thrown around the room. The room smelled like moldy books and rotten fruit. Apple cores and banana peels overflowed from his wastebasket, silver candy wrappers scattered across the floor like dried leaves. An iron clock hung above the file cabinets, clicking away the seconds.

"Ugh, I'm waiting in the hall." Sara pressed her hand over her mouth. She stepped to the little recess beyond the door and sucked in a deep breath.

"Why didn't someone empty his waste basket? This is awful." Priss pinched her nose.

I went over to the reeking container. The apples had shriveled into ugly brown knobs, as if no one had entered his office for days, but he arrived at our house before dawn on Friday. Today was only Saturday. Well, technically today was Sunday morning. This was weird even for Professor Noble.

Brett angled behind the desk and picked up bank reports typed on pale green paper. They were partially hidden under a jumble of rubber bands, silver paper clips, and pink absentee slips. Someone had emptied the entire top drawer on his desk.

"They're the bank accounts from Natchitoches Central Bank. These reports go back three years," said Brett.

Leaning over the desk, I found a checkbook in the pile. When I lifted the heavy leather book, paper slivers fell from between the pages. Someone had ripped out the last ten pages.

"Did the bank reports Professor Noble waved around look like they were from this checkbook?" I asked Brett.

He shifted the square book studded with metal teeth toward him. "I didn't get a good look at them."

"The mint-green paper is the same. I'm sure the pages came from this checkbook."

Priss went to the file cabinets. She had difficulty picking the lock with her nail file. When she turned, it was obvious she wasn't holding her nail file; instead she held the key. "This doesn't go to anything in here. Not the door, the desk, or the file cabinet. And it's sticky."

"Let me see it." I said. "Where'd you find it?"

She handed it to me with two fingers. "We shined the light underneath his desk, and saw a glint of metal. At first we thought it was part of the desk leg. When I reached for it, it was sort of stuck to the floor, like it was glued."

When the key hit my palm, I noticed something sticky and brown coating the metal. I lifted it to my nose and sniffed. It smelled like iron.

"What's on it?" asked Priss.

"Smells like blood," I said.

Priss shuddered and took a step closer to the door.

"Whoa... blood changes everything." Brett backed away from the desk. "Maybe we shouldn't be looking through this stuff."

"You have to admit he acted pretty bizarre when he came over the other night." I flipped through the financial reports. They were all out of order. It looked as if someone tossed them high in the air and let them fall haphazardly all over the room.

"You got that right." Brett said.

Sara stuck her head into the room. Her voice quivered and was so low I could barely hear her. She pointed to the hall, then to her ear for emphasis. "I heard something."

Immediately, we clicked off the flashlights. Brett pulled Sara in beside him and closed the door. She stumbled into to me. I slipped the key into the secret hip pocket of my jeans.

"Don't say a word," I whispered.

Her head rested beneath my chin. Even with her back to me I felt her chest rise and fall. She would hyperventilate if she kept breathing so fast. I stroked her hair, trying to calm her, even though my own guts were coiling up inside me.

I pressed her against me, keeping my arm fastened across her, inching away from the door farther into the room. Brett and Priss were skewed behind the door so if it opened they wouldn't be seen. Once I was across the room, I stood statue still, Sara's breathing picked up. She hid her head in the crook of my arm. We listened for a long time, but didn't hear anything.

"What did you hear exactly?" Brett asked in a low voice from the other side of the room.

"One of the doors opened and closed." Sara whispered, her breath blowing across my arm.

Everyone was silent, again. Listening. Waiting.

I turned my head to the window. Magazines stacked in the windows, pushed the curtains to the side, and I stared out over the campus through silvery green oak leaves. They fluttered, but not from a breeze. Someone had jumped from the tree. A figure stood on the ground below.

"Shit!" I moved across the room, grabbing Sara's hand.

"What?" Brett was at my side by the time I made it to the door. "Professor Noble?"

"The Shadow Man." I literally lifted Sara so she stood next to Priss. "He's been watching us through the window. I'm going after him. Stay here."

"No way." Priss almost tripped me getting to the door.

"Get out of the way. Stay here." I growled at her.

Brett was almost on top of me. I felt him at my shoulder. We pounded down the stairs. The girls were close behind. Why didn't they listen? Didn't they understand?

When I reached the door I swung it open hard, immediately regretting the noise. I bounded down the few steps of the building and raced to the tree. Sounded like elephants wearing lead boots behind me. So much for stealth. I guess that didn't matter anyway. No telling how long he'd been watching us from the tree.

I spun around and glimpsed the back of a black shoe rounding the corner. Brett must have seen it too cause he leapt ahead. We sped along the building, slowing at the corner. Brett craned his neck to see, and I heard the girls panting, coming up on us.

"Anything?" I asked so low it wasn't even a whisper.

Brett shook his head. I came up even with him. "We need to split up."

I looked back at Priss and Sara. "Stay together. Go to the front of the building and see if he doubled back. Brett you take the back, and I'll head to the parking lot."

Everyone nodded and ran in separate directions. I humped it over to the parking lot. It was empty, except for a plain vanilla car used to transport students across campus. Boxwood hedges ran parallel on either side of the lot. I started there first. I thought about turning on my flashlight, but that would make me a bright white target. One single streetlight poured its light over the parking lot. Beyond it, the campus was dark.

Running my finger over the boxwoods, I entered the lot. The pavement released heat, and it coursed over my shoes, sweat popping on my forehead. I methodically checked over each hedge and then around the car. I heard a squeak, metal on metal, from the next building, the Science Building.

I jogged over to a bank of windows, staying low. I peered into one of the labs, but there wasn't enough light to see in. Someone grabbed me from behind, gloved fingers clasped around my neck. I attempted to pull away, but an arm slammed across my shoulders, pulling me backwards. I squirmed and bit down on the forearm, twisting the fabric into my mouth.

Sharp cold steel pressed against my throat. I stopped struggling.

"Don't move, and I won't hurt you." It was the Shadow Man. He spoke in a high-pitched voice.

My hand fell to my side, and I felt his clothes, smooth, yet bulky. His wool hat scratched my ear, making him about my size, which ruled out Professor McKnight since he was over six feet tall. He breathed against my shoulder. His breath was steamy hot and smelled like day-old bread.

"I saw you searching Professor Noble's office. Why?"

"Nothing. We were looking for something of my dad's." Unbelievably, my voice was strong, not even a small quiver.

He pressed the knife deeper, tiny, wicked teeth stinging my skin. "What were you looking for?"

"Clues. Clues to why Dad fell."

"What did you find?" His voice was calm. He thought he was in control.

I gulped. "Nothing."

He grunted and patted me down, momentarily lowering his knife to use his hand. This was my chance. I tried to wrench my shoulder out from under his other arm and jerked forward, stomping on his foot at the same time. He didn't flinch.

He bashed my shoulder joint with the knife handle, hitting a pressure point; pain and numbness shot down my arm worse than a jab to the funny bone. I couldn't pick up my arm. I swayed. He steadied me with one hand and jammed his other hand into my pocket. He pulled out the mug pieces, tossing them to the ground. He rifled through my other pocket and patted me down, again. A trickle of sweat dripped off my ear, a memory shivered near the edge of my brain, threatening to break through. I bit my lip and thought about the secret pocket containing the key. Stay in the present, stay in the present.

He pressed the knife tip where my ear met my jaw and flicked a sweat droplet. "Stop looking. There are no clues. You won't like what you find."

He kneed me, and my legs gave way. I had one good arm, and I tried to punch behind me. He jerked the knife toward me, nicking my jaw. I jumped but not fast enough. A swift kick knocked me down. Another kick jabbed me solidly in the ribs. I rolled on my side, gasping for breath. Once I pulled in a good one, I scooped up the ceramic pieces in my good hand and jumped to my feet, but the Shadow was gone. I chased after him, around the corner of the building, but he had vanished.

I yelled, "Brett over here!"

I turned on my flashlight, scanning the campus in front of me. Brett was at my side in seconds, followed by Priss and Sara.

"He was here. Pulled a knife on me." I panted. "He's been watching us. He's after something."

We combed past the building, washing the area with light and walking four abreast, almost as if we'd been trained. It was eerie the way he just disappeared.

"You believe me." I looked over at Brett.

"I saw his leg. The black pants and the black shoes, just like you said. Did you get a look at him?"

We slowed down, standing in a circle. "No. He grabbed me from behind. But it was the Shadow Man. He held a knife to my throat and asked what we found in Professor Noble's office, then he searched me."

"You couldn't get away?" Priss asked, rubbing her hands together and looking around.

"I tried. He hit me then kicked me to the ground. Before I could get up he was gone."

Sara touched the nick on my jaw. "Oh my God, you're bleeding."

"Yes." I'd barely registered the cut. I dabbed my jaw, then pressed along the bone to stymie the bleeding.

Brett blew out a string of air. "We have to tell the Chief."

"And what?" I stepped back. "What will he do? He has men driving past the house every day and every night. And don't even think about telling Mom or Tudy. They'd have Chief lock us in a jail cell for our own protection, and we'd never find out what's going on." I wiped more blood off my chin with the back of my hand, now that it was working again. "This guy is wearing thick clothes in the summer. He's covered from head to toe, definitely doesn't want to be discovered. He disguised his voice, too."

"So it's someone we know," said Priss.

I shook my head. "He's either afraid I'd recognize his voice or that I'd be able to identify him later. If we only knew what he wanted, we might be able to catch him."

Priss started walking across campus toward Russell Hall. "Do you think it's the key? Where is it? You didn't drop it, did you?"

"It's in my secret pocket." I fished it out of my pants and palmed it. I would have shown her, but the Shadow Man might be watching.

"What if it isn't the key? What if it's something else?" Sara was close to me. I smelled her hair, fresh shampoo, lemony, as we walked past Russell Hall.

What did he want? What was he looking for? Something he was willing to hide in the shadows for, hold a knife to my throat to get, and possibly kill to obtain. And what the hell did this have to do with my father? This brought me back to the last code. There was no doubt, I had to solve it.

"Whew. Too close for comfort." Priss crossed her arms and hugged herself. "I should have known better than to come with you inexperienced bozos."

"You were the one who insisted," said Brett. "Besides, it's the most exciting thing to happen to you all summer."

"Humph." Priss sneered. "I hardly think so."

All I wanted to do was get out of there. I didn't want to listen to Brett and Priss bicker. How could they argue at a time like this? If the girls hadn't been with us, I'd have doubled over and thrown up. *So much for being a thief.*

Sara swayed into me as we walked. She wrapped her fingers in mine. They were cold, even in the summer heat. I squeezed her hand, and she squeezed back. Finally, we made it to the house. Priss had parked her mom's car behind Woody.

I wanted to drive Sara home, but Priss insisted. I walked Sara to the passenger side.

"I have to say, Julian James, I've never been on a date quite like this. You know how to show a girl a good time." She smiled. Her hand tightened around mine, and I noticed her fingers were warm now.

A car slowed as it drove past the house. It was one of the Natchitoches policemen doing his nightly drive by. He tipped his hat and sped away. I glanced at Brett. He nodded; he knew I was right. We were on our own. The police wouldn't be any help.

"Pretty scary." I brought her fingertips to my lips.

"Maybe we can try again." Sara leaned toward me, her face upturned. She tilted her head slightly to the side and licked her lips.

"Oh, God. They're going to kiss." Priss plopped into her seat. Brett closed the car door and hunched down beside the driver's window so his head was the same level with Priss. She rolled the window down with a buzz and mumbled something, but who wanted to listen.

"Talk about ruining the mood," said Sara. She scooted into her seat and pressed the power button for the window. It sped down, and she rested her arm on the cracked padded ledge. "The book on codes. The one your father gave you?"

"Yeah. What about it?" I asked.

"Can I come by and pick it up tomorrow? I want to study it." Sara dropped her chin in the crook of her arm. "All the pieces are coming together. Maybe I can help you figure the last code."

"Sure." I'd memorized the entire black book, but something teased the back of my brain. Did I really want Sara's help? She'd solved the first code, but things were different now. There was something wrong about Dad's death. Somehow Professor Noble was involved. Exactly how I didn't know, but I didn't want her in danger.

The doorbell rang at least fifteen times, waking me up from a sound sleep. The front door opened and slammed shut. At first, muffled voices rose up the stairs, then someone screamed. I jumped out of bed. I peeked over the stair railing; Rebecca Sharp was standing in the entry, shaking like a baby deer by the highway. I tried to make out what she was saying. Her words spewed out like the rat-a-tat-tat of a machine gun.

My mind rolled in on itself. What did she want so early in the morning? And why was she so upset? Then I remembered last night. I'd stayed up until dawn going over the last code. Hoping something would break, but no progress.

"They called from campus security and demanded I come to Russell Hall. Chief Hendricks was all ready there when I drove up." She ran her index finger around her collar, loosening the silk bow of her blouse with a single pull, as if her clothes were choking her.

Mom smoothed her striped shift around her emaciated hips before hugging Rebecca Sharp. "Tell me what happened."

"His office is a mess. Smells like a garbage bin. Oh Caroline, he's gone insane. All this business about your husband's death has driven him mad. Poor man."

"Who?" Mom sounded sincerely confused.

"Professor Noble, of course." Miss Sharp tugged at the fabric around her throat again and acted as if she were swallowing thumbtacks. "Chief asked when I'd last seen him. No one's set eyes on him since yesterday evening."

"Maybe he went out of town." Mom was being pragmatic. A small wonder since she wasn't used to all the hysteria surrounding her these days.

"No. He left a note."

"A note. What did it say?" My mother led Miss Sharp into the great room, patting her hand.

"Chief Hendricks wouldn't tell me." Miss Sharp sniffed. "But he did say as far as he was concerned, Professor Noble was considered either missing or dead."

XXIII

Tudy rushed home from a friend's the minute as she heard about Professor Noble. She, along with Mom, answered one phone call after another. Rebecca Sharp camped out in the great room, drinking hot tea mixed with ginger and cloves, a drink Tudy swore calmed the nerves. The entire house reeked of it. When Miss Sharp wasn't drinking tea, she was pacing a ring around the coffee table.

Professor Noble's disappearance was worrisome. Finally, the Chief was asking questions. They'd checked his house, and when he wasn't there, it seemed like the whole town just started wringing their hands. Since I was in his office last night, I knew something was wrong. He wouldn't leave his office in such a state unless he was stark raving mad. His disappearance was connected to Dad, had to be.

Later someone knocked at the front door. I barely heard it above the same repeated phrases: *Unbelievable. Don't know a thing... I'll call you back as soon as I know something. No, no. The Chief is looking into it.*

Since it didn't look like anyone else heard it, I slipped downstairs. Sara stood at the front door. Her long hair was pulled back in a ponytail. She held a black notebook against a white eyelet shirt and distributed her weight evenly over red canvas shoes. Clearly she came here to work.

"Hey. You look surprised. Did you forget I was stopping by?" She asked.

"No." I didn't want to discuss anything in the entry where we might be overheard. "Hold on. Stay here. I'll be right back."

I left Sara and raced into Dad's study. Mom had hung Dad's rare butterfly collection on the main wall. The shadow boxes looked out of place, and their presence nagged at me, but I didn't come in here to gawk at the butterflies. I wanted the old codebook.

I went to a box labeled DESK. The cardboard corners overlapped to form a top. I tugged them open and lifted out the small black book even though I still had serious doubts about giving it to Sara.

Professor Noble's disappearance, the Shadow Man, and Dad's death were somehow strung together, and the Chief was looking for answers, but my gut instinct told me the solution was in the last code. I cupped the small book in my hand and went to the entry.

Sara stood by the front door. The corners of her mouth slowly curved upwards when she saw me coming back. I ushered her out the door and onto the porch. A thunderstorm was brewing overhead and kicked up a slight breeze. I cradled the codebook in my hand, directing Sara to a corner of the porch.

"I guess you heard Professor Noble's disappeared." I thumbed the tattered book. The leather separated at the corners, crumbling along the edges.

"That's all Mrs. Dupree has talked about since she heard this morning. I'm surprised she isn't here. I guess Miss Sharp's upset. Everyone she works with is either missing or..." Sara stopped talking and looked into the sky. "It's frightening to think we were there in his office last night. Why is the Chief so sure he's missing?"

"He left a note. Only Chief knows what it says, but he has the impression Dr. Noble may have harmed himself. Miss Sharp was at the college this morning. They asked her a million questions."

Sara reached up and touched a pea-sized St. Christopher hanging from a delicate gold chain. "If my father knew how boring this little town really was, he'd make me come home."

"Yeah. I forgot. The real reason he sent you here. Boring and safe. Letting you spend the summer with Priss is about as safe as sleeping with a crocodile. Where is she, by the way?" I asked.

"You won't believe this, but Jack showed up with flowers, Priss's favorites, daisies. The reason I'm so late. I wanted to come earlier, but they wanted to talk things over. Anyway, they dropped me off." Sara rubbed the tiny medal between her thumb and forefinger.

"Ahhh. Priss and revenge, best friends since kindergarten." I had difficulty feeling too sorry for Jack, though. Payback actually felt good.

"Well, I don't think he's completely off the hook just yet." Sara stopped fiddling with the medal and held out her hand. "Can I see the codebook?"

"Are you sure you want to help me with this last code? It could be dangerous." I was more convinced than ever of Shadow Man's involvement in Dad's death.

"I want to help. It's obvious the last code is some kind of clue."

Last night really frightened me. I was certain something happened to Dad. Sara had it right, and I agree. The code was a clue or led to a clue. But I didn't want her involved, didn't want her mixed up in something this dangerous. Big Red's prediction rang in my ears.

"You gotta be careful. You're gonna search for answers. Your decisions will put others in danger."

My lip stung. I had bitten it pretty hard and focused on Sara's amber eyes. She leaned toward me, concentrating so deeply I swear she could see my mind working.

"What did Big Red say to you?" She leaned in even closer.

"Nothing."

"You've been avoiding the subject of Big Red since we went to see him. Why do you get so testy when anyone asks?"

"I don't want to believe his idiotic prediction. I'd have to throw everything I was ever taught out the window. But the weird thing is… he knew. He knew Dad left me a clue, the diary."

The whole idea made me bristle. If he knew about the clue, could his warning come true? No way I would have to give up reason and hard facts to believe him. I wanted to let it go, wanted to forget the whole prophecy business. But I couldn't.

"Tell me what he said."

"I can't." My head still hurt from the brief memory.

"What are you afraid of?" Sara crowded me.

"Nothing." Was I afraid? Afraid everything could suddenly spin out of control like last night and put someone else in danger?

"Then if you aren't afraid, why not tell me what's bothering you?"

"I don't know." I hedged, squirming under her gaze.

Sara tilted my chin toward her with two fingers. Her eyes were hypnotic.

"Oh… all right." Completely against my better judgment, I started talking. "He reassured me the same way he reassures everyone, using information from the past. He said some incident had recently changed my life. Common knowledge, but then he revealed that my father left something behind to help me. He was purposefully cryptic. He didn't like me from the minute I walked in. I doubted him, and it made him mad."

"I'm surprised he told your fortune."

"He almost didn't. I pretty much begged him. Then he said the craziest thing. He said I'd make decisions and put others in terrible danger. He was wrong." My body went rigid.

"He didn't say anything else?" Sara's fingers still rested on my chin.

She'd brushed right over the danger business. "Sara, didn't you hear me? He thinks I'll make some kind of stupid decision, maybe more than one and harm someone. Possibly put them in so much danger, they'll die."

"Yes. I heard. But what can you do about it? You don't even know what he's talking about. For all you know, you've already made the decision. He could have been talking about last night. And the danger's passed." She tapped my chin. "Think. Think. What did he say when you walked into the room?"

"He made some crack about me being a traitor to my own beliefs. Then he ordered me to leave. It took some persuading to get the rest out of him."

"Hmm. Not much help. It has to be in the diary. He told you your father left something behind, something to help you. There has to be something we're overlooking? Why don't you give me the codebook?"

My fingers tightened on the book. I couldn't give it to her. "I don't know, Sara."

"Then what is it?"

"I don't want anything to happen to you." I backed up and hit the porch column. So many things could have gone wrong last night. The Shadow Man could have stabbed me to death. If any of the others had found him, he could have hurt them. One of us could have ended up in the hospital. No, Sara didn't have to be involved.

"You're not making the decision. I am." Sara's frowned, her brows arched as a new idea formed. "You don't trust me. After all we've been through."

I held my hand up between us, hoping she'd slow down. But Sara plowed ahead. "I've helped you and have never said a word to anyone. Sometimes you act as if you're the only one to lose someone. I want to help you *now*... I thought you trusted me."

"You don't understand. I do trust you." I reached out for her. She reached for the book. I pulled back. "You can't give it to anyone. Not even Priss."

"I wasn't. You aren't giving it to me, are you?" A hurt look crossed her face, and her hands dropped to her sides.

Jack's jeep jostled up the drive. Priss yelled out the window. "They're forming a search party for Professor Noble. Down at the riverfront. Come on."

Sara ran down the porch steps. I started to follow, but she spun around and gave me such a harsh look, I stopped. "Don't think you're coming with us. We don't need *your* help, either."

The entire town turned out for the search. But no one saw any sign of Professor Noble. He'd vanished and left nothing but a cryptic note behind. I looked for Sara at the riverfront, but she and Priss left when the first group formed. I wanted to explain, but she was more than angry. The look on her face told me she was hurt. However, things were more dangerous than before, and I couldn't change how I felt.

I was on to something. I'd collected a few clues, but there were still so many questions.

Everyone who saw him the day he died said he acted strange, even depressed. Why? Was it because he knew about the forged bones? Was it because he knew someone, the Shadow Man, was after his research? And what about the money?

Professor Noble's disappearance was associated with Dad's death. Was he behind all forged bones? His office didn't look like some master criminal. It looked like someone who'd lost his mind. But I had to be more careful than before. Brett had to help me. Where was Brett, anyway? He wasn't in his room earlier. And I hadn't seen him all day. More than ever, I felt alone. It was partly my fault, though.

Chief had called Mom earlier in the day asking questions. I couldn't hear what he said, but I heard Mom's answers. It was obvious, he was beginning to rethink Dad's death. Chief Hendricks had created a command center on Front Street under a plain white tent. As long as he looked for Professor Noble, he couldn't finish the report on Dad, and it gave me an extra day to gather clues.

I was assigned to a search team that combed the upper part of Cane River and the lower end of Camitte Bayou, below the Crawfords' camp. We looked until well after midnight. We didn't find anything, and neither did anyone else. I returned home and crashed.

On Monday, instead of going to the clinic, I called in sick and concentrated on solving the last code. I'd checked Brett's room, but he must have left at dawn, which was weird. He must have gone out with another search team.

But I couldn't let anything distract me. I had to break the last code. Methodically, I'd started with the easy keywords Dad might have used: family names, pet names, birth dates, special dates, names of places we'd lived. Nothing worked. Then I read through the entire diary, looking for underlined words or phrases. I searched the top and bottom of each page, hoping for some magical word or number to jump out. But nothing worked. I searched his desk, the shelves and boxes in his study, and all his drawers. Again, nothing helped. Exhausted and cotton-headed after work-ing on the diary all day I took a walk around the block to clear my head. I missed Sara. Maybe I should have let her help me. What harm would it do? Then I thought about the Shadow Man. No, it was better to leave her out of this. I trudged up the porch steps. I wasn't ready to admit defeat.

XXIV

When I opened the front door, it struck me right away the house was unusually quiet. Tudy wasn't banging around in the kitchen, and Mom wasn't bustling about setting the dining table for supper. Instead, a note was taped to the refrigerator.

Chief Hendricks came by. He called off the search and thinks Professor Noble might be dead. Professor Noble left a note and confessed to tampering with bones at the archeology site. He implicated your father in the fraud. I don't know what to think anymore. Tudy and I will be at the church praying.
MOM

I sagged against the refrigerator. Mom didn't known about the bones because she didn't know about Dad's codes. With all the evidence stacking up against him, even she'd lost hope. Brett still wasn't back. I wondered if he knew about this.

My mind should have been on the codes, but I couldn't focus. I wanted to talk to Sara. I called her, but no one answered. Since the search was off, where was everyone? I was lost. My head buzzed. I needed to pull it together and tackle the last code. Time had run out.

On the way upstairs I forced images from Dad's diary to appear in my head. I was positive he used a keyword for the last code. He'd always said unless the decoder knew the keyword, the code was unbreakable. He wouldn't use a keyword that Brett and I couldn't figure out. The problem is I'd tested every keyword I'd ever known him to use. None of them worked. In all my life, I'd never felt so much pressure to find the right answer. This wasn't some science fair or a math problem. Someone was responsible for Dad's death, and the last code was the answer.

My argument with Sara encroached on my thoughts again. If I didn't believe in Big Red's prediction, why was I allowing it affect my decisions? I should have let Sara help me. What was the harm? We weren't going anywhere. We'd be safe in the house. Bitter cold clamped around my brain, drifting into my chest, an aura. I resisted, but the argument I had with Sara wanted to surface.

I plopped on my bed, trying to forget the argument. Big Red's words came back to me about being a traitor, and for some reason, the memory of the day I came home from the science fair drifted into my brain. I could do this… I could control the memory. I opened my imaginary hands and let the memory fly.

The train squealed into the station. The smell of hot greasy fumes filled my head. Lila Dupree paced the platform. I dreaded hearing her. Her voice grated over me…. "Your father didn't make it." Nausea bit the back in my throat, and I swallowed. I couldn't stand it.

As if pushing a button, I fast-forwarded to the house then raced through it until I reached my parent's bedroom, the familiar gray room with lumps of ashen colored furniture, everything spotless and orderly. But was everything orderly? Something nagged at me. I looked at Dad's bedside table. Odd, his diary wasn't there. His glasses were on top of The American Revolutionary War instead. For a moment, I hovered there. The book. His glasses were on top of the book… like a clue. Then a thought struck me, the idea so strong, I mentally doubled over like I'd been slugged.

I vaulted out of the memory. The hollow in my head ached, and I pulled the memory of Big Red, stuffing it into the space.

He stood before me in his overalls, the tobacco tin bulging in his chest pocket. The earthy smell of the little room nipped at my nose. He stared at me. "A traitor to your own way of thinking."

My heart almost pounded out of my chest as the memory dissipated. I'd mistaken Big Red's words for contempt, but they were actually part of the solution. He'd been trying to tell me something from the very first. I wasn't the traitor.

I reached under my mattress and grabbed Dad's diary. I dashed to his room, straight to his bedside table. I jerked open the upper drawer. There, exactly where I'd left it laid *The American Revolutionary War*. It was yellow, two inches thick and dense like a block of cement. I automatically flipped open to a narrow, cardboard bookmark shoved into the chapter on Benedict Arnold.

I could have kicked myself. Dad always told us stories about spy codes and secret signals used during all the famous wars. The flag signals used by Horatio Nelson to help defeat Napoleon's navy, quilts hung with messages for runaway slaves using the Underground Railroad, and of course, the thousands of codes used in WWII. But the most famous code used during the Revolutionary War was the code devised by Benedict Arnold.

Nicknamed the traitor's code. The code word was buried in a book and unless the code breaker knew which book, it was impossible to figure out. The problem was Benedict Arnold chose *Blackstone's Commentary,* a cumbersome book, so the British refused to use it and instead sent messages in plain English. Dad still said it was an unbreakable code, and if the British hadn't refused to use the book, then maybe Benedict Arnold's name wouldn't be synonymous with the name traitor, today.

It was a smart choice. An obvious clue. He left the book on his bedside table where he normally left his diary. He even left his glasses on top to draw more attention to the book. Why did it take me so long?

The bookmark fluttered to the ground. When I picked it up, I noticed a fold at the bottom. Flattening the crease, three numbers appeared, 263-2-12.

I opened the book to page 263, traced my finger down to the second paragraph, and slid it over to the twelfth word. **Across** nearly jumped off the page. Such a simple word; no one would have ever figured it out.

I went to my room and sat at my desk, pulling paper from a drawer. This was it, the final clue, had to be, I'd run out of time. I turned to the last code in the diary. It was three lines long.

Op Isahsy raiiso. Vspfbfso clksq aps klt jlps teak bsw ysapq lio. Aqhso Jrhkfdet tl pstpfsvs tesj. Wfii rlkbplkt Pscsrra Qeapm tljlpplw. Quqmsrt qes eaq arrljmifrs.

The only way to know for certain if **across** was the keyword was to set up the cipher. I wrote the keyword **ACROS** on the tablet, *minus the repeated letter S,* then followed it with the remaining letters in the alphabet. The new alphabet looked like this:

ACR OSB DEF GHI JKL MNP QTU VWXYZ

Next, I copied the standard alphabet underneath it.

ACR OSB DEF GHI JKL MNP QTU VWXYZ
ABC DEF GHI JKL MNO PQR STU VWXYZ

Matching the top letters to the corresponding letters below, I converted *Op* to *Dr* and *Isahsy* to *Leakey*—**ACROSS** was the key word!

I converted the remaining letters of the first line: *Op Isahsy raiiso. Vspfbfso clksq aps klt jlps teak bsw ysapq lio.*

The sentence read: *Dr. Leakey called. Verified bones are not more than few years old.*

I jumped and shouted loud enough for the whole town to hear. This was the proof. Dr. Leakey was the ultimate expert. He was world famous, and he'd confirmed the bones were forgeries. A trill jumped up my spine. Dad didn't fake the bones!

So why would Professor Noble accuse him of tampering with bones and stealing money? Did he kill Dad? I wanted to share it with Brett and Sara, even Priss, but I had to finish. If the Chief finished his report tomorrow, all this was for nothing. *Snap!* I committed the code to memory and started to exchange letters.

The doorbell rang. A wrinkle formed between my brows. Who could that be? My mind shifted and stored the new letters in the side pocket of my mind. I folded the paper into Dad's diary, and pressed it into my top drawer. Whoever it was, better have a good reason for coming by. I didn't have time for company.

When I opened the door, Sara stood there, holding out a bag of peanut M&M's. "I brought a peace offering."

"Peace. Good idea." My heart tapped my chest. She was back. Honeysuckle filled the space between us. God, she smelled so good.

"I was pretty mad at you yesterday, but it's not completely your fault." Sara's voice was tight, but she didn't seem angry.

"I tried to find you, but you left with Priss and another search group. I brought the codebook with me. I was going to give it to you." I scratched my ear just to have something to do with my hand, because I really wanted to wrap it around her waist.

"I'm sorry, too. You don't know why I was really mad, and it isn't fair to blame you. It's because of my mother."

"Your mother?" Whoa. What did Sara's mother have to do with this?

She bowed her head. "It made me angry you didn't trust me. I've told you about my mom. I thought you understood. When you didn't want my help it was like all the anger and frustration I've tamped down for years just exploded."

I knew what she was talking about because until a few moments ago I was beginning to think finding the truth was hopeless, and I wanted to punch every wall in my room.

"I made Priss swear she wouldn't tell anyone about my mother. I didn't want anyone's pity." Sara looked at me through her lashes. "I've never let anyone close to me. I don't want to go through losing someone, again. I can't. The pain crushes your heart flat so there's no room for feeling anymore. I tried not to like you. I really did. But I think about you all the time and wish I were with you. And you seem to really want me around…."

Sara squashed the space between us. "…most of the time."

Explained a lot. Why her father was so overprotective, and why she sometimes seemed like a snob, using it as a shield to protect herself from pain. She was more vulnerable than she let on. I leaned into her, put my hand on her waist and pulled her to me. I suddenly realized her pain was my pain.

"I'm sorry." My voice was low. "I know what it feels like to want answers and not find them."

Sara pressed her body to me, and heat flooded into me like a hot cider on a winter's day. Her face was turned up, and her mouth was so close I had to kiss her lips, softly at first, then harder, tasting her breath on my tongue, Spearmint. I started running my hand down her back when the codes broke into my thoughts.

I backed away. Sara's lids fluttered open like she didn't understand, and she touched her lips.

"I broke the last code." I gulped to get a breath. Letters jiggled out of the corner of my mind, and the two alphabets stacked one on top of the other. Letters changed places, and I couldn't focus.

"What?"

Before Sara could say another word, I grabbed her hand and raced up the stairs. Once we were in my room, I opened the diary and unfolded the paper on the desk.

"How?" Sara bent over the desk, examining the page.

"Look." I ran my hand over the codebook and explained about *The American Revolutionary War*, Big Red, and Benedict Arnold. "I just started. You're just in time to help me finish the last code. It's got to be the final clue."

Sara dropped into the chair and opened the bag of M&M's. She broke one in half with her front teeth, popped it into her mouth, and then traced the original message with her finger.

ACR OSB DEF GHI JKL MNP QTU VWXYZ

ABC DEF GHI JKL MNO PQR STU VWXYZ

Then she traced the first decoded line.

Dr. Leakey called. Verified bones are not more than few years old.

"We should get started." She looked back at me and winked. "We can do this."

She wrote the entire message on the page, leaving a space below each letter, just enough room for the newly decoded letter. My mind calmed, but my throat tightened, and three-dimensional letters linked one behind the other until the entire code was a chain so real it almost breathed. I mentally touched each letter.

Sara scribbled away. My foot tapped, faster and faster as my mind busily flipped and replaced letter. We finished at the same time.

Sara dropped the pencil. Her mouth formed a perfect *O*. "Not what I expected."

I stared at her. I couldn't speak. I shook my head. "Had me completely fooled."

Now what? Where did we go from here? Did we turn this over to the Chief? The air pressure changed. I felt it in my ears. Someone had opened a door in the house. Must be Mom and Tudy. I had to tell them the truth. My pulse picked up. It was time to hand over all the clues and let Mom decide what to do. I grabbed the diary.

"We have to tell Mom." I clasped Sara's hand. "Come on."

From the corner of my eye, I saw her pick up the paper from the desk and scoop up the package of candy with her free hand. We ran down the stairs, but no one was in the entry.

"Mom?" I yelled. "Mom, I have to show you something."

Sara hung back on the stairs while I plowed through the entry. At the door to Dad's study, I smelled ether. What the heck? Before I could turn, someone grabbed me from behind and shoved cotton over my mouth and nose. Struggling, I tried to pound them with the diary, but my hand swung wide, connecting with nothing. *Don't inhale any more ether.* I clenched my teeth, and felt my diaphragm stop. The ether had started to affect me, and a dizzy ocean roared in my ears. I barely heard Sara scream. My brain was closing down, my vision clouded, my legs wouldn't move, the roar took over. I needed to breathe. I couldn't save her.

My face hit the floor. Pain shot through the side of my head. I tasted a rope of blood where my teeth cut my cheek. Silver flecks spiraled between the wall and me. M&M's scattered over the floor, several rolling against my cheek. A beige-brown shoe crunched the candy into the floor and walked away from me.

I blinked, bringing the shoe into sharp, brief focus. The right heel was made of rubber and had a crack running through the middle. When the shoe lifted, the sole was exposed. The letters **LUPI** were on one side of the crack. Two letters were on the other—**N E**. I stared at the letters until they blurred to darkness.

XXV

A strong smell like gasoline seared my throat. My stomach roiled with each breath, stirring up sticky loops of hot saliva. I tamped down the urge to vomit and opened my eyes. At first, the room spun and colors blurred together like a Jackson Pollack painting. The mentholated taste gagged me, and I scrunched into a ball as best I could with my hands tied close to my chest, fighting the need to puke. My jaw was heavy and swollen. What was going on? I squeezed my lids shut. Even though my brain was in a fog, I knew it was dangerous to move.

I heard someone breathing and lifted my eyelids. Sara. She was peacefully sleeping on the ground next to me, but her breath smelled ketotic, like secondhand ether. The urge to vomit contracted my stomach again. I wanted ice or water, something to wash the taste away.

I stared at Sara. Her hair was matted and tangled with dirt, her clothes stained with grass and mud like someone had dragged her through a field. I noticed my own clothes; they were covered in brown muck. Someone drugged us. Dumped and abandoned us on a packed dirt floor.

We were inside though, beside a wooden table. The light was low, but I made out two cloth camp chairs next to the table and about six others folded in a single row against a wall made of hewn logs. Archeology tools: shovels, brushes, trowels, screens were stacked near my feet. I knew where we were, the storage cabin at the excavation site.

Rolling to my side, I looked through the open door. Beyond it a soft earthen mound at least twenty feet tall rose beneath an army green waterproof tarp. A triangular wedge cut through the center, exposing earthen bands like a rich chocolate layer cake, the bottom layer crisscrossed with white string. Dogwood trees bracketed a dirt path leading from the site to the small cabin. I heard two people arguing.

Golden evening light streamed through the trees. It gave Rebecca Sharp a heavenly glow, but I knew she was anything but a saint. Fear zipped up my spine, shivered up my neck, and coiled at the back of my head. She was the monster responsible for Dad's death.

Sara and I had finished the code. Dad suspected Miss Sharp of tampering with the bones and trying to steal the research. She was why the date was circled in red on the calendar. Dad planned to confront her. But something went horribly wrong.

Miss Sharp paced from one edge of the tarp to the other, and I remembered the shoes. They clinched the deal. Mostly, she wore high heels. It had thrown me off. I suspected everyone else. I never dreamed she left the shoe print in Dad's office. I'd never seen her wear anything close to a brown oxford.

"I can't believe you talked me into bringing them here." Rebecca Sharp yelled at someone beyond the door.

"Look, let's just leave them." A man's voice. "By the time they're found, we'll be long gone."

"This is all your fault."

"My fault? I wasn't the one Dr. James suspected. I wasn't the one who called in a panic. You were sloppy. I told you to wait...." The man's voice cut deep and angry.

"Yes. And that turned out so well." Rebecca tossed her hair. "We've been through this before. You said it was easy. Slip him a Mickey Finn in his coffee. He'd black out for hours. But he didn't, did he?"

"Look, it wasn't me he suspected of tampering with the excavation site."

The man moved into the fading light, and my lungs shriveled, squeezing out all the air. I couldn't see his face, but he was dressed completely in black. So Rebecca Sharp and the Shadow Man *were* in this together.

"I told you to put in the knockout drops *after* he came back from the snack room." He moved closer to Miss Sharp. "You didn't think the situation through."

"Things changed. You'd have done the same thing." She stiffened, then closed the space between them. "I had no choice. I had to act fast."

"If you had just waited."

"Wait for what? For him to regain consciousness and then call the police?" Her voice was sharp, sneering. She tapped her index finger on his chest. "How can you possibly criticize me? *You* were almost caught at his house. Just slip into his study and steal the research file. Great job!"

The man pounded the hood of Miss Sharp's car. She jerked her hand back, curling it into a fist.

I was fully awake now. Miss Sharp and the Shadow Man obviously had plans for us, and they weren't good. We had to get out of here. The rope cut into my wrist, and no matter how hard I tried, I couldn't reach the knot. Then I remembered the stack of tools at my feet. If I could just reach a trowel and cut through the rope. The two figures outside the door were pacing, not looking inside. The biggest danger was one of these callous killers spotting me through the door. I'd have to be quick.

Keeping one eye on the Shadow Man and one eye on the pile, I slid my feet into the mish-mash of tools. The toe of my shoe barely caught a trowel leaning against a rectangular sifting screen. Trapping the flat blade between my toes of my shoes, I moved the trowel toward me. The screen tipped forward. Oh no. It rocked back, nearly crashing to the ground, then swayed forward with a clatter. If they looked in, I was sunk. I closed my eyes and held my breath.

"You had to get into an argument with him. He only suspected you faked the bones. But no... you had to announce you found a ceremonial knife. Now look where we are." His voice reverberated off the cabin walls.

I lifted my eyelids a crack. The screen was still. I pulled my knees to my chest, bringing the trowel into reaching distance. The wooden handle dragged in the dirt, leaving a snail-trail. Wrapping my fingers around the handle, I eased the trowel into my hands.

For a second, Miss Sharp and the Shadow Man stared at each other, two fighters stalking each other in a ring, hesitating just before the bell. He slapped his thigh and turned toward the cabin, pulling a lantern from the outer wall. I didn't dare move. I saw his face. His Chiclet-shaped front teeth glinted like a rabbit. Sam, the security guard. Chill bumps chattered over my skin.

"Why didn't you just come clean? Why couldn't he know about the discovery?" Sam wiped his forehead with the back of his hand and turned back to face Miss Sharp. "When you called, I didn't think you'd pour a half bottle of ether down his nose. You killed him, Rebecca. Whether you meant to or not."

I flipped the flat blade, using the sharp corners to saw the rope binding my wrists. What were they talking about?

"Look, let's not lose our heads. Remember, no one else knows about the knife." I heard Miss Sharp speaking, but I concentrated on severing the last few strands of rope. I glanced back at the door.

Sam made a half turn, and the lantern light gave him a sallow look, but he didn't look into the room. "Pushing him out the window was the hardest thing I've ever done. Why, Rebecca? Why do we have to go to such lengths?"

The rope loosened around my wrists, falling in the dirt. I scooted next to Sara and worked on the rope binding her wrists, watching the door the entire time.

Miss Sharp stepped into Sam's path. She lightly stroked his cheek, then slid her hand to his neck and purred. "Your life was boring before I came along. You love living on the edge. Remember, we're in this together. In case you forgot, you were the one who found the human bones in the woods. It didn't take much to convince you not to turn them over to the Chief. And when I sell the knife... well let's just say we'll never have to worry about money again."

"But it's gone way too far." Sam's jaw hardened. She kissed his neck, and his jaw relaxed. He covered her hand with his and brought it to his chest. "We've covered our tracks, but two people are still dead. Where does it stop?"

She ran her finger down the side of his face to the cleft in his chin. I quit sawing at the rope. How could she be so calm? I hated her. We had to get out of there, but Sara hadn't budged. How was I going to carry her out? I chopped at the remaining frayed rope fibers, watching Miss Sharp and Sam every other second.

"Don't worry. The Chief thinks Noble lost his mind. I forged a note, making him confess to everything, even accused Dr. James of helping him. No one will ever find him at the bottom of that old well."

"I should have never let you talk me into going to Professor James's house today. You're obsessed with finding that safe and his research notes." Sam's hands dropped to his side. "You said this would be it. One last look. Why in heaven's name did you think there wouldn't be anyone at the house today?"

"I ran into Caroline James, and she told me no one was home. She and that nosy maid of hers were going to the church." She put her head on Sam's chest. "I had no idea the kid was there. We'd have gotten away, but *the girl* saw us. We couldn't leave them."

The last thread of rope slid off Sara's wrist. I moved back to my original spot, tucking the trowel under me. I watched Sara for any signs she might be regaining consciousness. She slept on. The room was completely dark; night hugged the woods, the only light thrown over the two murders from the lantern.

Miss Sharp pushed her hand into Sam's chest, pivoting so that her butt brushed against him in the turn. Then she walked to a black on white Ford Fairlane and opened the car door. She picked up Dad's diary and something wrapped in black velvet. "I never thought about a diary. He wrote about the argument I overheard between him and Dr. McKnight. And he knew something was going on at the site, but he hadn't figured it out."

"At least until he confronted you, and you lost it."

Miss Sharp slipped the diary in the front of Sam's pants, letting her hand linger, her fingers sliding against his skin.

So she didn't understand the codes or she would have known Dad was one hundred percent positive *she* faked the bones. But Sara had the last decoded message in her hand. I saw her pick the paper up before we went downstairs. How did Miss Sharp miss it?

I glanced at Sara's form, willing her to be all right when a soft moan left her lips. She was coming around.

My eyes darted back to the door. Miss Sharp and Sam were just outside now, not ten feet away. She stroked Sam's arms, kissing him with her sickening red lips. Planting several kisses down his neck, she slipped her hands under his shirt and over his ribs. I hated her so much I wanted to beat the life out of her.

A jagged line appeared between his brows. "We can't stay in Natchitoches. There'll be too many questions."

"Don't be silly. If we leave now, everyone'll be suspicious. If we stay, everyone'll blame Dr. Noble and Dr. James for the forged bones. We'll be heroes. We'll travel the world, and I'll give lectures on forgeries and how to spot the difference. It puts us in the perfect position to find a buyer for the knife. Wasn't exactly my plan, but nothing's perfect." She wrapped a leg sensuously around Sam and licked his ear.

He grabbed her wrist, pulling her back. "Not now."

"Fine. Go remove the well cover. We need to get rid of them before they wake up." Breathless, Rebecca Sharp tapped Sam's chest. Her face glistened pink, and her eyes tilted upward at the edges when she smiled. She enjoyed this.

Sam stepped away, handing Miss Sharp the lantern, then aiming a flashlight into the woods. The moment he left, Miss Sharp rounded the door and knelt in front of a peeling metal footlocker. Flickering light filled the room. I remained motionless and dropped my eyelids to half-mast so I could watch her. She bent over the locker, and a little brass key dangled from around her neck. It looked like the key from Professor Noble's office. With a little jerk, she lifted a gun from the locker and stuffed it in the back of her pants. She placed the item wrapped in black velvet on the floor near the locker.

Miss Sharp spoke under her breath. "He's a fool. Going to be a crowded well tonight."

All the air in the room vanished, and I couldn't breathe. My lungs burned, each tiny air sac screaming for air. She was going to kill Sam, too.

I had to find a way out of this. I felt the trowel underneath me. It was all I had.

My gaze shifted to Sara. When I was sick, Dad used to say he wished he could take the pain away. Nothing was worse than watching someone you love hurt. I knew what he meant. If we made it through this, I would make sure she never hurt again.

Sara coughed. I prayed she didn't move, but Miss Sharp was on us in a flash. She shoved Sara with her foot, rolling her under the table legs, then hovered over at me, scowling down at me. I wanted her dead.

The key around her neck dangled above me. It definitely matched the key from Professor Noble's office. I leapt up, surprising her, pushing her off balance, grabbing the key, snapping the chain.

Miss Sharp screamed and punched at my face. Luckily, I'd lived with Brett too many years. I anticipated the jab and turned my head so the punch glanced off my cheek. I saw movement from the corner of my eye. Sara was on her hands and knees, coughing up thick silver mucous and shaking her head. I pushed Miss Sharp so hard she flipped over the table. I lunged for the trowel. But when I stood up, Miss Sharp was already on her feet with the gun barrel pressed to Sara's head.

I dropped the trowel next to my feet just as Sam came in the door. My hands were slippery with sweat. I checked them, but it wasn't sweat, I'd reopened the cut on my jaw. I wiped my hands on my pants. Miss Sharp didn't notice me slip the key in my pocket on the last swipe.

"Damn it, Rebecca. What's going on?" He looked at me and then at Miss Sharp's arm fastened around Sara, the gun still pressed to her head. "Where'd you get that gun?"

"We keep one here. Wild animals and all." Miss Sharp glared at him. "Is everything ready?"

Sam rubbed the back of his ears. They were scarlet. "We can't do this."

"Do you want to spend the rest of your life in jail or have your head snapped off at the end of a rope? Not me. We've come this far. Now let's finish it."

Miss Sharp motioned me next to Sam, then directed Sara toward me with the tip of the gun. Sara tripped coming toward me, falling near the locker. I helped her up, and she hugged me to her so hard I thought I might fall over. Her hands were at my waist. She slid something metallic into my pants–the trowel. I felt her tremble and looked into her eyes. They were bright with fear.

Sam grabbed me by the arm, pulling Sara and me apart. I felt like my heart was being ripped out. Big Red's prediction bounced off the sides of my heading, echoing louder than my thumping heart. If I hadn't let her help me, she wouldn't have been in the house, and she wouldn't be with me right now. I had to make this right. But all I could do was wait for my next chance.

Miss Sharp held the gun on us. "Aw. How sweet. Look at it this way. You're getting what you want. You'll be with each other forever."

Sam slammed his hand into the center of my back, forcing me out the door. Once outside he passed me, shining the flashlight ahead of us. I heard Sara file behind me, and Miss Sharp after her. We walked past a scruff pine forest. Pine straw matted the forest floor, muffling our footfalls as we padded toward a desolate area beyond the excavation site.

I knew where we were going: a vine-strangled farmhouse at the back of the property. An old well jutted from the ground just behind the house. Above us the night sky loomed black with only the basic stars. It was like an eerie omen.

I shuffled along, trying to come up with a plan. I had a metal trowel down my pants, but I couldn't shoot with it, and it wasn't large enough to cause any major damage. Really, I had nothing. Then Miss Sharp's words came to mind. I picked up my pace until I was next to Sam. I glanced over my shoulder. Sara had slowed almost as if she read my mind. She grabbed her ankle. Miss Sharp nearly stumbled over her.

"She's gonna kill you, too." I whispered to Sam.

He grunted and pushed me away. I loped back beside him. "You know she talks to herself. She called you a fool. Said you were next."

His head cut toward me. His brows went up like he knew, knew exactly what I was talking about. Then he looked back to the path, his face silent and sullen. His fingers gripped the aluminum flashlight.

If Sara and I could just get away, we could run through the woods to the main highway. We walked a few more feet. Sam ran the light over a large concrete cap shaped like a giant Roman coin, tilted to the side of the well.

Miss Sharp chucked a rock into the well. I listened until it plunked into the water. It didn't take long. A tremor clamped my jaw.

Sam stopped at the lip of the well. "Give me the gun."

He held out his hand, but Miss Sharp raked her teeth over her lower lip. "I didn't think you wanted more blood on your hands. I'll keep the gun."

"There's no reason to shoot them." Sam kept his hand out. "It'll leave blood and attract vultures. Someone may investigate."

"True. Fewer bullets, fewer questions." She pushed Sara and me forward, herding us next to the well.

I slid my hand along my waistband. My fingers touched the trowel, but the handle felt lumpy, not smooth. Unexpectedly, Miss Sharp sidestepped Sara and me, aiming the gun directly at Sam.

"Did you really think I'd give you the gun?" She fingered the trigger. "Such a fool."

Now! I jumped her, pulling the trowel from my pants. My fingers were so sweaty they slipped on what I thought was the handle, but it wasn't wooden—it was metal, bright and gold. I tightened my grip and struck her wrist with all my strength. A gunshot cracked the night. My ears rang. I could hardly think. The gun hit the ground with a thud. Sam slumped beside the well.

"Run!" I yelled. Adrenaline shot through me, overpowering the sluggish ether effects.

I bolted with Sara beside me. We ran straight for the scrub pine forest and made it to the perimeter, darting behind the first thick tree. I inched my head around the scaly bark and looked back. Miss Sharp was screaming, pointing a crisp beam of light on the ground, searching for the gun. I clenched my hand around the metal rod or stone or whatever it was. I couldn't see anything but a faint glimmer in the dark, but it felt like a spade, yet the shape and weight were off. I tucked it back in my pants.

Sara and I moved farther into the forest. Stumbling over downed limbs, we felt our way from tree to tree. It was slow going with so little light, but we didn't stop. Once we were well into the forest, we hid behind a mother-oak tree. I didn't want to think about how fast I was breathing. Didn't have the time. We stepped out from behind the tree.

Light swept over us. Miss Sharp screeched like a wounded owl. We heard a whiz go past our heads. She'd spotted us.

"Stay low." My ears still hurt, but the incessant ringing now sounded like a never-ending waterfall. I took Sara's hand and prayed my voice didn't carry through the woods. "We'll head to the main highway. It's a couple of miles ahead."

"We'll never make it." Sara caught her feet in the understory; her fingers clung to my hand. I dragged her a few feet before she was up again.

"Sara, focus on Polaris, the North Star. You can see it above us through the upper branches." I pointed to the sky, and she glanced up. "It'll lead us to the highway."

She nodded, then tightened her fingers around mine, pressing our palms together. Her hands were slick with sweat. I wasn't sure why I sounded so calm, but all I wanted to do was make sure Sara was safe.

Another whiz. Another scream. We darted to the next tree large enough to hide us, working our way north. Light crawled up our backs each time we left the safety of a tree, declaring open season on Sara and me.

Miss Sharp damned the darkness and closed the distance between us. But we kept running forward. After several minutes, we ducked behind a thick confused jumble of bushes.

"We're coming to a ravine. It's wide, but it narrows a little ways down. I think we can make it." I could just make out Sara's head. I ran my hand over her hair and pulled her to me, kissing her forehead. She smelled slightly of honeysuckle, but mostly of fear.

"Will we have to jump?" Her head burrowed into my shoulder.

"Yes." I pulled her closer. "Don't look down and don't jump short. We have to make it across. I'm positive she doesn't know about the narrow part. We'll have to hurry so she doesn't see us. Hopefully, she'll try to cross the ravine on foot."

I gave Sara one last squeeze and ran my hands up and down her arms. "Stay close and follow me. Ready?"

"Yeah. I'm ready."

When we reached the ravine, we stopped. Trees were outlined with low light, but the ravine sucked up all the remaining light. I tracked the edge with my foot, moving to the left about fifty feet until I could just make out the trees on the other side of the jagged split. The neck was barely narrow enough, but we had no other choice and had to make it across.

"This is it. We'll need a running start." My legs had started to shake. I spoke with more confidence than I had. "Let me go first. Then you'll know the distance."

"Okay." Sara sounded a little unsure.

"We can do this."

Miss Sharp wasn't far away. Light spookily filtered through the trees, making them look as if any minute they'd rip up their roots and start chasing us. I took a running start and sailed across the ravine, landing on the other side. My feet slammed into the ground and my ankles vibrated from the strain. I went back to the edge. Sara's turn. I held out my arms.

"Jump!"

Sara charged toward the edge, jumping at the last minute. Her arms spread up even with her shoulders on either side, helping her balance, but her foot landed short. She propelled forward, just not enough. She struggled like a broken windmill, sliding into the ravine. I grabbed for her, felt cotton brush my fingertips. Warm air filled my hand. I'd missed. Her hand snatched my pant leg. My hand wrapped around her wrist. Her feet scrabbled up the side, and I pulled her to me. A rattlesnake sounded. The pine straw undulated along the sides of the ravine.

Sara gasped. Now she knew why I said we *had* to make it across. A fresh wave of light landed near us. We dove behind another tree just as another bullet whizzed over our heads. We stood locked together, chest to chest, our hearts thumping out of sync. I counted the number of times Miss Sharp had fired the gun, once at Sam, three times at us–four times in all, four bullets spent. If the gun had been fully loaded, she'd have four left.

We zigzagged between six more large pines and stopped. We were well past the ravine. I hugged Sara to me, running my hand over her back. She leaned her head into me, holding my waist.

"She should drop into the ravine soon." I felt Sara tense. "The deep end is full of snakes."

"What if we'd fallen in?" Her face was tilted up to me, and her voice was soft. "I almost did."

I touched her lips with mine. "But you didn't."

We watched the light waver near the edge of the ravine. Then it dipped and was gone. Miss Sharp was as noisy as a bull, trudging through the leaves and pine straw, but there was an unmistakable rattle, then another, another, and another. Sara's hands clenched my waist. I felt the tang of cool metal between us.

Miss Sharp screamed and fired into the ravine. A flash. One shot. Another scream. Another flash. Then two shots: one behind the other. She'd used four bullets. She was out.

"Quick. We can make it to the road." I took Sara's hand, and we sprinted to the highway. We never looked back, though Miss Sharp continued to scream and thrash around inside the ravine. Who cared? A part of me felt lighter. I wanted her to die.

We pounded through the pines, following the North Star until we reached the highway. The asphalt was hot and steamy, but I was never go glad so see a chunk of road in all my life. We panted to a stop. I grabbed Sara and kissed her hard, crushing her to me. Her lips were salty and sweet.

"Someone will come along." At least that's what I hoped. We started walking, hand in hand, keeping to the shoulder of the road.

In the distance, sirens wailed and it wasn't long before flashing red lights appeared along the horizon. Soon headlights scanned us, and three cars screeched to a halt. The Chief was out of his car, but Brett and Priss bounded past him to reach us first.

"Are you all right?" Brett clasped me, then pushed me back at arms length, checking me head to toe. Priss was all over Sara, smoothing her hands over her shoulders and asking rapid-fire questions like a news reporter.

"Yeah." I chuckled, actually chuckled. Part of my mind wasn't sure if I was in a memory or not, though. For just a second, my brain sort of spun like it was suspended in a whirlpool, not fully understanding this reality.

Everything else happened almost at once, so fast that I had to shake my head to keep up with it. The Chief was beside me asking overlapping questions, and Priss was cooing over Sara. I caught Sara's eye, and she gave me a semi-smile laced with relief.

"Holy shit, boy. Are you all right?" The Chief and his officers were gathering around us.

"Yeah. Miss Sharp and Sam from campus security tried to kill us."

"Where are they now?" The Chief was all business. He didn't even have a toothpick wiggling in his mouth. "Still at the dig?"

"No sir. She's in the ravine. She shot Sam near that old farmhouse. He fell near the well, but I don't know if he's alive." I was starting to shake, a delayed reaction from adrenaline overload. My teeth chattered between sentences. "They killed Dad... and Professor Noble. They dumped his body in the old well."

The Chief shouted orders. Car doors slammed and spotlights lit up the woods. Two officers swerved around us in a cruiser, red lights flashing and sirens blaring to the archeological site. The Chief darted around his car. When he closed his door, he lugged a rifle.

He clamped me on the shoulder. "Looks like I owe you an apology. There was a snake in the hen house after all. I'll need a statement from you, but we can do that later."

"Chief... Sam has Dad's diary in his waistband. It explains some of it."

"I know, son. Your brother told us." He clapped my shoulder once more.

He tromped into the woods, aiming his flashlight above his rifle. By this time, Mom was next to Brett. Her eyes glistened with worry. Not like when Dad died. Not sad and uncomprehending. I'd underestimated her steeliness. She thrust out a blanket and hugged it over me.

"You're hurt." She ran her hand over my jaw.

"It's nothing. Just a cut from earlier."

Mom tucked my hands under the blanket, talking as she gently touched each hand. "Brett found the paper with the last coded message in the entry. He told me all about the diary, and the man watching the house. When we figured out Rebecca Sharp was behind it all, we could only think of one place she might go, the excavation site. It was our only hope. We called the Chief right away."

I looked at Brett. He ran his hand over his hair. "The entry was a mess. Tudy and Mom had just gotten home when Priss and I arrived. Candy all over the place. Tudy had a fit. Then she picked up a paper off the bottom step. You and Sara obviously broke the code."

"Yeah. Good thing you came home when you did."

Brett smirked. "Yeah. About that. I've been working overtime. Trying to bring home a little extra. Priss brought me home."

Sara and Priss slipped over to us, and I wrapped my arm around Sara, draping her with the blanket. Despite the heat, she quivered as if she were freezing. I felt the brush of metal at my waist.

Priss pinched me. "Okay, mister? Good thing Brett was at our place. I was supposed to pick up Sara when I dropped him off. I could have missed the whole thing."

I drew out the metal object from my pants. Light flashed over an ancient knife. The handle was heavy, pure gold. Three lozenges of green jade rode down on side. I'd seen pictures before in Dad's office. How did Miss Sharp come by this?

"Oh My God. What is that?" Priss asked.

"I grabbed it so fast, I didn't know what it was." Sara placed her hand near the waistband of my pants, where the skin was still cool from the knife. Her face was bright with discovery. "When I tripped. I saw metal, but I didn't really look. Just grabbed it and hid it in your pants."

I turned the knife over in my palm. The handle flared at the top into an elaborate headdress. The priest's head and body formed the shaft and were carved from dark jade. Then end was rounded much like a shovel. It was beautiful. Mom studied it without touching it.

"Dr. McKnight will need to see this." His name brought up several images–keys: the one in my pocket, the one around Miss Sharp's neck, the one in Professor Noble's office, and the one taped to the underside of Dr. McKnight's bed.

"Oh Lord, I forgot. He called before the Chief showed up. He's in town. Tudy's waiting for him at the house." Mom's voice came out in one long stream as if she had to get it out in one breath.

"Back from his honeymoon?" I wrapped my free arm snuggly around Sara. Maybe if we were closer together we could stop shaking.

Mom shook her head. "It's all so strange… he didn't elope with Penny, after all. He called as soon as his plane landed in Shreveport. Said he'd been in London this entire time."

XXVI

When Woody's headlights scanned the house, three figures quickly rose from rocking chairs on the front porch: Tudy, Lila Dupree, and Dr. McKnight. He ran a hand over his suit; clearly, he'd been traveling, since he never wore anything but khaki pants or hiking shorts.

Lila was first to the car waving a flimsy scarf in her hand. She sounded like Blanche DuBois after she drank perfume: sickeningly sweet. "Oh my goodness, where is my baby?"

Tudy scurried in right behind her, waiting to be whatever help she could. "Lord, Lord… I been praying for everybody to get home safe and sound."

I sat in the back seat with Sara. She rested her head on my shoulder. She lifted her head, then wearily exited the car, her lack of energy a sure sign of ether overdose. I avoided Lila Dupree while she flapped and fussed over Sara and Priss. Dr. McKnight stood at the top of the steps. He offered Mom his hand.

"Tudy was kind enough to fill me in on Dr. James's death. I'm so sorry. I had no idea." He bowed his head like he was saying a prayer. "I should have stayed, but he insisted I go to London."

My mother directed everyone into the house. "Let's talk inside. The kids have been through enough tonight. They are thirsty and surely want to rest awhile."

Sara took my hand and wiggled her fingers to get my attention, then gave me a tiny smile. I couldn't believe what we'd been through. It was surreal to come back into the house. The entry was spotless, as if nothing had happened.

Tudy made for the kitchen. She always said it made her feel better to have something to do. The minute she stepped into the house, Mrs. Dupree dabbed her flimsy scarf against the tip of her tongue, then rubbed it on Priss's cheek. She batted her mother's hand away. Dr. McKnight followed Mom into the great room and sat down beside her.

"Before we start, I need to tell you something." Mom brushed a stand of hair off her face. "I'm sure Tudy told you about my husband, but Miss Sharp and the security guard, Sam, killed Professor Noble, too. Julian overheard them talking. They threw him down a well."

"Miss Sharp shot Sam before she fell into a ravine. She might be dead, too," I said.

Professor McKnight didn't say anything, just rubbed the side of his face. It was as if he rubbed it hard enough all the information would sink in.

Mom smoothed her skirt while looking Dr. McKnight in the eye. "What's really going on?"

"Penny didn't elope with me. She was a cover story. She had a boyfriend in the Air Force from Barksdale and ran off with him when the semester finished." Dr. McKnight cleared his throat. "Tudy said Dr. James died on Monday, May twentieth. He'd called me into his office the sixteenth, the day after classes ended. He suspected someone had tampered with the bones from the excavation, making them look older than they were, thousands of years older. He'd wanted an expert opinion and sent the bones to Dr. Leakey for inspection. After Dr. Leakey examined them and verified they were forgeries, he didn't want to risk shipping them. He was at a conference in London and asked your father to meet him there. However, your father sent me."

Tudy came in with a tray painted with magnolias and passed around glasses of iced lemonade. I wanted to gulp it down; my throat was so parched it felt like I was swallowing liquid smoke. Sara raised her glass, watching me over the rim. A chill ran over me thinking about how close I'd come to losing her.

Dr. McKnight continued. "Your father suspected Rebecca broke into his office. He felt she was more than likely behind the fraudulent bones. Clearly ambitious, she joined our department and soon accused us of being sluggishly backward. It goes without saying, she loathed being an associate professor and was determined to make her way up the ladder as rapidly as possible."

For some reason, it relieved me Dad had confided in someone. I just wish he'd had that same confidence in his family. All the secrecy and clues almost killed Sara and me.

"She criticized the way Dr. James ran the department and accused him of keeping the limelight to himself. When the bones were found, she prodded him to go public. But he told her if they'd been in the ground for thousands of years, a few more months wouldn't matter. She was furious, claimed no one appreciated her, threatened to quit." Dr. McKnight set his glass on the fireplace mantel; moisture clung to his fingertips and a narrow wet ring formed at the base of the glass. "All along she was setting us up. She would accuse us of forging and planting the bones, then she would become famous. She thought we were a small college, and she could get away with it, but she forgot one thing—your father was well known and respected for a reason. He was meticulous and everything with his signature was carefully checked."

"The day he explained everything to me, we had a heated argument. I wanted him to confront her. Why wait? He reminded me she could say the entire department was complicit in the forgery. She'd ruin us all, everything we'd ever worked for. He said proof was imperative." Dr. McKnight paused and looked down at his feet.

"Normally, the day after finals, I leave for the most remote part of the planet I can afford, but this year I was going to stay in the states. My plans changed the minute you father explained everything to me. Penny left on Friday, so her elopement was the perfect cover. I told a couple of key people who couldn't keep a secret if their lips were sewn together. Then, Dr. James arranged for me to fly to London and pick up the faked bones from Dr. Leakey. Any information I gathered was kept secret. He gave me a check for expenses and instructed me not to call or talk to anyone until I returned."

Finally, the reason Dad wrote the check. I glanced over at Mom. Her shoulders were drawn up to her ears she was so tense. She had so much information to absorb. Her gaze never left Dr. McKnight's face.

He tugged on his lower jaw. "The saddest part is Dr. Leakey divided the bones into two sets. Ironically, Rebecca planted bones never realizing there were actual bones dating to the Bronze Age in the next level. There was no need to plant them."

"She may have planted the bones, but she found more than she expected. More than anyone expected." I had placed the knife in my pants for safe-keeping. I raised my shirt and showed Dr. McKnight.

His hand went to his head like it might explode into a million pieces. When he recovered, he held out his hand. "Where did this come from?"

"Miss Sharp found it at the excavation site."

Dr. McKnight looked confused. "How could she keep this from every-one? As far as I know she was never alone at the site."

"I heard her talking about the knife to Sam. She must have found it later, after she planted the bones. She planned to sell it."

Dr. McKnight's mouth opened but his words came out in a whis-per. "This changes everything." He made a small whistle. "Dr. Leakey confirmed the real bones came from around 1000 BCE. If this is true, then this knife means the society living here either was associated with the Olmec civilization or traded with it. This knife is an Olmec sacrificial knife. It's priceless."

"Sacrificial. Like killed humans?" Brett boomed. His voice contrasted with Dr. McKnight's soft-spoken manner.

"Possibly. There's no definitive evidence of human sacrifice, but we don't know what else we'll find in this mound. They were the precursors to the Aztec and Mayan cultures. If this is true… I can't take this all in, but… well, nothing's ever been discovered this far North. It would change how the world views the culture and migration patterns in this area. It's quite the find." Dr. McKnight ran his fingers over the tiny round jade stones embedded in the gold headpiece. "Magnificent."

"Dad found out about the knife. That's why she killed him." My voice shook so, the words sounded garbled.

My Dad truly believed in honor before self. It was his credo, but he'd placed it before everything else. Part of me admired him, but another part resented him. In his zeal to protect his department, he'd placed himself in a deadly situation. And now he was gone.

I stood while everyone else just sat in bewildered silence. I went to my room and pulled the rabbit skin bag from under my mattress. All heads turned to me when I reentered the room.

"Follow me." I said, pouring the key, and mug pieces into my hand.

Everyone mutely followed me down the hall to Dad's study. When I walked into the room, my mind churned and images flashed so rapidly I felt bile rise to the back of my throat. Cold snaked through my brain and memories collided, creating sparks. Leaning against Dad's desk, I automatically bit the inside of my lip, pulling it together. No one sat down. We held one long collective breath.

"On the day Dad planned to confront Miss Sharp, he left his bedroom the same as always, except for one thing… his glasses. I noticed right away Dad's glasses weren't on his diary. He kept it by his bed because he wrote in it every night. Instead, his glasses were on a history book, *The American Revolutionary War*, a clear clue. He must have felt there was some danger because he wrote parts of his diary in code."

I walked to the wall where Dad's butterfly collection now hung. An open cardboard box rested on the floor beneath the collection. Beside the box laid an empty ether tin and a crumpled box of cotton. A memory cut across my brain. I pushed it back, but it pushed forward. I could do this. I could control this. I need it.

I let my eyelids drop and breathed slowly in and out. The memory opened. *The medicine cabinet behind the door in my Dad's office came into focus. Through the glass door I tried to read the red tin, but it faced the back wall. Two boxes of cotton sat on the shelf beneath the ether. One was pristine, a gold seal smoothed over the top. The other box was dented and crammed in front of a jagged row of specimen jars. I slowed the image enough until it was three-dimensional and examined the tin. I picked it up and turned it to the front, then I checked each specimen jar.*

I bit down on my lip and zipped back to the present. I looked around the room at all the anxious faces and started.

"Dad was very particular about how he stored his things. He kept his books in order by genre, his research filed by date, and the supplies for his butterfly collection arranged by use. Until tonight, I didn't know how Miss Sharp subdued Dad long enough to push him out the window. When Sara and I came downstairs after solving the last code, I smelled ether."

I picked up the metal tin and a box of cotton, grouping them with the pieces of broken mug on Dad's desk. I slipped the key from Professor Noble's office into my pocket with the other key.

"Miss Sharp suspected Dad knew about the altered bones, but he hadn't written anything in the research notes they all shared. That meant he must have written something in his personal notes. She had to have them. She had to know how much Dad knew." I ran my hand over my face. This was much harder to do than I thought. It was one thing to think a crime through, another to describe it to others.

"Dad planned on confronting her the day he was killed. He either called her to his office or she came by intending to go through his stuff. She knew he drank coffee every morning, several cups. So she spiked his coffee with knock out drops. I'm not sure how it came out, but she slipped and told Dad about the knife. She panicked. While Dad was unconscious she changed her plans."

The empty red tin made a screech when I scooted it to the center of the desk. "She called Sam. While he was on the way to help her, she opened the ether, saturated a wad of cotton, and shoved it over Dad's face."

Mom gasped, and Tudy's cheeks glistened with tears. But I had to get it all out. I couldn't stop now. I plowed ahead and held up the broken pottery pieces. Images of the window in Dad's office eased into my mind.

"When Dad passed out, he dropped his coffee mug, it shattered. Miss Sharp was in such a hurry she didn't clean up the mess right away."

I stared over everyone's heads, thinking out each terrible step.

"No one knew Sam was helping her. By the time he arrived, Dad was dead. Sam had Miss Sharp return to her office so she'd have a credible alibi while he cleaned, but he missed the piece of mug near the baseboard and the heel print next to the desk. Then he dragged Dad over to the window and pushed him out."

I held up the mug piece Brett and I found on the ground outside Dad's office "Somehow this was wedged under Dad's body and gouged the window sill as he was pushed out. Brett and I found this on the ground where Dad landed."

The box of cotton still rested on the desk. It was crushed, as if opened in a rush. I scooped out two rolls wrapped in blue and white paper. But where one was neatly wrapped and sealed with a gold sticker, the other was rumpled and tattered.

"Dad used ether for his butterfly collection. He soaked cotton pledgets and dropped them in the specimen jars." I unfolded the neatly wrapped cotton coil.

"See where he took tweezers and twisted the cotton? It left a neat little trail of holes about the size of dime."

I held up the only specimen jar with anything inside, a beautiful Southern Flannel Moth; beside it was a dried, crinkled pledget. "Miss Sharp needed more than a tiny pledget for humans and grabbed fistfuls of cotton to use on Dad, Sara, and me. I think the only reason Sara and I are alive right now is because Sam must have talked her into taking us to the excavation site."

Lifting up the scrunched roll of cotton, I peeled back the wrapper. Sure enough, it gaped where someone had torn off half the roll. I glanced over at Sara, then to Brett. "She helped Mom hang Dad's butterfly collection and knew the cotton and ether were in the study. I recognized the smell before she rammed it over my face."

Sara nodded while I was talking and cupped her hand in front of her face, then blew out a breath. It obviously smelled like ether. She wrinkled her nose and said, "She came out of nowhere. She crammed something white over your face, and you started sinking right away. I screamed and tried to attack her, but Sam grabbed me. You dropped to the floor. I fought him but Miss Sharp held the ether over my face until I passed out. I vaguely remember dropping the paper with the decoded message on the steps. Sam didn't notice because when he yanked me up, my bag of M&M's ripped and candy spilled everywhere. It's the last thing I remember."

Lila Dupree clutched Sara to her chest. "All the things you've suffered at the hands of that woman." She wagged her finger at Mom. "Rebecca Sharp was a charlatan. She didn't take sugar in her iced tea, and she made fun of little boy babies in day dresses. Can't trust a woman if she isn't Southern."

Of all things to think about, Mrs. Dupree had a different take on life, that was for sure. But it gave me a momentary distraction, enough time to restructure my thoughts. I knelt by Dad's desk and picked up the manila envelope I'd left there earlier. I tugged out the beige packing tape, holding it high for everyone to see. "Miss Sharp left a heel print when she stepped in Dad's coffee. I brushed it with white alum before saving the impression on this tape."

Pointing to the print, I said, "You can see a split and the letters **N E**. The letters spelled out a name, probably a brand. I knew this heel print belonged to the killer, but I wasn't certain until tonight. The shoes belong to Rebecca Sharp. When she knocked me out, they were the last things I saw before my face hit the floor. If the Chief checks her shoes, he'll find they match the tape."

Dr. McKnight rubbed his forehead against the cuff of his shirt. "How did you figure this out?"

"I suspected something was wrong from the start. My dad was afraid of heights and wouldn't just fall from a window. I remember things in detail, so I can recall all kinds of images other people forget. Like the way Dad positioned the ether tin on the shelf. He always had the labels facing the outside, easy to read. Rebecca Sharp was in too big a hurry and pushed the ether tin back on the shelf with the label facing inside. I didn't understand it at the time. The first thing that caught my eye was the crooked shadow box. Someone ran into it, tipped it sideways. Anything crooked or facing the wrong direction would have driven Dad crazy; he would have had to straighten it. Little hints were all over. I just had to piece it together. But there's one thing I haven't solved."

"What?" asked Dr. McKnight.

I pulled the keys from my pocket, one stained with Professor Noble's blood and the other shining brass. Other than that, they were identical. I held the keys high above my head.

Dr. McKnight asked, "Is that the key I hid under my bed?"

"Maybe. I found the black clothes Sam wore at your house. He must have been staying there. He must have given the key to Miss Sharp. We found the other one in Dr. Noble's office."

"Your father gave Noble and me the keys. They aren't duplicates. They go to a safe. Unfortunately, I have no idea where."

Tudy shook her head with a chuckle. "Lord have mercy. Been right under us the whole time."

She shooed us, and we moved away from her like the points on a star. She flipped back the carpet. Two small recessed locks had been drilled into a trap door on the floor.

XXVII

Everyone went home sometime past midnight. It was the most depressing, yet exhilarating night of my life. The keys opened a metal safe hidden under the floorboards. Inside were the missing research folders. Dad had thought of everything. He set up the hidden safe like a bank security box. He gave one key to Professor Noble, and one to Professor McKnight, but never told them what the keys opened. He probably hid another set somewhere. A later mystery to be solved.

Dr. McKnight quickly scanned the reports and told us everything was painstakingly documented. Dad had suspected something more was going on than the altered bones. He's intercepted a letter from a wealthy collector a couple of days before he died. He couldn't imagine what the man was talking about. Maybe he had asked Miss Sharp about it. Maybe that was what started the argument the day he died. Maybe he'd figured it all out before he died. We would probably never know.

Dr. McKnight said he'd give the files to Chief Hendricks. It would clear up everything about the excavation, the doctored bones, and Dad's murder. He said it was the least he could do. I think he felt he'd let Dad down somehow.

Lila Dupree zipped out the door before she said a proper goodnight, shuttling the girls ahead of her. I never had a chance to say goodbye to Sara. But if Mrs. Dupree had anything to do with it, all of Natchitoches would know the entire story within a few hours. I still needed to give the Chief my statement, but the adrenaline had finally drained from my body, and all I wanted was to sleep. My mind stuttered with exhaustion.

The following morning, Chief Hendricks's voice drifted up the stairs, waking me from a rough sleep. I crammed my pillow around my head, but it didn't help. I was awake. I wandered downstairs, dreading my interview with the Chief. Everyone sat in the dining room.

Tudy cooked a tremendous breakfast: scrambled eggs, fried bacon, buttermilk biscuits with butter, and cheese grits. Mom wiped the corner of her mouth and smiled. The Chief sat at the table with the biggest cup of coffee I'd ever seen. Just as I dropped in my seat, I heard a commotion outside.

"Who's out there?" I asked.

"Reporters." Tudy handed me a pitcher of milk. "They showed up 'fore sunup. I was gonna give them some biscuits and coffee, but Chief says don't even start." She giggled. "He says them men'll descend on us like hungry locusts once they taste my cooking."

I stood up and pushed the curtains aside. The lawn was peppered with photographers all dressed in black suits, white shirts, and black ties.

"Why're they here?"

"Once word got out on the Teletype last night, the phones started ringing nonstop. Forgery, theft, and murder are sensational news, son. Didn't get a wink of sleep." Chief held up his cup like a salute. "Dr. McKnight brought the research papers and the other evidence you found. He explained it all, but asked to keep the knife. National treasure and all. I'll need your statement, but there's no hurry."

His words should have been reassuring. Everything was taken care of, but somehow I didn't feel any better. It didn't bring my Dad back, which is what I really wanted.

"Sam's gonna be okay. Once he was in the ambulance he started spewing like a gal durned oil well. He told us Rebecca Sharp had him bewitched. It was all her idea." Chief nodded like there was nothing truer. "Rebecca Sharp is another story. She was bitten several times and is in a coma. Dr. Pasquier thinks she's already at the pearly gates."

Chief leaned forward, his chest almost touching the table. "I don't want to scare you, but you might want to lock the back door when you leave. She had Sam break into your house a few times. He said he watched the house, and when no one was around, he just walked right in. I shoulda believed you, son. But my deputies never saw hide nor hair."

Mom put her hand to her throat. "Monsters. They're monsters."

"Sam confessed to *helping* kill Professor Noble. Said Noble caught onto Rebecca while investigating the financial records. At that point he remembered your dad had given him a key to a safe." The Chief slurped his coffee, mixing it with air to cool it. "Good stuff. Thing is, poor man couldn't remember where he hid it. Unfortunately, Rebecca came by his office while he was looking. Now we all know Professor Noble's elevator didn't always go to the top floor. He was under a good bit of strain when she came into his office."

Chief chugged the rest of his coffee, then thumped his chest to release a burp. "She knew Professor Noble would turn her in, so she called Sam. They tied him up tighter than a tick before driving him to the excavation site and throwing him down the abandoned well."

"How horrible." Mom hung her head, staring at her hands in her lap.

Chief Hendricks turned to me. "You're lucky Rebecca didn't know about your dad's diary. Scary to think what she mighta done to get it. Promise me next time you and your brother decide to solve a murder, you'll let me in on it. Better safe than sorry, I always say."

He could have read me the riot act, but he didn't. He could have arrested me for withholding evidence, but he didn't. I think he respected me for believing in Dad and pursuing the truth. Maybe he hoped, deep down, his kids would do the same for him.

He picked up a canvas bag off the floor and pulled out Dad's diary. He thumped it on the table. The back cover was dark and damp to the touch. Must be Sam's blood.

"We've copied the passages we need from the diary and the pages you left inside with the solved codes. Thought this might be the safest place for the time being."

I touched the diary, then passed it to Mom. I knew she'd want to go over it. Maybe not right away, but someday.

"Well, time's a wasting. Hate I gotta wade through those reporters." Chief snuck a bad-boy grin, then grabbed his hat off a vacant chair. "Thanks, Miss Caroline, Miss Tudy. Mighty fine breakfast. Oh, before I forget. I talked to the Coroner, and we're gonna send out the reports to the insurance company right away. No sense in stretching this thing out any longer."

Chief clamped his hat on his head and swaggered to the door. Mom and Tudy didn't move a muscle. Normally they would have walked him out, but they just sat there.

"Praise the Lord," Tudy said.

Mom folded her hands together and looked up as if God were in the very room. "We'll be fine."

The atmosphere changed after the Chief walked out. We'd never stopped mourning for Dad. A hollowness no one else could fill sat in Dad's chair at the end of the table, expanding through the room, closing around my heart. However, a healing began, and our confidence in each other was restored. Dad believed in honor and truth. His love for us kept us going. I'm certain he would have been proud. And despite all our doubts, we never truly gave up.

After Brett heard the good news, he snuck out disguised in a tweed vest and a gray felt fedora from Dad's closet. He carried a box of old newspapers right past the reporters to meet his friends. Yeah, things were pretty much back to normal.

In the afternoon, the doorbell rang. When Mom called me, I was reading in my room. I bounded down the stairs. She handed me a note written on basic lined composition paper folded into a perfect square.

"The mailman said someone asked him to deliver this with the mail." Mom peered sideways at my name written on the outside. She ruffled my hair. "Seems this young lady told the mailman she couldn't get past the reporters."

I nodded then headed straight to my room. I unfolded the paper. Right away I knew Sara had written it. Who else would send a message written in mirror image? I immediately flipped the sentence in my mind and felt my lips curve into a smile that stretched all the way to my ears.

.thgindiM ta egdirB hcaeB llehS eht ta em teeM
Meet me at the Shell Beach Bridge at Midnight.

I pushed Woody down the drive just before midnight. I didn't have to be quiet, but I enjoyed the intrigue. All the penguin reporters had evaporated with the sun. I rolled down the window and drove to the highway. The air was dry and light for summer, and for once, I wasn't sweating. When I turned onto the gravel road leading to Sweet Magnolia, I glanced through the windshield at the moon, a fingernail clipping punched into the deep night sky.

Woody chortled past the Duprees' house. Blue light from the television flickered across the walls of the living room. How could that be? The station signed off with the national anthem at twelve. Who watched a blank screen? Then I spotted Jack's jeep parked by the glass bottle garden. He and Priss were probably enjoying the grainy static or else they'd escaped through the not-so-secret trap door. They didn't occupy my mind too long. Woody trundled onto the trestle bridge. Sara stood in the middle with one hand on her hip and the other shielding her eyes from the headlights.

She was simply beautiful. There was no other way to describe her. Even after I clicked off the headlights, a glow made from millions of illuminated dust particles hovered around her. I eased out of the car and walked to her.

"Hey." After all we'd been through, it seemed like I could come up with something better, a clever greeting or cool line, but we were beyond all that. Somehow solving secret messages and being kidnapped and nearly killed by vicious criminals brought us closer together than the average teens.

"Hey, yourself." She reached out and touched me. Her fingers slid over my arm, leaving a searing trail. She stepped closer to the bridge railing with me in tow. "I'm glad you came. I guess you read the newspaper. You and your dad are heroes."

I hadn't thought of myself as a hero. "I never realized how hard it is to stay true to someone when no one else believes you. But my dad would have done the same for me. He would never have abandoned me willingly."

"He formed a bond with you that'll never be broken. You're truly lucky." She hooked her index finger into mine. "I had to see you one last time."

"Why?" I asked, not quite understanding. "Are you leaving?"

"Mrs. Dupree called my dad's office. He's out of the country and didn't call back until this afternoon. He went ballistic." Sara looked past me into the water below. Star shapes sparkled and skated along the dark water. "He's sending his plane for me tomorrow morning."

"You're leaving in the morning?" This was another of those times I repeated what I'd heard so it'd stick. "Wait, did you just say your dad was sending his plane for you? Like in an airplane?"

Sara's gaze left the river and turned to me. She nodded.

"You never said you were rich."

"You never asked." She ran her hand along the bridge struts. "Let's not talk about that now. I have a question. Why haven't you asked me about Big Red's prediction?"

"What?"

"You asked Priss, but you never asked me." She gave me a pouty look.

"You and Priss thought his prophecies were a lark. But if you remember, I didn't want to believe in Big Red. Thought all his predictions were mumbo jumbo. I should have paid attention to his predictions. Maybe I could have prevented our kidnapping and Professor Noble's murder."

"Well, since you believe." She squeezed my finger. "Do you want to know my prediction?"

I smiled. She was so earnest. "Yeah. What did he tell you?"

"He said I'd meet my perfect match this summer." She tilted her head. "What do you think?"

What did I think? I felt a familiar crinkle across my forehead as I tried to work it out.

Sara giggled.

"I–"

Sara touched two fingers to my lips.

"Shh. Don't worry. I just wanted you to know." She moved her fingers away. "This has been the best summer of my life, even though it almost killed me. It would have been so different if I hadn't met you. You made me feel special, clever and pretty…. Who knows, by the end of the summer, you might fall in love with me."

I laughed and pulled her to me. She smelled like honeysuckle and rain. She looked up at me, and my heart swelled, displacing my lungs and halting my breath. How could anyone be so beautiful?

"There's just one thing left to do."

What did she say? She leaned in toward me. Her face blurred, her cheeks red with heat. If I'd learned one thing this summer, it was not to overthink things. She lightly brushed her lips against mine, then her body pushed against me, her breasts pressed into my chest, her hipbones against me. She fit.

She stood on tiptoe and wrapped her arms around my neck. She kissed me full on the lips, then flicked her tongue along my bottom teeth. A fiery chill ran through my body, every nerve popping. She pulled back.

Sara stood still in the moonlight, my hand at the arch of her back. She took a deliberate step back and slipped off her flip-flops, handing them to me, first the left, then the right. Next she unbuttoned her shirt, slowly, one button at a time. She had definitely taken control. I couldn't take my eyes off her. The white border of her bra and the curve of her breast peeked through the shirt's opening.

She let her shirt fall off her shoulders. "What if all Big Red's predictions come true?"

Before I could answer, she playfully tossed me her shirt. It covered my face before tumbling into my arms. With a little shimmy, she pulled her shorts off and shoved them into my chest. She stood before me, a goddess in white lace underwear. The light fell on her shoulders like a faint snow dusting. Then she reached up, grabbed a metal strut, and hauled herself up on the bridge railing. I couldn't focus. What was she doing? She unclipped her bra and threw it into the water.

I almost lost it. She was the most stunning thing I'd ever seen. Sara looked back one last time, gave me a two-fingered salute, and dove off the bridge.

I couldn't move. My stomach dropped. What did she do? I didn't hear a thing. No scream, no whoosh. I shucked her clothes and sprinted to Shell Beach. As I rounded the bridge, I heard a splash. I couldn't see beneath the dark surface, so I hammered on and ran over the slippery shells to the river's edge, breathless and terrified.

Suddenly Sara's head popped up a little downstream. She waved her arms over her head and yelled, "I did it. I did it."

For the umpteenth time since my Dad's death, my knees were the consistency of putty. I wanted to be mad. However, at the same time, I knew how she felt. I'd had the same feeling after I captured the gator, super charged on an adrenaline high.

I'd always heard you couldn't live life without changing. Had this summer changed us? Had my father's death made me a stronger person? Had it taken a kidnapping for Sara to let people close to her? Who knew? All I knew was I wanted to figure out the answers with her. Big Red didn't have to tell me she was my perfect match.

Sara swam toward me. Gentle waves lapped around her. A glimmer reflected off the water, outlining her face. She tipped her head back while she treaded water, and her hair fanned out, forming a circle around her. She stopped treading water and swam into the shallows.

"Well Julian James, do you need written instructions or are you going to come skinny dipping?"

She didn't have to ask twice. I jerked my shirt over my head, ripping off my pants and shoes faster than Clark Kent in a phone booth. Then just as swiftly, I dove into Cane River.

Acknowledgements

No book is written in a vacuum. If not for the help and encouragement of several incredible people, Skinny Dipping never would have been written. It is a work of fiction; yet, even fiction must have real world references.

Without Sam Haynie, this book would still be just an idea. She took me to Natchitoches and showed me *her* town: the streets, bridges, beaches, and even the plantation she called home. From her memories many places sprang to life, and I was able to make a realistic world for Julian and Sara.

A special shout-out to Andrew Crawford and his amusing, sometimes tense insight into brothers, tricks, teens, and alligator hunting. A hug and a kiss to Dr. Megan Conway. Without our first foray into screenwriting, I wouldn't be writing, period.

From the very start, my friends supported me, sometimes reading unfinished chapters just to make sure I was on the right track. I am beyond grateful to Mary Young, Bryan Sullivan, Laura Crawford, Sharon Waddell, Rae Ann Ebarb, Darla Rackozy, Dottie Reeser, and Wallace Rackozy for reading the first manuscript. God, y'all are saints.

I also want to thank my Critique Group. We have laughed together, cringed together (over the most ridiculous lines), and celebrated even the smallest victories together. I hear your voices in my sleep. Special thanks go to Eva Contis, Sam Haynie, Scotty Comegys, and Vona Weiss.

Plotting and walking each week with Amy (Liz) Talley saved my sanity. There is no encouragement like that of a published author. I owe her so much— thanks, Amy.

I also want to thank the patient people who helped me with self-publication: Melissa Ringuette, who made the awesome cover, Megan Records, editor of the first degree, who made the book deeper and more accurate, and Melissa Schroeder, self-pubbing guru, for sharing her infinite wisdom of the publishing world.

No woman would be complete without a posse, and I fell into the arms of the most loving posse in the world. With deep thanks to Mary Thoma, Melanie McCook, Diane Busieck, Sherri Skrivanos, Lee Collier, Elena Duke, Melissa Burford, and Lory Evensky. Wonderful women, gracious hearts.

Great appreciation to my fellow NOLA members, published authors willing to give time and advice to novice writers, especially Winnie Griggs and Connie Cox.

Of course, I owe my biggest, deepest, most heartfelt thanks— this can't be written without a lump in my throat— to my family: David, Stephen, and Kathryn. I couldn't write a word without them. They support me without reservation and create the yummiest meals when characters won't shut up long enough for me to cook.